A Diamond in My Pocket

The Unaltered series: Book One

Lorena Angell

Lorena@lorenaangell.com
or

Fantasy Books Publishing, LLC
631 Riverside Dr.
Washougal, WA 98671

ISBN-10: 0-9795248-7-3
ISBN-13: 978-0-9795248-7-5
Library of Congress registration number: TX0008138965

Cover art designed by Lorena Angell and Luna Angell.

Other titles in The Unaltered series, by Lorena Angell:

A Diamond in My Heart, book 2, The Unaltered
The Diamond of Freedom, book 3, The Unaltered
The Diamond Bearers' Destiny, book 4, The Unaltered
The Diamond Bearer's Secret, book 5, The Unaltered
The Diamond Bearers' Rising, book 6, coming 2017

Visit: **http://lorenaangell.com** for more information on upcoming books and other books written by Lorena Angell.

Special thanks to:
My family and friends for unending support and encouragement, my daughter Luna for her plethora of ideas and creativity, and to Larry, for believing in me—thanks, honey.

Contents

Chapter 1 – Olympic Dreams

I don't understand what's happening to me. Something strange and inexplicable is going on inside my body, and there isn't anyone I can tell about it. I wouldn't know where to start.

I just crossed the finish line in first place for the 100-meter race. No one else is even close, I'm sure. I turn around to verify this and can see the other runners are still racing towards the finish line. The crowd has grown eerily silent. I glance up at the stands to find nearly every face looking in my direction.

The other runners finally reach me and halt nearby, panting as they walk in circles to cool down while throwing suspicious glances my way. I watch the lips of a couple of the competitors and listen to their low whispers. They debate back and forth about whether I jumpstarted or not. The shorter of the two girls hammers her point home by asking why the starter's gun didn't fire twice to indicate a false start if that's what happened.

The answer: I didn't leave the starting blocks before the other runners.

Coach Simms jogs over to me with his clipboard papers flapping in the wind. His overly round waist bounces to and fro, throwing off his balance. "Calli! Wow! How did you do that?"

I respond to Coach Simm's question with the puzzled truth. "I don't know, Coach." I've never won a race before—and to win by such a long shot without feeling the least bit tired doesn't seem right. I'm beginning to wonder if winning the race was all a weird dream. "What was my time?"

Coach hands me his stopwatch and grins. The time shows 9.3 seconds. "Of course, this isn't the official time," he says. "I'll find out what it was."

My brain struggles to grasp the incredibly fast time on Coach's stopwatch. It has to be a mistake, I think.

We are ordered off the track so the next race can begin. Coach Simms and I walk towards the bleachers where my personal belongings set in a pile. As we reach the bleachers, one of the officials pulls Coach Simms aside.

I climb the stairs towards my half-frozen bottle of water, winding through the gaps between fellow athletes. Their stares of question and suspicion prickle my skin. They probably think I'm on steroids.

I'm not a track star or a spectacular athlete in any sense of the word. I tried out for the team last season in my sophomore year because of the encouragement of Coach Simms, who is also my algebra teacher. I figured it would be better for me to join an extracurricular sport than to stay home alone after school. I am the youngest junior and, until today, I was one of the slowest on the track team. I haven't performed very well. In fact, my best time for the 100-meter was 13.9 seconds, not 9.3. Looks like I'm not the slowest anymore.

I pass through a group of senior boys and one of them teases, "Hey, Courtnae, wanna share some of your 'speed' with us?" His buddies chuckle. I don't even know his name, and frankly, I'm shocked he knows mine. I sit down by my things and take a long swig from my water bottle. The boys are still staring at me—something I'm not used to—so I raise my water in a toast-like fashion, smiling half a smile, and drink some more.

I'm doing my best to appear like I'm another tired athlete, yet I can't ignore the sensations racing through my body. My muscles feel pumped and ready to run again, which is completely the opposite of how I usually feel after giving the 100-meter my all. Maybe Coach had been slow in starting his watch and I didn't actually have such an unthinkably fast time—but that would mean the other runners were incredibly slow. I rub my face with my hand, trying to transfer some of the moist coolness from the bottle to my skin. Now would be a good time to awaken from this dream.

Coach Simms climbs the bleachers and heads in my direction. I take another drink of water so my hands have something to do. Will Coach ask if I'm using drugs or steroids? He sits nearby, fatigued and sweating profusely from the climb. He looks like he could be having a heart attack.

"So, Calli, what in the world did you eat for breakfast?" He grins, as if he's come up with an original line to express his amazement.

I shrug my shoulders.

"You broke the record!"

"Oh?" I try to act surprised.

"No, I don't think you understand. You broke *the record* for the 100-meter. Well, I mean, it's unofficial. We'll have to hold an officially timed run."

"Excuse me," a female voice breaks into our conversation. On the other side of Coach Simms stands the most beautiful, elegant woman I've ever seen. She has a kind of soap-opera look about her, with everything coordinated, right down to her manicured and polished nails. Not one hair on her head is out of place. I fleetingly wonder if she has a stylist who follows her around, primping her to look exquisite. "My name is Clara Winter,"

3

she says, reaching in front of Coach Simms to shake my hand.

I grasp her feathery-soft hand and shake it. "Calli Courtnae," I respond politely.

Coach reaches up to shake her hand too. "Gerald Simms, Calli's coach."

She briefly shakes his hand, then focuses on me. "That was an amazing run you just completed, Calli."

"Thanks, Ms. Winter." I try my best to sound formal. Years of introductions to my parents' professional associates has taught me to do so.

She takes a seat on the bench, her eyes never leaving my face. "Calli, I operate an athletic training facility in Montana called High Altitude Sports. After watching your performance, I want to invite you to come with me to train for Olympic qualifications."

I cough on my sudden inhalation of saliva. "Excuse me?"

"Of course, we need your parents' approval," she continues, "but all your expenses will be covered. When would I be able to meet your parents? Are they here today?"

My insides clench. Olympics? Montana? That's a far cry from Northern Ohio. "My parents couldn't make it today," I say. "I'll have to call my mom and see when a good time is. Both my parents are doctors and have pretty jammed-up schedules."

"I'm scheduling an official timing for Calli," Coach Simms says, interrupting us, "so she's going to have to wait to go anywhere." He then goes back to accessing the internet on his smart phone.

Ms. Winter ignores his comment and tries harder to sell me on her invitation. "Calli, there's only a small window of time to qualify. Any delays will cost you four more years until the next round of Olympic qualifications."

"Do qualifications even work that way?" I ask. "I mean, I always thought the athletes who made it to the Olympics had also won other competitions. Besides, how do we know this race wasn't just a fluke?"

Coach interrupts. "Here, see this, Calli." He excitedly shows me the statistics on the screen of his phone. "You broke the *men's world record* with your time."

Ms. Winter asks, "Calli, are you taking any—"

"No!" I cut her off. "I'm not taking steroids or any other illegal substance. I don't even take a multivitamin."

"All right." She holds her hands up as if fending me off. "I had to ask."

"If you don't believe me, get a cup and I'll pee in it." My blood pressure seems to rise with my voice. Beautiful or not, she isn't going to accuse me of cheating. Part of me *wants* to pee in a cup to see if anything can explain why I feel a deep molecular change within my muscles and bones. What's wrong with me?

Coach Simms says to her, "I should hear back sometime next week about setting up an official timed run."

"She'll be in Montana by then," Ms. Winter says confidently, which surprises me.

Coach Simms frowns. "What about her studies?"

"Our facility is equipped with teachers and tutors to keep the athletes current on their studies." She turns her attention to me. "Calli, call your parents and see if we can meet tonight or tomorrow morning. Time is of the essence. Qualifications are only a few weeks away. I want to get you on a plane as soon as possible."

I retrieve my cell phone from my bag. I feel more than a little nervous as I call my mother's office number and leave a message asking her to call me back.

Coach Simms and Ms. Winter continue debating the need for another timed race. She is against it, while Coach Simms adamantly insists on holding one in Ohio, and he isn't backing down.

I stare off in the distance, watching the runners on the track as they strategically manage their strength and endurance while running the 1600-meter. My next scheduled race isn't for another hour, yet my body and mind feel like I should get up and leave. A voice, not my own, sounds inside my head, saying I need to leave. I look around at the people nearby to see if someone has actually said those words. Plenty of faces are turned in my direction, but I don't think anyone has spoken. I'm beginning to think I might be going crazy. Well, if that's the case, I am in good hands.

My mother is a psychiatrist and my father is a brain surgeon. One could say both of them work on head cases. I like to think of their work this way: one deals with the thought processes and the other deals with the brain's functionality. So if I am in fact losing my mind, they'll take care of me. They already did so once before, when I lost my hearing in middle school.

Someone had rigged a bathroom stall with a firecracker, and I'd been the unlucky one to find it. When it exploded, the small, all-tile area amplified the noise so much the sound ruptured my eardrums. I still remember the intense pain. The agonizing waves felt like someone was pounding an ice pick into my ears. In a blink, my hearing disappeared. As my parents expected, I developed severe middle-ear infections. They were on top of my situation every step of the way. But even with all their combined knowledge and expertise, only so much could be done. I endured months of pain, injections, surgeries, and speech therapy. I had to be taught how to read lips in order to communicate. For a long time no one knew whether or not my hearing would return.

I gradually healed over a year's time but never lost my lip-reading ability. In fact, I still practice all the time to keep up my skills. My mother has said on several occasions that I can read lips better than anyone she knows. I don't know how I learned so quickly, or why the ability came so easily to me. It just did.

My mother advised me against letting my classmates know I could understand their whispers for fear they might take advantage of my abilities. She worried I'd become a circus act.

"They may ask you to read lips that reveal secrets," she told me. "Not many kids can do what you can, Calli. In fact, not many adults can either. Trust me, it's better to keep this ability a secret as long as possible."

As soon as I returned to school, I picked up on conversations in the lunch room typical of the age range, and the cafeteria seemed noisier than before. *Did you hear what she said? Do you know what I heard about him?* I got so sick of all the gossip and backbiting on the lips of others, I had no choice but to bury my face in books. That's how my interest with science and the medical field came about . . . well, besides hearing about medical stuff every night over the dinner table.

Once I began reading and learning about how the human body works, I couldn't get enough. I'm pretty sure I've read every book in the public library and off my parent's bookshelf on the subject. My father often jokes I'll only have to challenge the test at medical school and they'll give me my doctorate. I know my parents are pleased their only child is interested in a career in medicine, but the interest is quite real on my part.

My extensive knowledge of how the human body works brings a pressing question to the front of my mind. How can I have run so fast when I haven't trained and built the necessary muscles to do so? This mystery will have to wait. I don't want the same experience all over again with the 200-meter. The voice in my head encouraging me to leave apparently doesn't want me to run either. I need to come up with a plausible excuse to leave. I look over my shoulder again to see if I can figure out who's talking, telling me to go. No one is near enough to be the culprit. I lean forward, resting my elbows on my knees, and massage my temples with my fingers. What's happening to me? This isn't the first time I've wondered why I'm so different than other sixteen-year-olds, but this is the first time I've heard "voices."

My cell phone rings, revealing my mother's number on the screen.

"Hello?"

"Calli, you called?"

"Yes."

"Did you improve your personal time?" she asks excitedly. She's been actively following my personal time for the 100- and 200-meter all season.

"Yeah, Mom. I won!"

"You won? What was your time?"

"9.3 seconds."

I expect to hear some kind of exclamation—or a thud, due to fainting—instead her voice is calm.

"That is definitely an improvement."

Huh? That's it? I figure my mother must be preoccupied and my incredible running time hasn't registered.

"Yeah, it is," I reply.

"You'll call me with your time for the 200-meter, won't you?"

"Um . . . Mom, a woman has invited me to go to a training facility in Montana . . . to train for Olympic tryouts." I scrunch my eyes shut. Saying the words aloud sounds so unbelievable.

"Excuse me? Is she with you now?"

"Yes."

"Give her the phone so I can speak with her."

I hand the phone over to Ms. Winter. "My mother wants to talk to you." She takes the phone and begins talking to my mom.

I think about my mother's inattentive and unfazed reaction to the news about my time for the 100-meter. That's *so not* like my mother! Learning my time was 9.3 seconds should have made her shriek or something. Where are all the usual questions, especially concerning the strange woman who wants to take me to Montana? And why is this woman here in Ohio, at a high school track meet, looking for Olympic athletes?

After speaking for a few minutes, Ms. Winter hands the phone back to me.

"Your mother is coming to pick you up. We will then go to her office so we can discuss my invitation."

That sounds more like my mother. She isn't about to let me get in the car with an unknown adult. She would rather drop everything and come get me herself. I can't help but smile . . . now I won't have to invent a lie to get out of the 200-meter.

"Hold on. She can't leave yet," Coach Simms says. "She still has another race."

Ms. Winter calmly replies, "You can tell that to her mother when she gets here."

A DIAMOND IN MY POCKET

I'm still amazed at how easily my parents accepted the notion that I'm the fastest human being on the planet, heading off to train for the Olympics. Neither one of them acted normally yesterday when we met with Clara Winter.

My father was already waiting at my mother's office when we arrived. Ms. Winter gave a brief explanation about the Montana facility and presented paperwork for them to sign that gave their permission, along with authorization for my medical care in case of an emergency. That was it. My parents didn't so much as blink an eye or show any signs of suspicion or doubt.

I looked at the three adults who were making decisions that would affect the rest of my life and wondered if they were thinking of my own wishes at all. I don't want to be an athlete. I want to be a doctor.

When I expressed my feelings to my parents, my father said, "You'll have plenty of time to pursue your dreams, Calli. For now, follow this road and see where it takes you. You can always come home if you change your mind."

Change my mind? It wasn't my decision to go to Montana in the first place! Changing my mind would be deciding I want to *stay* in Montana.

My mother said, "This is the experience of a lifetime, Calli. You never know, you might decide you want to be a doctor to professional athletes."

After I reluctantly agreed to go, Ms. Winter instructed me to stay at home for the night and remain indoors. She told me she would be arranging plane tickets for the two of us, hopefully for the morning.

When I questioned her about not going outside, she said, "There's a darker side to being a super-star athlete that I don't think you're ready to cope with just yet. You'll be protected at my facility from the paparazzi. Please stay indoors, pack your bags, and spend time with your family."

So that's exactly what I did. Then early this morning Ms. Winter called with the itinerary and told us where and when to meet her at the airport.

"Oh, Calli, I've always known something like this would happen. This is your moment to shine," my mother says as she gives me a big hug. I pull her close, not wanting to let go. The gate attendant announces our flight is boarding, and I release my grasp from my mother and fling my arms around my father.

"I'm proud of you, Calli." The sincerity in his gentle voice almost brings tears to my eyes. "Now, go show them how Ohio girls run."

"We'll take good care of her. There's no reason to worry," Ms. Winter assures my parents.

Leaving my parents behind, Ms. Winter and I continue through security and walk to our gate.

In the company of what I think of as the world's most beautiful woman, I can't help but notice how many heads turn her way. I've always been a people watcher. What can I say? I'm fascinated by the way people behave when they don't know they're being watched. Here in the airport these people, mostly men, but a few women as well, are shameless with their double-takes. Ms. Winter is obviously used to the attention and doesn't seem bothered at all. No one is giving me a second glance, but I'm used to that, probably the same way she's used to all the attention.

It's never been my desire to be the center of attention. I didn't try out for cheerleading or drill team, and I never joined any clubs. I'm fine with being plain ol' Calli Courtnae, void of the limelight and undiscovered by the boys. I help the "lack of attention" thing along, though. I don't wear the current fashions or sport the latest hairstyles and my jewelry is kept to a minimum. In my opinion, teenage popularity contests are a waste of energy and I can do better things with my time than stress out about what others think of me. Besides, there aren't any boys in my school worthy of getting dolled up over. I suppose Brand Safferson is the most sought-after guy because he's Mr. Never-Fumbles-Always-Completes-The-Pass Quarterback, but he's not all that good looking in my opinion. I think the other girls fawn over him because they think he'll be a rich professional athlete someday, which only supports my theory that guys seem to be all about the looks and girls tend to be about the money. I'd like to think I'll be different in that respect, but I haven't actually been put to the test.

At sixteen, I've made a mental comparison of myself to other girls, to their body shapes and dimensions, in an effort to figure where I stand in contrast. I'm pretty sure other girls do the same thing . . . at least I hope they do and I'm not the only one. From a scientific standpoint, tinged with a bit of anatomy knowledge, my facial features are symmetrical and considered to be normal. I have average breasts and hips for my age, however, I think my thighs are too muscular. My conclusion is my physical appearance is a bit better than average in comparison to the girls at my school. I'm not ugly, but I don't know exactly how good looking I'm considered to be. I've never had a boyfriend to get the assurance that at least one guy, besides my father, thinks I'm beautiful.

I understand it's all relative—relative to what others think is beautiful. My parents will always think of me as beautiful, of course. I guess we're always beautiful to our relatives. Intellectually, I don't need to compare myself to others. Test scores tell that story. I've worked hard for my excellent grades and fully understand that good-looks aren't important when applying for college.

Ms. Winter and I find our seats and settle in for a long flight to Denver where we will be catching a connecting flight to Bozeman, Montana. From Bozeman we will drive to our destination and arrive by evening.

Once we are in the air, I ask, "Ms. Winter, what can I expect when we get there?"

"The training facility is a large building set high in the Rocky Mountains," she answers while retrieving her bag from under her seat. She opens it and pulls out a small laptop she sets on the tray table in front of her. "As of now, there are close to two-hundred residents living and working at the compound. The tutors who will keep you current on your studies will work around your training schedule so you'll be able to excel in both your sport and your grades." She presses the power button and her laptop fires up.

"Are there any other girls close to my age?" I try to picture the athletes who compete in the Olympics. The only images coming to mind are those of older, well-developed women.

"Why don't you rest? You have a big day ahead of you tomorrow and I need to do a little work." Ms. Winter isn't asking as much as telling me to quiet down.

I lay my head back to rest, trying to ignore my jittery stomach. I try to imagine how my introduction to the other Olympic candidates might go. Something tells me they won't be too thrilled to meet me.

I think about the phone call I had with my friend Suzanne James last night. She pointed out that the other athletes might as well go home now, because I have timed faster than all of them. There's no hope for any of them, she said, to get a gold medal. I had laughed and reminded her it wasn't official yet, that it's still possible the track meet was a crazy chance-happening.

Suz hadn't actually witnessed my race. She had been too busy flirting with some of the guys from the other school. She explained that when the cheering grew quiet, she turned to see what had brought the crowd to a hush. Some of the guys around her were in awe, saying things like, "Did you see that girl run?" and, "Holy crap, she was fast!" Suz told me she's proud to have been able to say she's my friend.

I know differently, though. Most likely, she saw the admiration in the boys' eyes when they looked at me, and she wanted some of that attention for herself. That's just the way she is.

I have a lot of people who talk to me and say "Hi" in the hall, but Suz is the only friend I hang out with. She befriended me in middle school and has stayed by my side ever since the firecracker accident, supporting me through my medical troubles. She's cute and spunky with a fun sense of humor and lots of friends. I'm not bothered by her spending more time with her other friends, but I'm amused when she comes to me after she's had enough gossiping, back-biting, and two-facedness.

Suz tells me all the time I speak and think differently than all the other girls and I'm "über-mature" for my age. I don't know about my maturity levels, I simply steer clear of the drama, that's all. Maybe my brain works differently because I've always been surrounded by adults who constantly speak in medical jargon and use big words. Plus, once I began reading medical books, my vocabulary went up several notches.

We like to hang out at the mall on the weekend and critique other teenagers' behavior. One thing never ceases to amaze me: jocks are jerks. It's one thing to be an athlete who cares about his grades and tries hard to achieve in his sport, but the arrogant, cocky, strutting, can't-get-better-than-a-C jock is a true degradation of the human species—only one step up from troglodytes.

The last thing I want to become is one of those conceited jocks Suz and I love to criticize. I'll need to keep that in mind at the training compound. I hope I'll fit in with the other athletes. I have to wonder what my future will hold now that I'm the fastest human on earth.

Ms. Winter and I make the connecting flight without a hitch and arrive in Bozeman at six o'clock. A valet brings her car to the baggage claim doors. Not surprisingly, it's a top-model sedan with a posh leather interior. I wouldn't expect anything less for a woman of her caliber.

We navigate away from the airport and turn onto the two-lane highway. The monstrous Rocky Mountains block the sun and cast a shadow across the valley. I stare out the window at the massive peaks, wondering how tall they are.

"Calli, would you tell me what your body felt like as you ran the hundred meters?" Ms. Winter asks without taking her eyes off the road.

Definitely a strange question. "Well, I don't quite know how to explain it, but I wasn't exhausted when I finished."

"Could you have run faster?" she asks, and I wonder if she's testing me.

"Faster? Well, I guess, um, yes, I think I could have." I'm not sure why I feel ashamed to be admitting this. Ms.

Winter seems relieved, as if a heavy load has been removed from her shoulders. I wonder why, but before I can figure out how to frame the question, she slows the car and turns into a restaurant parking lot.

"Let's go in and eat. Dinner will have already been served at the compound, and I can't have you going to bed hungry."

Any questions I have vanish. My stomach has been growling, and the thought of warm food sounds wonderful.

As we enter the diner, the hum of conversation ceases. Ms. Winter doesn't seem disturbed by the blatant stares of the locals who are attired in tattered overalls and plaid shirts. She acts as if nothing is out of the ordinary.

We seat ourselves, and a bubbly young waitress appears instantly.

"Ladies, how are we today?" Barb, as the label-maker nametag announces, cracks her chewing gum annoyingly while she prepares to scribble on her pad.

Ms. Winter smiles and answers politely, "Wonderful, Barb."

Barb hands us menus and leaves to "grab us waters." I glance over the photocopied sheet of paper.

I want a burger and fries, and the Big Sky burger plate sounds like the one for me. I don't know what is acceptable to order, so I ask Ms. Winter, "What are you going to have?"

"Calli, you can order whatever you want," she reassures me, almost as if she's reading my mind.

When Barb returns to take our orders, Ms. Winter requests a detailed special combination of foods consisting of mostly fresh vegetables. The waitress seems to be a bit put out with the particulars and looks to me to see what out-of-the-ordinary order I will place.

"Big Sky burger plate and a Coke," I say.

Barb smiles, jots some notes on her pad, then excuses herself.

Ms. Winter takes a sip of her ice water before she asks, "Are you nervous, Calli?"

"Yes, a little," I admit, feeling shy about saying so.

"I don't doubt it. Calli, there's so much to explain to you, but we'll do that tomorrow after breakfast. Tonight, you'll be shown to your room. You absolutely must not venture outside the building. Do you understand?"

"No going outside?"

"Correct."

"Okay. Who's my roommate?"

"I'm not sure. We'll find out when we arrive. The female hall and living arrangements are handled by Stella Wood. She oversees the assignments and makes sure everyone is getting along. Talk to her if anyone is giving you a hard time. My door is always open, but I prefer you take your rooming issues to Stella first."

"Why would anyone give me trouble?" I ask, knowing the answer as soon as the question passes my lips: I'm faster than everyone else. Of course they will view me as a threat.

"I'm not saying they will, only if they do. Also, any and all phone calls will be made through my office, and I will be monitoring them until I'm convinced you've grasped the workings of the compound. Oh, and there are no cell phones at the compound. We have a scrambler."

My head reels. Monitored phone calls? Workings of the compound? Am I headed to prison?

Ms. Winter continues. "You're going to be a bit overwhelmed at first, but I'm sure you will adjust to everything easily with time. Remember this important rule: no leaving the building after dark."

"Is it because the paparazzi are waiting to attack?"

"I'll show you why tomorrow night. This evening I have too many things to catch up on."

Show me? What does she mean?

We talk for a little while longer and then our food arrives. My burger and fries look heavenly and taste even better. Ms. Winter's plate, on the other hand, contains primarily raw vegetables without dip. Yuck.

Ms. Winter uses a carrot stick to point at my plate. "I hope your burger is good. Just so you know, burgers are not served at the training facility."

I figured as much. Coach Simms tells us repeatedly that what we eat and drink affects our performance. Things like carbonated sodas, he says, slow our running times, but that has never stopped me from indulging once in a while. Look at me now: I drink sodas, eat burgers, and still run faster than any human on earth. Go figure.

We finish our food, and Ms. Winter puts down a sizable tip before we leave the diner to start the final leg of our journey. The road takes us higher in altitude to where pine and fir trees grow. No more sagebrush, only lush and thick forest with twisting roads. Due to the pressure change, I have to pop my ears several times on the ascent. We round a corner, and the entire windshield fills with the view of the compound.

The huge building looks like an Alpine Chalet, designed similarly, with intricately cut eaves and trim. Many of the windows lining the exterior are illuminated from the interior lighting. Standing outside the tall windowed front doors, four adults wait to greet us.

We climb out of the car. A woman immediately pulls Ms. Winter to the side and gives her a hushed message. I don't mean to eavesdrop, but I read the woman's lips and am able to take in half of the conversation.

"Clara, they never made it. Chris is still gone, investigating their last known location with a Hunter. He's trying to determine who's responsible for this." The woman pauses as she listens to something Ms. Winter says, and then adds, "As soon as you left, the Seers reported a fog that remains fixed in place. The last time that happened, well, I don't need to remind you—"

My attention is pulled away by the remaining three adults as they welcome me to the compound. One of the women introduces herself as Stella Wood. I smile and nod, not really hearing what they're saying. I keep looking back at Ms. Winter. *What's going on?* Ms. Wood holds her hand out in invitation and says, "Let's get inside."

We enter the building and stand facing a giant staircase.

Ms. Winter ends her mysterious conversation and joins us, leading the way up to the second floor. She makes a swooping motion with her arm, "Calli, this is the girls' hall."

Ms. Wood walks ahead of us and knocks on each door.

Girls step from their rooms out into the hallway. Obviously they've been told a new athlete would be arriving. I make eye contact with the nearest girl and smile. She gives me a sour look. The girl across the hall has the same look. I'm confused because these two are younger than I am. Further down the hall, I note that not all of the girls are this young. One thing stands out though: every girl, whether twelve or twenty, is beautiful, not just pretty, but gorgeous, even with the crabby expressions on their faces.

"Come." Ms. Winter pulls me forward. "Everyone, this is Calli Courtnae from Ohio."

I greet everyone in my most cordial voice. "Hello."

No one says anything in return.

We continue down the hall and Ms. Winter tells me the name of each girl as we pass. I smile and greet each one. No one responds. I notice that every girl, has a perfectly proportioned body, with long legs and small breasts, accentuated by lean, toned muscles. Their bodies seem to be genetically perfect for cross-country running, regardless of their skin color or height. I realize I look *nothing* like them. The expressions on their faces and the whispers behind my back tell me they're thinking the same thing.

As we arrive at the end of the hallway, my eyes connect with a girl with heavy black eyeliner and unnaturally black hair. At least she stands apart from the other girls. She scrutinizes my appearance, looking me up and down, and then says to Ms. Winter and Ms. Wood, "No! No, I'm not rooming with that . . . that human!"

"Calli, this is Beth Hammond. She's your roommate," Ms. Wood informs me.

Beth focuses on my face and says adamantly, "No, I'm not." Then she turns to Ms. Winter and orders, "Find another room." Beth flips around and struts into her room.

Ms. Winter rolls her eyes ever so slightly and follows Beth.

Stella Wood places her hand on my forearm. "Give us a moment, Calli. Wait here."

Stella follows Ms. Winter into Beth's room, leaving me alone with the world's most stuck-up girls. I turn around, wondering how many girls are still staring. Everyone who's remained in the hallway gathers around me with expressions of derision plastered across their faces. The kids at my high school ignored me on a regular basis, and I was perfectly fine with that. But they never looked down their noses at me the way these girls do. These girls don't even know me. How could they hate me?

One older girl asks, "How fast can you run, Calli?"

I figure a vague answer might be the best bet at the moment, so I answer with, "Fast enough to be invited to come here."

She persists with a mega-snobbish attitude. "What's your time?"

"I'm sorry, what was your name?" I ask, trying to be polite.

Another girl steps beside her and takes over the drilling session. "She asked how fast you are."

Some girls further down the hall whisper to each other, and I read their lips. I can't make out the whole conversation, but I pick up on a few words: "spy," "lock your door tonight," and "don't talk to her."

I shoot the same question back at the girl who is interrogating me, "How fast are *you?*" From the stunned expression on her face, I can tell she didn't expect me to answer that way.

Ms. Winter and Ms. Wood come out of Beth's room and usher me in. I hear them tell the other girls to "lighten up on her" and "you know the rules."

"Calli, we'll go get your things while you make yourself comfortable," Ms. Winter says, leaving me to fend for myself against Attila the Hun.

"I'll help you," I offer, but Ms. Winter shakes her head and closes the door.

Beth stares me down with her darkly outlined eyes. Her eye color appears to be gray or perhaps watery light blue. It's hard to tell because her eyes are so narrowed. Her standoffish attitude leaves my skin cold as she says, "I don't want a roommate. Clara's losing her mind." Beth stands and stomps over to her dresser and brushes her hair while she stares daggers at me through her mirror. She lets out a huff of exasperated air and slams the brush down on the polished wood. "I finally move up in the ranking order around here, and I get stuck with the muck," she declares angrily.

"Thanks," I mutter. I walk over to my bed and sit down.

She wags her black-tipped pointer finger at me. "Don't be thinking I'm going to be your friend or anything. I don't like you! You've got *human* written all over your aura." Her arms make a sweeping circular motion. "Now, Clara brings you here, exposing our location to the world."

I've had enough. "Sheez, you're paranoid, but I guess that goes along with the hair." A rather daring comeback, I must admit.

"What does that mean?"

I imitate her circular motion with my hands. "Isn't that the look you're going after? The hair, eyes, nails, attitude— it's a complete paranoia package. Anyone who dresses like you is constantly aware of everyone around them, positive others are looking at them, judging them. You're paranoid." I take a breath and finish before she can interrupt, "Oh, and I'm not a snitch."

Ms. Winter enters the room, carrying my luggage. "Here you go, Calli." She sets my bags down and faces Beth. "Beth, will you show her around?"

"No."

"All right," Ms. Winter says to Beth in an exhausted tone. Then she turns to me and says, "Breakfast is at eight sharp in the dining hall on the main floor. Good night, girls." She leaves and shuts the door behind her.

Beth stares at me for a few seconds before asking, "How fast are you?"

No way am I going to tell her exactly how fast I timed out, or the fact I could have run even faster. "Probably not as fast as you."

"Well, we'll find out soon enough. A word of advice, showing off around here will only get you beat up."

"So, I should run slowly?"

"Yep."

"Would you beat me up?"

"Yep. I've worked and trained hard to get to where I am, and I'm not going to let you ruin that for me."

I realize she's afraid of me and, oddly enough, that calms me down.

"This side of the room is mine. Don't touch anything." Beth makes a chopping motion with her arm to draw an imaginary line.

I glance up at the walls on "my side" of the room, only to see her posters with things dark and mysterious covering them. I look back at her, hoping she'll say she'll remove them.

"Don't touch those either," she says, noticing my look.

Fine! "Where's the bathroom?" I stand, itching to get out of the room.

"Find it yourself." She points to the door.

I suppose a common bathroom must be down the hall somewhere, and as I don't want to stay any longer in her black cave of a bedroom, I leave. Everyone has gone back into their bedrooms and shut their doors, but it isn't like they would point me to the little girls' room anyway. Maybe this is some sort of initiation rite for newcomers. Well, that's just swell. I prefer to do things all on my own anyway.

The interior of the compound has a masculine feel with its dark woodwork and jewel-toned carpets and draperies. Dim lights, positioned every couple of feet in the ceiling, along with antique sconce light fixtures on the walls by every bedroom door, illuminate the hallway.

I walk the entire length of the girls' hall and can't find the bathroom. Climbing the staircase at the end of the corridor and rounding the corner at the top, I crash right into a rock-hard body. I instantly apologize, then look up and see my hands are planted on the bare chest of a dark haired guy with deep-set eyes. I remove my hands and divert my eyes to the floor, and find he wears only a towel around his waist. I've never been in a situation like this before. I don't know where to focus my eyes, so I look back up into his, hoping my cheeks are not as red as they feel.

"What are you doing up here?" he squints his eyes and speaks in a blunt tone.

"I'm, um, sorry. I didn't know this was the boys' hall." I take a step back. My eyes follow his hands as he secures the towel around his waist. I notice his well-defined chest and stomach muscles and realize I'm staring. I look back up to his eyes.

His head tilts to the side, with one eyebrow raised, as his eyes travel over my body. "You must be the new muck."

I'm unnerved to be called that again. I ask, "What does 'muck' mean?"

"It means I don't have to speak with you." He turns and walks away, calling over his broad, muscular shoulder, "You should leave the way you came in."

Okie-dokie. Oh, how I detest guys like him. Jocks! They think they are all that, and everyone else is inferior. If he's an indication of what all the guys look and act like at this facility, then I'm going to be miserable.

Descending the stairs, I notice a small sign on the door at the bottom of the staircase, designating it as the

24

bathroom. How embarrassing. I walked right by the door. If I'd seen the door earlier I could have avoided Hot Jock.

Minutes later I enter my room again. Beth makes eye contact with me for a second, then rolls away to face the wall.

I change into my night clothes and lie down on the remarkably comfortable bed. Staring at the ceiling, I think about the day. It started well enough, but ended miserably. My grouchy roommate refers to me as a human. I have been called "muck" twice. Even though I don't know the meaning of the word, the look in the eyes of both Beth and the good-looking guy when they use the word tells me the word isn't anything polite. Maybe it's some type of superior athlete's slang. The four-letter "M" word.

I miss my parents, Suz, and my little hometown. I miss the familiarity of my life, my usual daily grind, my comforts, even my distresses. At least they are normal for me and I know how to deal with them. This place, however, has "strange" stamped all over it. I'm unwelcome here. I've never felt more abnormal. Will I ever fit in? My stomach growls as I turn over and fall asleep.

Chapter 2 – Paradigm Shift

"You'd better get up, muck, or you'll be the last one entering the dining hall. And believe me, last is not a place you want to be." Beth makes her little pronouncement without looking at me, then leaves our room.

I jump up and hurry to dress. Unzipping my suitcase, I rummage through the contents looking for the bare necessities it will take to get ready in the quickest amount of time. I put on some clothes, run a comb through my hair, rub lotion on my face, and reach for my perfume, but then change my mind and set it back down. I don't want to appear to be trying too hard.

As I race down the empty hall to the stairs, I hear voices floating up toward me. The giggling and whispers of words like "muck" and "sloth" increase as I approach the door, then the voices quiet as I enter the room.

The huge dining hall is filled with large round tables and fellow athletes. Over at the nearest table, Beth sits next to Hot Jock from the night before. Her eyes narrow as she gives me the once-over. With the amount of black eyeliner she has on, she looks downright scary. The guy glares at me and makes me feel as if I'm the last person in the world who should be trying out for the Olympics. Obviously Beth has told him about me.

"Good morning, Calli," Ms. Winter says as she comes up beside me. "Everyone, this is Calli Courtnae from Ohio," she says, announcing me again. I suppose the introduction is meant for the guys and the other adults, since they weren't present last night.

No one says a word. I glance around the room at all the blank faces, imagining what they might be thinking. I have yet to find a face, female or male, that isn't strikingly handsome or gorgeous. Too bad their coldness seems to be equally distributed, too.

Ms. Winter leads me to a table filled with kids who don't look any older than twelve. One seat is unoccupied. I guess this is what Beth meant by not wanting to be the last one to breakfast . . . you're forced to sit with the children.

I sit and make eye contact with the curl-lipped faces of boys and girls. I figure I'd better show some kindness if I expect to get any in return, so I smile and say "Hello." They all quickly look away, as if even the sight of me is disgusting. *Is no one friendly in this place?*

Ms. Winter takes her position at the front of the room. "This is Calli's first day, and she hasn't had her orientation yet. I want to remind everyone about the do's and don'ts concerning new arrivals and the consequences of disobeying them."

A low grumble rolls throughout the dining hall, which only adds to my mounting confusion.

Do's and don'ts?

Ms. Winter continues. "We will be holding a time trial tomorrow morning as we've received a new assignment. Okay, let's eat."

Everyone gets up from their seats and starts filing toward the door to the kitchen.

I end up half way back in line, surrounded by boys and girls who won't talk to me or even acknowledge me. I face forward and find that the line moves rapidly. At least this torture will be over soon.

Once I enter the kitchen and view the spread of food set out in buffet style I am dismayed—fruits of all kinds, some vegetables and nuts, in fact more nuts than I've ever seen before, are the only foods to choose from. Several pitchers of different colored juices and ice water at the end of the table complete the selection. No bacon and eggs or French toast? No pancakes or waffles? Where is the real food? Needless to say, I don't end up with much on my plate.

I go back to my seat and glance around the room. Everyone seems to be staring at me, which I suppose is normal. I'm the new girl, after all. I indulge in a bit of lip reading to try to get an idea of what they are thinking. Other than standard questions about me, the only strange comment I pick up on is, "She's so *old* for a newbie."

Old? I'd figured the athletes training for the Olympics would be older than me. In fact, now that I think about it, where are all the older athletes? A quick inventory of the room reveals almost everyone is my age or younger. It makes no sense at all.

Ms. Winter comes over as I finish my food and invites me to follow her after I clear my plate. She waits for me as I exit the kitchen and then leads me down the hall to a private office and closes the door behind us.

"Take a seat, Calli," she says, motioning to the overstuffed leather sofa along the wall.

I sink into the luxurious, buttery-soft cushion. Right away I relax since I've gotten away from all the judgmental stares.

She sits in an extravagant executive chair behind her desk. "You must have questions for me by now. Go ahead and ask."

Where to start? "What is a 'muck?' "

"A muck is a slow Runner."

"Well, I guess I *should* have told them my time, then." I pile a heavy dose of sarcasm on my statement.

She smiles. "I believe the word 'muck' is used in a similar fashion as 'loser.' When you understand the nature in which you are viewed, it won't seem as harsh."

"Why did Beth refer to me as a human?"

"She doesn't think of you as being on the same level as her. Do you have any other questions, or shall we get started?"

"Let's start."

"Good. First up, feel free to call me Clara. Ms. Winter is too formal. Calli, I want you to keep an open mind and try to understand what I'm about to tell you. This may be hard for you to comprehend at first."

I nod.

"You are an extremely fast athlete, and your speed is only emerging. Not everyone is able to run as fast as you—your fellow teammates back in Ohio, for instance. But your burst of speed isn't, how should I put this . . . *normal.* Your ability comes from a cosmic energy blast originating in a distant constellation."

I stare at her for a second and then laugh. I can't help myself. How ridiculous!

Clara keeps talking as if she's used to being laughed at. "What we've found is the running ability surfaces during puberty, usually around twelve to fourteen years of age. Yours came a bit later. You are a Runner, Calli, but you won't be in the Olympics. I'm sorry I had to lie to you. You wouldn't have come here otherwise, nor would your parents have allowed you to, even though your life depended on it. I told you not to go outside last night because there are dangers in the nearby shadows, waiting for someone with cosmic powers to come along . . . someone like you."

"Paparazzi?" I roll my eyes. "You know, I haven't even seen one guy with a camera outside."

"Not paparazzi. The dangers I'm talking about are only found in absolute darkness where they wait for someone with powers to wander too far away from the light."

"Homeland Security Agents? Are they going to throw a net over me and haul me away?"

"No, Calli, the dangers in the shadows are invisible to the eye, but they are there all the same."

"Oh, like ghosts?" I lift myself up from my spot on the couch, laugh, and rotate a complete circle, letting her know I am looking for any suspicious objects. "Is there a hidden camera here or something? I'm not sure why you brought me here, but I'm not the kind of girl who believes in fairytales or spooky stories."

Clara doesn't move from her spot and remains unperturbed by my attitude. "Calli, I'm completely serious when I say you have an ability that originates from deep in the cosmos, one that's sought after by unseen forces that lurk in the shadows of the night. We refer to the forces as Shadow Demons."

"Of course you do." I throw my hands up in the air. "I want to call my parents. This is a big mistake and I want to go home."

"Calli, going home before you learn how to protect yourself will get you killed."

"Are you going to let me call my parents or not?"

"You can call your parents after I finish my explanation of your superhuman ability."

Superhuman? That's the last straw. I've heard enough. I shake my head as I back up toward the door. I turn to leave the office and am shocked to find her in front of me, blocking the way. I glance over my shoulder, convinced there must be two of her, only to see an empty chair.

I take one step back, afraid and shaking. "Please let me go."

"Calli, I'm not holding you captive. I'm trying to teach you about your gift and how to protect yourself from the evil waiting to harm you. I'm not trying to hurt you, and I understand how insane this must sound, but allow me more time to explain. Please."

I stare at her for a second, a million thoughts running through my head. I guess what convinces me to turn around and walk back to the couch is the fact I have nowhere else to go. I'm trapped in the Rocky Mountains of Montana, sixteen-hundred miles away from my parents, with a beautiful psychopath who operates a cult-like compound, surrounded by freakishly perfect-looking people with really bad attitudes.

She takes her place behind her desk once again and continues speaking.

"Everyone you know was affected in one way or another by galactic cosmic energy rays while they were in the womb. When a fetus is exposed to the energy blasts, some alteration to DNA will occur depending on the proximity to the hot zone, the area at the direct center of the blast. Those, like you, who are located in this area end up with a superhuman ability. Those on the outside edges of the hot zone will experience increased intellect, photographic memory, artistic or athletic ability; those further out will be affected with milder increases in their skills and abilities. The ones way out on the perimeter can end up with deformities and mental delays. Think about your own high school. There are probably a couple of highly athletic individuals, the kind who get scholarships, and a small handful of extra-intelligent kids who will become valedictorians. Also, a few who excel in the arts, I imagine. And then I would hazard to guess some in your school are a few bricks shy of a load, right?"

I have to cut her off here. "Clara, I haven't ever heard of this. These findings would be all over the news and in the scientific community if they were true. What about DNA testing? If my genes were changed, don't you think something like that would show up in my blood work? I think this is all hogwash."

"Calli, radiation hazards in outer space are well known. Astronauts are bombarded with radiation continually, and scientists have proven that a developing fetus subjected to x-rays can suffer damage. What they don't understand, however, is the same cosmic energy rays that fly around outer space also hit the earth in a pinpoint fashion, creating a ripple effect. Drop a small pebble in a puddle of water and watch the ripples form. Now, imagine the pebble is the cosmic energy blast that results in fetal DNA alterations, and the ripples represent lesser alterations. The further the ripples travel away from the center, the weaker they become."

"So, you're saying that as an embryo I was hit by some rogue cosmic ray that altered my DNA, and the alteration popped out two days ago?"

Clara leans forward, resting her elbows on her desk and interlocking her fingers. "The alteration simply reached maturity level. Calli, remember how your body felt as you ran and the fact that you could have run faster? You said so yourself. Now, put everything you felt into the perspective of a scientist. Would a scientist be able to explain your impressive burst of speed other than through performance-enhancing medications? You told me you were clean. Were you lying to me?"

"No, I wasn't lying, but—"

"Reflect on your own amazement. You hold the key to understanding this remarkable event, more so than any ordinary scientist. However, we have scientists in our community who are currently working on determining which galaxies or constellations the different powers come from."

"Different powers?"

"Yes, super-speed running is one of the several powers. There are also Mind-Readers, Healers, Seers, and even some who have over-sensitive olfactory abilities. We call them Hunters. They're easy to spot because of their oversized noses, the same way Runners are identified by their ideal genetics. The other types of powers do not have physical attributes associated with them like the Hunters and Runners do."

"Is that why everyone around here is unbelievably beautiful?"

"Beauty comes from the inside, Calli. Exterior appearances can be a gift and a curse. For Runners, it seems the DNA alteration affects the proportions of the body's structure making an ideal frame to handle the power. Unfortunately it results in an almost unnatural physical form . . . freaks of nature, if you will."

I wonder to myself why my physical form doesn't match the lithe bodies I've seen so far. Compared to the girls from my hometown, I rank myself above average simply because I don't have a crooked nose, my facial proportions are symmetrical, and my body-fat percentage falls in the normal range. Here at Models-R-Us, the bar has been raised and my above-average looks fall to the bottom of the barrel. At least my intelligence level and sarcastic attitude remain top-notch.

Clara continues. "We employ three individuals with power here at the compound: a Seer, a Healer, and a Mind-

Reader. This is a common practice among clans. I'm a Runner and I'm also trained in the art of spell-casting, which I use on foods and herbs for the benefit of the clan.

"Clan?" I ask.

"We refer to groups of individuals with the same power as a 'clan.' "

"Spell-casting?"

"Yes, there are Spellcasters who cast enchantments and such."

"Are you telling me there are witches and wizards too?"

"The ability to harness the energy around us, and utilize the benefits from certain plants and organic material, has always existed, Calli. This is not a cosmic ability but a learned one. Although I do not use witchcraft for my spell-casting, there are some who find it useful for theirs, and those Spellcasters would technically be considered witches and wizards. However, the clans believe that witches and wizards are the evil, underhanded Spellcasters who go against nature's will, who are actually known as sorcerers in the spell-casting world."

"Um, I don't see the difference."

"Spellcasters are aware of their natural limitations and do not push nature's boundaries. Sorcerers and sorceresses use their knowledge against nature's limits, not in conjunction with it, and not for the benefit of anyone but themselves. The clans erroneously mistake these people with witches and wizards thanks to cultural influences, but it doesn't matter. Any involvement with one is frowned upon. In fact, consorting with a 'witch' or 'wizard' can get you thrown out of our clan."

"You know," I interrupt, "the science stuff is almost believable in my mind. But to say that witches and wizards actually exist is not something I'm able to wrap my head around. I don't believe in that kind of stuff."

"Well, Calli, all I can say to you is your ideas and beliefs have been shaped by the limited information you've had access to during your upbringing. There's more to the world than what you've been taught. With time, you'll learn what I'm talking about."

I close my eyes and try to contain my erratic thoughts. I decide to focus on the running ability.

I ask, "What else can Runners do? I mean, do they only run or do they have other special abilities?" Not that I'm completely buying into anything, but after hearing her list all the other superhuman powers, I feel a little cheated that I can't be a Mind-Reader or Seer. How cool would *that* be?

"Calli, you are wise to question the value of our ability. Being able to run fast allows us to cross over the top of bodies of water or swim through them with incredible speed. We can travel as the crow flies—without roads—but that's not all. Our ability originates in our nervous system, causing our impulses to fire at extremely rapid intervals. We can catch a hummingbird effortlessly because of our enhanced reflexes. With enough distance from a shooter, we can even dodge bullets . . . well, that is if we know a bullet is about to head our way. Because of these supernatural abilities, we're able to avoid knife blades, steer clear of punches, and simply disappear in a flash. This is why we are selected to run errands. Not only can we run, we are our own security force and are not good people to be cornered."

I have to admit this description sounds pretty appealing. I ask, "What kind of errands are you talking about?"

"Other clans employ us to deliver goods and messages that are too high-profile to be trusted to standard delivery services. Even governments have used Runners for top secret assignments. In fact, during the Civil War, many orders were delivered by our clan."

"Civil War? These powers have been around that long?"

"Longer, Calli—since ancient Egyptian times."

"Well, how did they stay hidden? Why hasn't the rest of the world picked up on them?"

"The world *has* picked up on them. Think about all the big blockbuster movies that feature characters with superhuman powers. Consider the subject matter of popular fantasy and science fiction titles and comic books, and you'll recognize that these powers and abilities have been in the public eye for a long time. The clans have endeavored to fictionalize their powers throughout history because regular people function better when they think these powers are just a fantasy."

"What about vampires and werewolves?"

"They existed at one time, but not in the way you've learned about through fiction and movies."

"This is too much for my mind to handle. The next thing you're going to tell me is there used to be dragons, fairies, and leprechauns."

"Well, I don't know about fairies and leprechauns, but dragons definitely existed."

I roll my eyes. "Of course they did. And you know this because of all the scientific evidence that exists in the world today?"

"No, because I use powdered dragon bone in some of my recipes. There are no complete bones remaining for science to study. Anyway, Calli, try not to let all this information overwhelm you. Focus on this: our Seer *saw* you four weeks and two days ago. His vision revealed your powers would emerge at a high school track meet. I was there to collect you, to keep you alive. Once you learn how to protect yourself, and if you so desire, you can return home. But leaving too soon, without the knowledge we can give you here, would be disastrous."

I bend forward and put my head in my hands. This can't be happening. I definitely recognized a strange feeling in my body at the track meet, but superhuman power? Her description almost makes sense, but I can't help but think this is all a joke. Yet, I *did* feel the impulses she spoke of, experiencing them firsthand. Unless . . . unless I'm caught up in some kind of hypnotic session and my mind is being toyed with to convince me this is real. Yes, that would be more realistic. My mother uses hypnotherapy to help people in her clinic, and this woman might be using the same thing on me with evil purposes . . . but choosing me for some evil purpose seems just as unbelievable.

While I try to rationalize away the ridiculousness that threatens to make sense in my head, a knock on the office door pulls me out of deep thought. I glance over at the half-windowed office door to see the profile of an extremely handsome guy with well-trimmed blond hair. Not that seeing a good-looking guy at this crazy-house compound seems out of the ordinary, but this guy is much more than handsome or good looking—he's a stunning display of ultimate masculinity, a walking euphoria, and the total embodiment of every girl's dreams. My dreams, truth be told.

"Come in," Clara answers.

He enters and walks with purpose straight to her desk without even acknowledging my presence, his eyes firmly set on Clara. His aroma, somewhat like a combination of citrus and fresh-cut wood, drifts along behind, tantalizing my senses even further.

From my vantage point I again admire his commanding profile and strong jaw. He wears a uniform similar to a jogging outfit, which seems to be made of extremely thin material that purposely hugs his lean, muscular body in all the right places, accentuating his well-defined physique. His voice flows like liquid satin. "Clara, they never reached their destination. I searched with the Hunter for trails or clues, but they've simply vanished mid-journey."

"I've had word the Healers are missing three as well." Clara's eyes move to me, and then back to Chris.

"When did they disappear?" he asks, turning his head in my direction. Our eyes meet and lock.

Clara says, "Oh, excuse me. Chris, this is Calli Courtnae. Calli, Chris Harding."

I reach forward to shake his hand. Chris doesn't make any attempt to reach for my hand, so I lower mine to my lap. All the while, our eyes are locked on each other's. His eyes are blue, like . . . like the summer sky I used to gaze up at, dreaming of all things good and wonderful. I can't look away. His eyes hold strange emotions, however, emotions I can't identify as he looks my face over. Is he confused? Is he angry? He seems to recognize me, but that can't be. His mouth parts as if he's about to say something, and I wait impatiently to hear his voice again. Instead, he closes his mouth and slowly turns his head back to Clara. His eyes remain connected with mine until the last moment when he has to look away. As he speaks again, his tone is different. The confusion in his voice matches the strange emotions in his eyes. "Why did the Healers send *her*? Why not the leader? This is a highly unusual move on their part to send Cal—um, a beginner."

"Chris, Calli isn't a Healer. She's a Runner. This is her orientation."

He turns to look at me again, only this time his eyebrows are scrunched together, causing vertical lines to appear between his brows. His jaw falls open and he actually takes a step backward. What is it about my presence that causes such a physical reaction in everyone? Am I that out of place here?

"Clara, may I speak with you in the hall?" he asks through tight lips.

I watch as they both walk to the door. Chris holds it for Clara and then exits, pulling the door closed behind him. Through the window, he stares at me with an unreadable expression.

Clara's back is to me, but I can tell she's talking to him.

I read his lips as he replies, "She's not a Runner, she's a Healer." Clara says something else and he replies with, "I know she can't be both, Clara, but I *know* she's a Healer . . . well, they were wrong. She doesn't belong here."

Chris looks over Clara's shoulder at me. His eyes are narrowed and his jaw clenched. Why would my presence tick him off so much? Why would he think I'm a Healer? Is he confusing me with someone else? Before turning and leaving my sight, he says to Clara, "I don't like this one bit."

She reenters the room and forces a smile back onto her face. "Where were we?"

"What was that all about?" I try to sound innocent.

"Nothing. Let's get back to—"

"He thinks I'm a Healer. Why?"

"I'm not sure. I *know* you are a Runner. The Seer foresaw your powers emerging, I witnessed your speed, and *no one* holds more than one cosmic power."

I can tell by her facial expression that Chris's reaction bothers her.

She takes a deep breath and says, "You overheard information here that needs to be kept quiet or else widespread panic could erupt. Yes, we are missing three of our Runners, but we don't have enough details to make an announcement yet. I need to ask you to keep this quiet. Will you, please?"

"Yes, of course."

A thought comes to me. "Clara, why don't you ask your Seer what's going on?"

"Seers' powers are quite limited," she replies. "They can only view the future four weeks out. If something is going to happen sooner, they can't envision it. They can only spot the changes to the future roughly a month ahead. The problem is, there seems to be a cloudiness or fog where the future of our clan is concerned. Our Seer is unable to interpret our Runners' futures. He's communicated with his clan, who are also confused by the mysteriousness of the situation."

How frustrating would it be to have that kind of power and not be able to see things sooner? The Seers got the bad end of the cosmic-powers deal, in my opinion. I stop myself. Now I'm thinking as if this is all possible.

Clara's phone rings, interrupting our conversation. "Excuse me, Calli."

I sit back on the cushy couch while she speaks on the phone. So many thoughts are running through my mind. The new information from Clara spins wildly through my brain, bringing everything I've known and learned into question. I haven't witnessed anyone else exhibiting any significant power. Only the power within my own body helps confirm her information. Even without more evidence, the appearance of Chris and hearing of his investigation into the missing Runners has helped my mind begin to accept the reality of this new world.

Chris speaks of me as if he already knows me. I don't remember ever meeting him, and I know I wouldn't have forgotten *that!* Thinking back on the last look he gave me before leaving makes me slightly disheartened. Oh well, he's way out of my league anyway. Plus, he's older, in his twenties, and most likely has a significant other, what with all the beautiful girls floating around here.

"Calli, I need to take this call," Clara whispers, with her hand covering the phone. "Go on up to your room and rest. I'll come get you later."

"All right." I get up and leave her office and head to the main staircase, debating whether or not to call my parents later.

The daylight shining through the skylights in the vaulted ceiling illuminates the ornate, precision-crafted, beautifully polished woodwork of the main entryway and causes me to think of my father. He loves this type of architecture and would love to see it. I climb the large wooden staircase as a few girls head down in my direction. They pay me no attention, and that's fine by me. After visiting the ladies' room, I go back to my bedroom and find Beth studying at the desk.

"Got your head messed up, didn't you?"

Her smug question reveals she knows exactly what I've been through in Clara's office. I have to suppose every individual here has gone through the same emotional roller-coaster I experienced a moment ago. I nod at Beth and lie down on my bed.

"Well, don't go feelin' all sorry for yourself. No one here will waste any time feelin' sorry for you either. There are no pity-parties in the Runners' Clan Compound."

"What are you, the head cheerleader for team depression?"

Beth grunts some curse words and leaves the room. Even though she left, her attitude lingers. I recall Beth's words from the night before. She called me a human, then a muck. With the new insane information I've learned, I understand that to be called a human is worse than a muck. Even though a muck is a slow Runner, at least they have a cosmic power.

I close my eyes and try to imagine my life back in Ohio, but I can't get Chris Harding's face out of my head. I think about his perfect features and his determined scowl as he tried to convince Ms. Winter I was a Healer and not a Runner.

Information overload threatens to short-circuit my mind.

Chapter 3 – Shadow Demons

"Calli, wake up." Clara's voice pulls me out of my sleep. "It's time for lunch, after which we'll pick back up in my office." She turns and leaves the room.

I rub my eyes with my palms, and realize I've slept for three hours. I stand and walk over to Beth's full-length mirror to make sure no unruly hairs are standing straight up on my head. I study the face looking back at me in the mirror and run my fingers through my short hair to fluff it a little. Even though I don't look any different on the outside—my green eyes are the same, I still have the same high cheekbones, straight nose, and normal-sized ears—on the inside I have changed dramatically. According to Clara, I have superhuman powers.

I feel an unusual need to enhance my physical attributes before going down to lunch. I dig through my bags and pull out the makeup case buried at the bottom. I apply a bit of mascara to my lashes, then stop. *What am I doing?* I have an epiphany. No amount of makeup will improve the cranky attitudes and opinions of the other Runners. If there's any respect to be earned, I want it to come from my achievements, not my looks.

I head downstairs and take my place at the end of the lunch line, behind two guys. They glance over their shoulders at me, frown, and turn forward. Up ahead, several girls chat quietly, and I read their lips. They are talking about me. One says I lit into Beth as soon as our bedroom door shut, and the other says Beth told her I was bitterly cruel with my words and was probably a spy. They both make eye contact with me and then turn away, giggling. Idiotic female jocks.

A different girl, who's standing nearby, talks to her friend about Chris. She's infatuated with him because he touched her arm. The other girl informs the first that Chris's heart is already taken. He said so himself, she says. The first girl refuses to accept this information and admits to actively pursuing his attentions.

Oh, brother! This is the kind of stuff I can live without!

A group of guys, with Chris in the lead, enters the dining hall in a tight V formation like a flock of geese. A boy next to him whispers in his ear and points in my direction. Chris looks at me as he passes. His stare is deeper than innocent eye-to-eye contact. I can't tell if he's curious or upset, but his lingering gaze tells me something's on his mind. I smile at him hoping he might smile back, but instead he diverts his gaze back to the food line. His group inserts itself into the front of the line, and nobody seems to mind. I wonder what the point is of having a line if there's no order to it.

On second thought, I would let him cut in front of me. I'll admit, being the girl that I am, I'm willing to recognize undeniable attractiveness, even if it belongs to a jock. The fact his heart is already taken, like that other girl said, means I can look all I want.

The lunch menu includes some kind of disgusting cold soup—which could be mistaken for raw sewage—more fruits and vegetables, and broiled fish. I hate fish. What I wouldn't do for some sandwiches or a hamburger or fries—or ranch dip for that matter. The only dip available is hummus. Yuck!

"You'd better get the soup," a male voice says behind me. "It's called Muck Soup, and they made it just for *you.*"

"Because I'm a muck?" I answer without turning around.

"Bingo."

"Be careful, or I might start thinking you care." I glance over my shoulder to find the guy I ran into last night.

"The soup is made from enchanted herbs and energy-boosting vegetables. You should eat it because it helps you run faster—and because it's good."

"Are you sure? It looks like . . . muck."

"Exactly," he says with a diabolical sneer.

An equally good-looking, dark-haired guy smacks his arm, "Hey, Justin, you're not supposed to be talking to the newbie."

"Shut up, Will!" Justin looks at me once more and walks away with Will.

I accept my serving of muck soup and take my barely-filled tray to the table with the younger kids. They all stop talking as I sit down, and some of them turn around to see if they can move to another table.

I angle my head slightly to the left and see Beth, Justin, Will, and some other girl sitting at a nearby table, laughing—probably at something to do with me. Beth catches my eye and the smile falls from her face.

At a table to the right sits the flawless exemplar of manliness, Chris, who I can only assume is the best of the best, the Runners' king, the top dog. He's listening to the conversations at his table. I admire his stunning profile, and feel an incredibly strong attraction to him. His head turns in my direction, with his gaze coming to a halt when our eyes meet. His neutral expression turns to a grimace and he shakes his head a fraction of an inch. I don't know if his head-shake is meant for me or if he's responding to the table conversation. He redirects his gaze to the guy sitting across from him.

The others must have noticed his attitude change because a couple of them look over at me. One guy turns all the way around in his chair to find me. Their expressions are unmistakably negative.

My heart thuds in my chest. I look away so I don't have to feel their disapproval.

Why are all jocks such jerks? I've never been one to like the arrogant athletic type, and that's too bad for me because I am now surrounded by both female and male jocks.

The look on Chris's face, the whispers of other Runners, and Beth's constant icy stare sparks something inside me—a rebellious burst of energy. Beth warned me not to show off at the time trials, but I say to hell with her and all these egotistical jocks! I'm not scum! I'm a damn fast athlete, and everyone will find out tomorrow morning. They all hate me anyway. Why not bask in the glory of earning their hatred? I'll shake everything up and sit back and watch as they scramble to normalize.

After lunch, I head to Clara's office and she then ushers me down the hall for medical testing. Clara introduces me to Suki Kimura, yet another beautiful woman with dark brown hair and flawless skin.

Ms. Kimura explains the procedures I'm about to go through will take roughly three hours and are standard. Everyone undergoes them, she says. She draws my blood, x-rays me, hooks me up to all kinds of monitors, and places electrodes on my scalp to make sure I have a brain.

Good to get confirmation.

Clara moves me to another room. She attaches wires and electrodes to my chest and plugs them into a machine, then she flips a switch. A shrill noise echoes around the room and the thumping of my heart sounds as if it has been hooked up to a rock band's bass system. Startled, Clara jumps, then stumbles quickly to pull the wires and flip the switches off.

The door opens, and a middle-aged adult male with a name tag identifying him as Mr. Evans hurries over to Clara and shouts, "What did you do, hook a human up to the machine?" His eyes travel to mine and back to hers.

Ms. Kimura pushes her petite frame past Clara. "Clara, did you forget how to run the machine? Here, let me help." She proceeds to do the exact same thing Clara had already done. Again, terrible screeching and super loud thumping and swooshing sounds fill the room before Ms. Kimura unhooks the cords. "Well, clearly we have some damaged equipment. Bring her into my office and I'll evaluate her."

"I don't think that will be necessary," Clara says calmly. "She passed the rest of the exam. We'll address the heart evaluation later. Calli, come with me."

She ushers me out into the hall. We walk in the direction of her office.

"What was that all about?" I ask.

"I don't know. The machine worked fine last week."

Another woman approaches us. She looks to be older than anyone else. She says to Clara, "A group of Readers are here to see you. They say it's urgent."

"Thank you, Abby." Clara turns to me. "I'm sorry Calli, I must excuse myself. Go outside and get some fresh air. I'll find you later."

"Sure," I reply.

I could easily spy through her glass door to investigate what is going on, but I resist the urge to eavesdrop and head outside.

Ah, the outdoors of the Big Sky State. A spectacular view of the snow-tipped Rocky Mountains encompasses the giant compound/school/hotel/freak-show. I wander around the perimeter of the building and find some basketball courts and a large manicured lawn. Several teams of boys and girls spar off on the courts. Far off, near the tree line, I see a row of four small cabins with manicured lawns and trimmed bushes. They remind me of the ones at summer camp where the counselors slept.

I continue my walk around the backside of the compound, noting many exterior doors on the ground level and a large veranda on the second floor. Way down at the opposite end I find an indoor swimming pool. I didn't even know there was a pool. Cool.

I round the final corner and run smack dab into Chris. My abrupt appearance startles him, because he reaches out and takes hold of my arms to steady himself. I know he doesn't recognize who he's holding because I witness the realization hitting his brain with a boom. He lets go of my arms as if I'm contaminated with the deadly Hantavirus.

"Why are you *here?*" He clears his throat. "I mean, shouldn't you be with Clara?" he asks me with unjustified irritation.

"She's meeting with the Mind-Readers. They arrived a little while ago. I guess they have urgent business."

He opens his mouth to say something, but nothing comes out. Instead, he stares into my eyes for a few seconds, then looks away and steps around me.

"Talk to you later, Calli," I mutter under my breath as I rub my arms where Chris touched them. Oh great, now I'm like the ditzy girl in the lunch line, all goo-goo over a simple touch. His scent hangs in the air, and I can't help but take a deep breath. Regardless of anything else, his smell is darn near irresistible. His confused expression, however, makes me wonder if he wants to accept me into the clan or kick me out.

I make my way back into the building and up to my room, paying close attention to my surroundings to avoid running into anyone else. I'll wait for Clara to come get me.

Clara never came to my room.

However, Ms. Wood visited and told me to wear something nice tonight. Apparently, when visitors join the clan for dinner, we dress up and eat in the formal dining hall on the second floor. After she left my room, I heard her continue down the hall, giving the same message at each door, as well as a reminder to remember their manners. I wonder if that means being nicer to newbies. Probably not.

My seat at the little-kid table gives me a view of the entire dining hall and its occupants. I stick out like a sore thumb, being sixteen and sitting among kids whose voices haven't even begun to change. I feel as if I could be their babysitter.

As much as I stand out, the Mind-Readers stand out more. They look like a couple of pigeons amongst a flock of swans. I find it amusing how the adult Runners are hesitant to sit too close to the Readers, and they seem to not make eye contact with them either. Perhaps they're more like chickens than swans.

I glance around and discover Chris is staring at me. This time, he averts his gaze and continues talking to his friends. At the table next to Chris sits Beth, Justin, and

Will. I've seen Justin a couple of times since last night. Each time he sees me he mutters the four-letter M word. I ignore him. I've come to the conclusion Beth and Justin are an item.

My attention is pulled away to the main doors where food carts are being wheeled into the dining hall. Instead of the cafeteria-style lunch line, servers bring us our meals— but the food selection isn't any different. Nuts, nuts, and more nuts, plus fruits, vegetables, and fish. The Mind-Readers merely push their food around on their plates. They probably don't eat foods like these at their compound, if they have a compound.

I catch Chris looking at me on several occasions throughout dinner, and it makes me extremely uncomfortable. I wonder if he can see my cheeks heat up. *Hopefully not.* But a couple of times I peek in his direction and see him talking and laughing with his companions. Their topics of discussions don't include me, for once, but are about something funny that happened out on the basketball court earlier in the afternoon. Will makes a hand motion of something hitting his face, probably a ball, and the table bursts into laughter. Chris smiles a little, but he seems too distracted by his own thoughts to laugh aloud like his friends.

"May I have everyone's attention?" Clara stands and speaks loudly. "As some of you are aware already, three of our comrades are missing. Dirk, John, and Macey never reached their delivery destination three days ago. Our guests here tonight bring word of three of their own missing clan members, and the Seers and Healers are also missing three."

Alarmed and worried murmurs echo through the crowd and begin to grow in volume.

"We've yet to receive a ransom request and have not been given an explanation as to their whereabouts, but we will continue to investigate until we find them and bring everyone home. Please continue to use extreme caution when out of doors, and if you pick up on any suspicious activity, report it at once. Thank you."

The kids at my table start talking to each other, excluding me from their conversation, of course, but I sit and listen to them and gather as much information as possible.

"It's got to be the Death Clan behind this," one girl says.

"No, it's the CIA. They've been staked out, spying on us. They even have insiders here at the compound," another girl says.

A boy to my right exclaims, "You're crazy! Our Seer or Mind-Reader would have rooted out a spy."

"Not if the spy had really good blocking abilities," the first girl spits back at him.

Another boy, sitting across the table from me, points his finger at me and says, "Maybe she's the spy."

They all turn and look in my direction. "What?" I laugh. "Maybe all of *you* are the spies."

That gets them going. The bickering and name calling begins and grows rapidly until Clara has to come to our table and put a halt to the commotion. I can't help but laugh—until I raise my head and find Chris glancing in my direction again. *What is his problem?* I wish I knew.

"Please excuse me," I say. Not that anyone cares I'm leaving. I walk out to the floodlight-lit veranda. The sun is still low in the sky.

Beth comes out behind me and closes the door behind her. "Calli, you better not do anything stupid at the time trials tomorrow."

"Or what? You'll make my life even *more* miserable and make sure everyone talks bad about me behind my back? Oh, wait, I remember, you'll beat me up."

Her tone takes on a threatening edge. "This new assignment is most likely related to our missing friends, and if you go and beat out the fastest, you'll be placed on the team. You don't know crap about our world, so don't go screwing it up by being a showoff!"

I don't answer her. I just turn my back and wait until the door closes. The cool night air, along with the pure and fresh smell of the pine trees and cut grass, revitalizes my senses. Four adults, probably tutors or hired clan members, walk across the lawn to the four cabins. I turn back to the dining room, where almost everyone has filed out, except Chris. He stays in his chair, watching me.

Clara comes out to the veranda. "Are you okay, Calli?"

"As good as I can be, I suppose. When will you show me the Shadows?"

"Not for a couple more hours. The sun has to go all the way down before the Demons come out."

"Sounds like a bad dream."

"You don't know how right you are. Meet me in my office after dark, and bring the shirt you were wearing earlier."

◇ ◇ ◇

I walk the well-lit deserted hallways down to Clara's office. Her door is closed, so I peer around the edge of the glass window of the door. She sits at her desk, talking to someone on the phone and, unabashedly, I read her lips.

"I'm not comfortable with that. This will put our slowest in too much danger. Yes, he's right here, hold on." Clara extends the receiver toward what looks like an empty room. From out of my range of vision, Chris pops up and moves over to the desk. His back is to me as he speaks on the phone. Clara spots me through the glass and holds up a finger to indicate, "Wait a minute."

I move away from the door and rest my back against the wall. Soon the door opens and Chris walks out. He seems stressed. I look up at him and smile a little. His eyes lock onto mine for a second, then he turns and walks past me. I enter Clara's office as she pushes her arms into her extravagant coat.

"Calli, good—you remembered your shirt. Most kids forget and I have to send them back up to their rooms. Come with me."

I follow her out into the main foyer, where she turns and says, "It's vitally important for you to follow every direction I give you."

"I will."

We exit the front doors into the bright floodlights and crisp mountain air. She leads me toward what appears to be a toolshed at the edge of the property, where we stop beneath another floodlight.

"Calli, the Shadow Demons are found in absolute darkness after sunset. They are drawn to people with powers because they themselves once held powers. For some reason they are trapped in a suspended state of, well . . . hell. These lights are the only thing keeping us safe. Around the corner it's completely dark. That's where we'll find the Demons. Stay in the light," she admonishes, checking my face once more to be sure I'm taking her seriously.

We walk to the edge of the shed, keeping beneath the bright floodlight.

I peer into the darkness. "I can't see anything."

"Regardless, I know they are there. Many people with powers have been devoured by them. Now, I will demonstrate what happens if you wander into the shadows at night. Hand me your shirt."

I give my shirt to her and watch as she pulls out one of her own and wads the two together as if forming a snowball. She then tosses the wadded shirts into the shadows.

I gasp in terror at the sight of the unnaturally suspended shirts being shredded in mid air. The only thing I can hear is the woven cotton being ripped apart. The eerie sound reminds me of when my mother tore old sheets into rags. I stare in utter amazement as Clara's shirt is ripped into a small pile of confetti-sized pieces of cloth, which glide softly to the ground. My shirt has been torn into a few long strips and is already on the ground.

"What was that?" I cry out. "Was that a trick? What happened to our shirts?" No logical explanation can account for what I've just witnessed.

"Our scents on the shirts were enough to provoke the Shadow Demons to attack. Lesson number one: stay out of the shadows, or that will be the last thing you do. Oh, and that pile of shredded cloth is more than what would remain if they got their claws on you." She looks intently at me, appearing satisfied that I've gotten the message. "Let's get back inside."

She doesn't have to tell me twice.

Once inside the safety of her office, she begins to tell me more.

"A Runner's ability is the only power that surfaces during puberty, and is the only power-emergence a Seer can foresee. The other superhuman abilities can show up at any point in life and sometimes manifest slowly. We try to have a representative of the Runners' Clan present when a new member's power emerges. I was there for you. Other people with powers are not so fortunate, and aren't taken under someone's wing and taught about the Shadow Demons and how to avoid them. However, one consistent element with all people with powers is they are afraid of the dark. It's as if they can sense the danger awaiting them. Their instinctual hesitation actually saves their lives, but sometimes incapacitates the individual, leading to the development of nyctophobia—a severe fear of darkness. There are therapists, who are also people with powers, who help the patients by introducing them to their appropriate clan.

I think to myself for a moment, wondering about my mother. Many of her patients are deathly afraid of the dark. Wait! Does my mother know about the superpowers and Shadow Demons?

"But Calli, there's another reason I was present at your track meet. I was there to prevent you from being kidnapped."

"What? Kidnapped?"

"There's a splinter group that broke away from the Healers who call themselves Immortals, in reference to an ancient legend of clansmen who couldn't die. Almost everyone else refers to them as the Death Clan, due to the fact they can bring about your death merely through thought. Some call them the Death-by-Thoughts or DBTs. As a group, they constantly heal each other's infirmities, keeping each other alive longer than nature's laws allow. They can't heal themselves, the same as a Healer cannot heal himself, so they need to have another Death Clan member around to make sure if anything happens they will live on. As for bringing about the death of others, they have one major restriction to their abilities: they need to see you to be able to kill you."

"Are they really immortals?"

"That's a matter of perspective, I suppose. Most of their group is over two-hundred years old. Try not to confuse the definition of immortal with invincible. I think they could be killed if they were separated from one another. Well, if they didn't kill you first," she amends.

I ask, "Why would they want to kidnap me?"

"The fact is, the DBTs have a history of capturing emerging Runners and forcing them to be their slaves—to use the Runners' abilities as if their powers were their own. When another person with powers holds hands with a Runner, the running ability is passed on to the tethered person. We've lost more than a few clan members to the Death Clan and also to the Hunters."

"Hunters kidnap Runners too?" I ask. "Why don't Runners just run away from the Immortal-Death-Dudes or Hunters?"

"The captives are restrained to prevent escape, and are killed if they try to flee. Quite often they are threatened their loved ones will be harmed, so they stay put to save their families. You would obey, too, if you thought one wrong move would threaten your parents' lives. The Death Clan also kidnaps people from the other clans, using whatever emotional control they can find to keep them from fleeing."

I nod and a tight knot forms in my throat.

"We employ other people with powers, as do the other clans. We don't kidnap them and force them to do our bidding. Their abilities are respected and they're compensated for their help."

"So you were there at the track meet because I'd been 'seen' ahead of time?"

"Yes."

"You prevented me from being kidnapped and protected me from the Shadow Demons?"

She nods her head.

"Thanks for that."

Clara smiles.

I have to wonder how many times she receives thanks for the job she does. I change the subject. "Clara, what exactly do you do around here?"

Her perplexed expression tells me she doesn't understand the question.

"I mean, generally speaking, normal people get up and go to work, or go to school or something. Their lives revolve around jobs and schedules and events. But what do people with powers do?"

Clara sits all the way back in her chair and rests her head on the plush headrest. She takes a deep breath and exhales. "Well, they live life as they know it, the same as anyone else. You have described what normal life is to you, but what do the members of the aboriginal tribes of Australia do from day to day? How about the African tribal communities—what do they do? Consider the people in Thailand or China or Norway. What do they do every day? Are you following me, Calli? Your question is a matter of perspective. What's normal for you isn't normal for others."

"Oh." *Wow.* I've never thought about life from that perspective before. I guess I've never really looked outside my own narrow world. Caught up in my own life and viewpoint, as Clara so eloquently points out, my life naturally feels normal for *me*. I decide to be more aware of other human beings and their daily struggles. The discussion brings a different question to mind. I say, "What do you think the percentage is of normal humans to people with powers worldwide?"

"At present, it's estimated there are around one million people with superhuman abilities."

"That's a lot!"

"No, not really. With seven billion individuals populating the world, people with powers averages out to be only one in every seven-thousand. I believe seven thousand is around the population of your hometown. Imagine if you were the only person in your whole town with powers. Our clan is the only one that can keep an accurate count of new members because of the fact that Seers can foresee when someone's power will emerge. For whatever reason, we've seen stagnation in the number of new Runners over the last ten years. I fear we're on the decline. But that's beside the point."

I say, "Clara, you said you're a Runner. Do you ever go on assignments?"

"I don't run assignments anymore. There's still new blood coming into the clan, younger blood who can run the assignments. I chose to help at the compound. I'm an instructor and administrator along with the other adults. At some point you'll have to make the personal choice to step away from the elite group of Runners and either help here at the compound or return to the life you knew a few days ago, forever keeping your ability a secret." Her voice doesn't hold any enthusiasm.

I don't want to press what appears to be a sensitive topic for Clara, so I change the subject. "What does your husband do?" I ask.

"I'm not married."

"You're not? I've heard people call you Mrs. Winter—" The realization hits me that she must be a widow. Oh terrific! Open mouth, insert foot.

"I was married, but he discovered my ability and left. I keep the name because we never officially divorced. So, I guess I am technically married."

I pick up on her bitterness. "I'm sorry. It wasn't my place to ask."

"No, it's fine. I guess my advice would be that if you decide to get married, find someone with abilities in order to avoid heartache later. It's hard enough to stay married without the extra challenge of having powers."

"I bet. Marriage is a long way off for me, but I'll keep that in mind."

"Sometimes it's closer than you think, Calli. Many girls your age have already met the guy they will eventually marry."

"Well, I'm not the kind of girl who goes looking for guys, and they certainly don't come begging for me," I scoff at myself with a chuckle.

"I don't believe you. You're a beautiful girl, Calli. You'll be fighting off the boys with a bat, but I need to remind you that promiscuous behavior at the compound is not allowed."

"I can totally imagine myself smacking boys with a bat," I laugh, "but not because they're interested in me. And as far as promiscuous behavior goes, well, you don't need to worry about me."

"Good. Now I'd like to tell you what to expect tomorrow. Whenever we are given a delivery assignment, a leadership trio is selected to carry out the task. Time trials determine the fastest and the slowest of the clan, and then those two decide together who the third member of the team will be. My approval of the trio is needed. Often a team of protectors or running companions is selected to go with the trio if the mission is dangerous. There will be an accompanying team with this mission because of the fact our last trio came up missing. The fastest and slowest from tomorrow's competition will hand-pick the team. No breakfast will be served before the trials, and once the trial is completed, the selected team will be quickly outfitted and sent off."

I figure she's telling me this because she knows I will be the fastest and will be going on the assignment tomorrow. I appreciate the heads-up. "Clara," I say, "some of the others suspect this delivery is connected with the missing Runners. What do you think?"

"The timing is right. Anything's possible." She stands, giving me the cue our session is over for the night. "In the morning, dress in the workout clothing Stella will give you. The trial begins at eight o'clock sharp."

I stand as well.

"Calli, do you still want to go home?"

"Not at the moment."

"You'd better go on up to bed to get a full night's rest." She smiles knowingly.

Yep, she knows I will be on the delivery team. I leave her office and head straight up to my room. Beth is already asleep, fortunately, so I don't have to endure the torture of her attitude. Thank God.

Tomorrow will bring a new adventure my way. Like my parents encouraged me to do, I am going to go down this road and see where it takes me.

The next morning I awake to find Beth gone. I hurry and dress in my training outfit and look myself over in the mirror.

Movement out on the grounds catches my eye and I walk to the window to see a small gathering of adults out by the same toolshed Clara and I visited the night before. One of them wears similar clothing to mine, and upon closer inspection I recognize Chris.

The group talks as they look at the place where Clara threw our shirts. I can't tell what's being said until they begin to head back to the building.

I watch Clara's mouth as she says, ". . . and her speed is" —Clara turns to the side and I lose her conversation until she faces forward again— "than any I've seen." She moves out of sight.

My eyes move back to Chris, who still stands by the toolshed. He bends and picks up my shredded shirt, carefully folding the strips of cloth, and tucking them into his pocket before turning back toward the school.

Chapter 4 – Maetha and the Sanguine Diamond

The time trials are not what I expected. I guess I figured we'd run on an oval track with a starter's gun telling us when to leap forward, and a finish line showing us where to stop. It's not at all like I imagined.

The first event is an individual run through the trees to the top of a hill and back down. There is no trail or even an outlined course, only the simple instruction to run up and back. I'll be one of the last to go, so I'll use the opportunity to watch the others to see what they do.

I'm amazed to watch this display of agility and speed for the first time since arriving here. Runners are graceful and fluid in their movements, not to mention quick. However, I know I can run faster than the Runners I'm watching.

Beth is next in line. Ms. Kimura holds a stopwatch and gives the order to begin. Beth runs like a deer, gracefully bounding over fallen trees and weaving in between boulders and brush. Sometimes she jumps from tree trunk to tree trunk without her feet hitting the ground. She has cat-like grace and speed that's mesmerizing to watch. She reaches the top of the hill, having been out of sight for some of the run, and doesn't pause a second before turning around. When she runs back down the hill, she takes a different route than any of the others. I think she likes being different.

A few more Runners take their turns. Soon it will be Chris's turn. I notice his size and muscle development is more advanced than nearly every other male. His only contender in that department is Justin. However, the younger boys seem to be more agile simply because of their smaller frames and trim bodies.

Standing in front of me are a couple girls who are evidently smitten with Chris. They giggle every time he moves and they whisper comments that make me blush. After hearing some particularly inappropriate and disrespectful words and phrases, I clear my throat and say, "Do you mind?" They both turn and give me the stinkiest stink-eye, but at least they stop.

Chris starts his run up the hill. His moves are different than Beth's, naturally because of their gender difference, but also because of his muscle mass. His powerful legs take him over the ground Beth bounded over. I understand how this makes his time faster after hearing Coach Simms instruct the hurdle runners to just skim over the hurdles and get their feet back on the ground as soon as possible. I once heard him say, "Your strength is in your legs. Anytime you're in the air, you're slowing down. You don't have wings to propel you forward." Observing the difference between how Chris runs compared to Beth is proof enough the laws of physics are alive and well. I'll keep my feet on the ground as much as possible when I run the race.

When Chris completes his run, he jogs past me. He doesn't look at me when he runs by, but somehow I know he's quite aware I'm there.

Now it's my turn. I'm glad most of the Runners are gone so they won't witness my incredible speed. I'm determined to carve myself a niche in this group, no matter how much they end up hating me in the process. Ms.

Kimura tells me to go. I launch forward and swiftly bound over the first fallen tree, getting my feet back on the ground immediately. I want to run faster, but I can't because of how many trees and rocks I have to dodge. I wonder to myself how this is considered to be an effective way to test a Runner's speed.

Near the top of the hill, I come across a cliff about twenty feet high that I'll need to climb. This must be where I lost sight of the other Runners. I'm not sure exactly how to approach this obstacle, but my intuition tells me to avoid the cliff and run around it to the other side where Beth came down on her run. That's exactly what I do, and I feel I made a better choice than slowing down to climb.

When I reach the bottom of the hill, Ms Kimura says, "Very good, Calli."

I feel like I did well.

The next event resembles a military obstacle-course, complete with a string of tires and a climbing wall. I wonder if this is a speed test, or combat training? What difference does it make if we can swing from a rope? We are Runners, after all.

Three of us run the course together. I hurry through as fast as I can, keeping an eye on my opponents. They seem to be taking care to place their feet directly in the center of each tire and to make their movements rhythmic. I just want to win, and I do. Well, at least I place first in my group. I don't know how I performed overall.

The final race takes place on a dirt road that winds up through the mountains from the compound. We walk up the road for several miles and then prepare for the race back.

This is my moment to shine, to run as fast as my legs will take me, and blow their socks off, I think to myself. I catch Beth's eye as we are preparing to begin. She shakes her head as if to warn me not to win. *Yeah, right.* The starting gun sounds and I run as hard as I can . . . and yet I watch the backsides of everyone else get further and further ahead of me until I can't see them anymore. When I finally cross the finish line, they all cheer, or more like jeer. Some of them say I'm faster than any human, insulting me further.

One girl comes up to me with a genuine smile and pats me on the back. "Thanks, Calli," she says. "Now I'm not the slowest muck anymore. I won't have to go on the assignment."

What just happened? I shake my head in confusion. I ran so fast the trees blurred as they flew by. The skin on my face had been blown back by the g-force because I moved so rapidly. But I was the slowest! I certainly didn't hold myself back like Beth told me to do. No, I went into the race determined to kick everyone's butt. However, the only butt that got kicked was mine.

I feel crushed and humiliated. *I* am *a muck*, I think.

Clara comes over to me. At first I think she's going to chastise me for going so slow, but she congratulates me on my speed and instructs me to head to her office and wait there for her.

As I enter her office a few minutes later, I'm caught off guard to find Chris sitting there. Even after the exertion of the course, he still smells wonderful. He stands, seemingly nervous, when he sees me. I stop and take a step back and say, "Sorry, I didn't mean to—um, Clara told me to meet her here."

"Because you finished last," he states, then sits back down, his body language tight.

"Well, yeah, I guess." I sit down in a chair next to him to wait for Clara. My brain explodes with the realization: Clara *did* know I'd be going on the delivery, but as the slowest.

Chris must have placed first, and that's why he's here in Clara's office.

He confirms my thoughts by saying, "We're supposed to select a third for the assignment. I've chosen Justin Macintyre."

"Justin? Beth's boyfriend?" I cough out my response and turn halfway in my chair to face him. Of all the people in the clan, Chris and Justin seem to be the ones who have some problem with me. "Why?"

"I don't need your approval."

"You just said *we* have to choose the third," I point out. "*We* means both of us." I'm not in the mood to take his attitude.

He glares at me. "You don't know anything about what's going on here, Calli. You don't know the other guys like I do. You shouldn't even *be here* at all."

"Who peed in your Cheerios?" I mutter.

Ms. Winter enters the room, ending our conversation. "Have you two come to a decision on who'll be the third?"

"Justin will be the third." Chris glances at me as he informs her.

"Are you good with Justin, Calli?" Clara asks.

"I guess."

Chris pulls a piece of paper from his pocket and hands it to her. "Here's my list of the preferred twelve for the accompanying group." His tone is all business.

She looks over the list. "It's evident you've planned this out well, Chris. You have a good equal representation of different skill levels." She looks at me. "What do you think, Calli?" She passes the list to me.

I find this interesting, considering I still don't know most of the people in the compound as Chris has so arrogantly pointed out. The names all run together in my mind, except for Beth's—that name stands out real well. Near the bottom of the list, one name has been crossed out and another added. The crossed-out name is mine.

I hand the list back to Ms. Winter and say, "This list looks good to me, except for the fact Chris obviously didn't want me on the team. He scratched my name out."

Chris answers my retort before Ms. Winter can. "You came in last and that automatically put you in the trio. I *had* to add someone else."

So he originally wanted me on his team. The fact he'd already drawn up the list beforehand means he knew he'd be the fastest. That doesn't escape my attention. He also didn't think I'd finish last, so he was expecting me to be faster than a muck.

I'm not sure what to think about that, given his behavior towards me.

"All right, Chris," Clara says. "Alert everyone else and be ready to run in thirty minutes."

Chris stands and leaves the room in such haste I can't help but be offended. Not even a "see you later, Calli."

Clara turns to me and says, "Calli, don't worry about your speed. You'll get faster over time. Your powers are still developing."

"Clara, this doesn't make any sense. Why send me on a running assignment when there are so many others who could do this better? I'm so slow compared to them."

"Everyone starts out slow, Calli, and everyone starts out by going on an assignment. There's a reason for this procedure. What better way for you to learn how your new world operates?"

"But my slow speed could jeopardize the safety of the other Runners."

"We've always divided up the responsibility of assignments by using an equal representation of the fastest, the slowest, and an average Runner. This way, if a trio is ever overtaken and lost, the clan will still have members who can replace those who are lost—we can't afford a total wipeout. Our missing clan members right now are a prime example of this. Chris was already on a delivery when we received a second assignment, so we held another time trial and a different trio was selected: Dirk, John, and Macey."

Doesn't she realize she isn't giving me any comfort at all? "Do you think this assignment could end badly?" I ask.

"Every assignment is dangerous, Calli, this one no more than the next. I know you're worried about your speed, but your position in the trio is non-negotiable. You'll need to hold someone's hand to draw upon their speed for a while."

"What? Are you serious?"

"Of course I'm serious. Your participation in this assignment is non-negotiable. That's why we held the trial."

"No, not that part—you're saying I have to hold someone's hand when I run?"

"Yes, either Justin's or Chris's. They can both boost your speed."

Oh, brother. This just keeps on getting better and better!

"Here." Clara hands me Chris's list. "Learn the names of your teammates."

I soon find myself in a community changing room, similar to a locker room, with the six other girls on the list:

Beth Hammond, Shanika Williams, Ashley Bryant, Kayla Cooper, Lizbeth Morales, and Jessica Harper.

According to the list Chris created, our entire team, the guys included, ranges from age thirteen to twenty-three. I am shocked to learn two thirteen-year-old girls, Shanika and Ashley, are even allowed to go on the trip. Don't their parents have to give approval for such a thing? If they were at my school and about to go on a field trip, they would need a signed release form. Somehow I doubt that is the case here.

Shanika and Ashley look like they're close friends. They both have short, pixie-type haircuts, however Shanika is a brunette who looks to be part African-American and Ashley is a blonde with freckles. They aren't much smaller than everyone else, but it's obvious they are younger. Jessica is a stunning redhead. Her smooth complexion and green eyes complement her long curls. I think she's probably eighteen. Kayla is the girl from the lunch line who thinks Chris likes her. She has light brown hair and looks to be close to my age. Lizbeth is the oldest girl on the team at twenty-one. She's Hispanic with beautiful dark skin, brown eyes, and long black hair. Beth stands out like a sore thumb with her black hair and pale skin. I'm thinking she's a year older than me.

Clara and Ms. Wood bring in several piles of running clothing, all in a forest-green color. I figure there must be some wisdom behind this choice.

The running outfit is similar to the one I saw Chris wearing in Clara's office the day before. The fabric consists of a strange material that is kind of a cross between silk, gossamer, and finely spun steel. The outfit has virtually no weight and is designed to endure excessive friction and not wear out. The form-fitting design of the suit makes me extremely self-conscious. The cut fits the contours of my body like a glove fits a hand—a very thin, silky glove. My father wouldn't let me leave the house in this outfit—it's *that* scandalous. Clara explains the fabric keeps moisture off our bodies but also acts as a thermal insulator to keep us warm. I catch my reflection in the mirror, astonished at what I see. A different girl with an hourglass figure stares back at me.

Our specially-designed underclothing is made of the same material. Our bras fit tight, like sports bras, to prevent bouncing, yet don't flatten us down to nothing. The boxer-brief underwear ensures no snuggies will have to be pulled out. Sweet.

On the jacket, the front pouch has zippers designed to prevent accidental opening. Individual pockets inside the pouch allow space for personal items, such as Beth's black eyeliner, I think, smiling to myself, and additional hair bands for Lizbeth's and Jessica's long hair. A detachable hood folds neatly in one of the pockets, not taking up any more space than a folded dollar bill. On the back of the jacket, near the collar, another pouch contains an incredibly thin blanket, no thicker than plastic wrap. I assume this, too, will keep us warm if needed. Our running shoes are a slipper-type design with a firm bottom. They remind me of high-tech ballet slippers. Socks don't seem necessary with these shoes.

We will each carry our own four-day supply of food, consisting of nothing more than four individually wrapped granola bars formulated to give us energy and fill our stomachs. Each bar has three pieces, one for breakfast, lunch, and dinner. The kind of granola bars I'm used to eating certainly wouldn't have lasted all day—I can eat four normal bars and still be hungry—but these are special. We will be able to obtain water from rivers and streams using a collapsible cup, and we can purify the water using a small bag of purification tablets. Each tablet is the size of the head of a pin.

The basic idea here is to take only the bare necessities without adding extra weight or wind resistance. Therefore, no jewelry, wallets, or unnecessary items are allowed. Clara also emphasizes there are to be absolutely no phone calls except to communicate with the other team members in adjacent rooms once we are in hotel rooms.

Clara explains further, and I feel this is for my benefit more than anyone else's, "Remember, once this party leaves here, you'll be on your own. The leadership trio will make the decisions for sleeping accommodations every night. No reservations have been made in advance for any motel, since that would mark your trail if anyone is watching the clan's credit card transactions. You may find, at some point, many of you could be crammed into the same room due to limited room availability. If that happens, I expect maturity and consideration from everyone, and no inappropriate conduct."

A few girls giggle, while others groan. At least that part of my new world is normal.

Clara continues. "There have been missions in the past where hotel rooms were unavailable, and quick decisions had to be made about where to stay for the night. I expect you to act without question if you find yourselves in such a situation. Chris has the responsibility on his shoulders to make sure the Runners are safe at all times. Do exactly as he says. Am I understood?"

A collective "Yes ma'am" echoes throughout the room.

Clara begins talking with each individual girl, inspecting and approving what they've placed in their pouches. A few personal items don't pass inspection. I watch the other girls intermingle with one another, and wonder if they will ever include me. Beth is the only one who will even speak to me at this point, and that isn't saying much.

The door opens, and I swear fog rolls in to dramatize the entrance of the eight guys. I'm pretty sure they walk in slow motion with a spotlight trained on Chris—at least that's how my eyes see them. They wear similar dark green running suits which enhance their physical shapes even more than seems humanly possible, with Chris winning grand prize in my book.

Chris is the oldest of the team at twenty-three, according to the giggling girls. It's only appropriate he's the leader, I suppose. The youngest boy on the list is a fourteen-year-old named Jonas Flemming. He's easy to spot in the group because he's the shortest. He has dark hair that's trimmed short like most of the other guys. The next oldest is Yang Chan. He's fifteen with thick, black hair, and still has a smaller, lighter, more agile frame. I think he's Chinese. Ricky Chavez and Michael Fields are my age. Ricky is Hispanic with dark features and black hair. He's one of the few Runners who smiles often. Michael looks like a California surfer with blond hair and tan skin. Justin and Will Malone are like the dynamic duo: dark hair, dark, deep-set eyes, and sharp jaw lines . . . and rude to the core. I've heard Beth say they are eighteen. Then there's Tyler Beck. He's nineteen and on the whiney side, in my opinion. His overgrown blond hair is always in his eyes, well, except for when he's running.

My assessment of the guys comes to a halt when I make eye contact with Chris. My heart rate jumps a notch. I think about how, only a few days ago, I was nothing but a normal girl at a regular high school with only a couple of semi-good-looking guys there. None of them could hold a candle to Chris's looks or . . . "assets."

Suz would kill to be in my position.

My position. What's my position? Oh, yeah, that's right, slowest muck around, the loser who will be the tag-along and slow everyone else down on this assignment.

As the boys near, I watch Chris's expression change, and the look isn't attractive. I feel like I represent failure in his eyes. After losing the time trials this morning, I feel completely inadequate around him. I hope my day will end on a different note. It can't get much worse.

"Sir, the Runners are here." The secretary announces our arrival over the intercom.

The forty-five-minute run to the office complex was rather pleasant. I held hands with Chris, but only after Ms. Winter insisted he cooperate. Humiliated, I had assured him I didn't have any diseases and have had all my shots. He scrutinized me with his intense blue eyes, then reluctantly took my hand. I concluded he'd rather have surgery without anesthesia than touch any part of me.

We flew, or at least it seemed like we did, through the forest and over the lakes. Clara was right. When you run so fast you don't sink in water, you can go anywhere. The special shoes apparently have water displacement properties that help us stay on top of the surface as long as we don't slow down.

Chris's running power is much more intense than mine. I actually found myself having fun running hand-in-hand with him. What made the journey the most pleasant was the fact I couldn't talk or read lips while running. I didn't hear any snide remarks or degrading comments as we wove our way toward the destination with the other members of our team following closely behind.

When we arrived at the office complex, the rest of the team waited outside while we entered the building to receive the package. The secretary seated us in the foyer.

I look at Chris and Justin as they sit across from me in uncomfortable contemporary-style armchairs in the foyer. Chris fidgets, shifting side to side. Justin has his arms stretched out on the armrests and his feet spread apart. He stares back at me. A short coffee table covered with magazines sets in front of us. I glance down and notice the magazines are normal ones, the type I would have read only last week. The sign on the door says, "Harold Bates, Master Gemologist." I deduce from the kind of reading material set out in the waiting area Mr. Bates is a normal guy without powers.

The secretary at the front desk is busy filing her long and elegantly-colored nails. The sound reminds me of Velcro being pulled apart over and over. She is pretty, well put together, and probably close to fifty years old. If only everyone's appearance could be as favorable when they reach her age, I think.

"Send in the fastest," a male voice booms over the speaker at the secretary's desk.

She glances in our direction. Chris stands and walks gracefully to the door and goes in.

I feel a whoosh of air and turn my head to find the secretary standing beside me.

Before I can even voice my amazement at her speed, she says to Justin, "Your task, Justin, is to deliver the Sanguine Diamond to the Death Clan." She extends her hands, cupped together. They hold what looks like a huge diamond, about the size of a small orange. "They have hostages from every clan, and this stone is what they've demanded as payment to gain the hostages' release. This must be delivered by the very best of the Runners' Clan."

Justin fidgets in his chair.

She thrusts her hands a little closer to him, reaching over the coffee table. "You must take this, Justin."

"No!" He presses his back into the chair. "I'm not the best Runner. Chris is."

"You know he's not," she insists.

"He's the fastest."

"He's not."

"What makes you think that?" Justin asks. The flash of trepidation in Justin's eyes makes me wonder what's behind his question. Is he asking, "Why are you assuming I'm the fastest?" or, "How did you know?"

"Will you carry the diamond, Justin?" she presses.

"No!" He barks his answer and looks toward the door Chris entered a moment ago.

The secretary turns to me. "Will you carry the diamond, Calli?"

Justin's head snaps back to me, as if he is torn between wishing Chris would come out and take the lead position, or making sure I don't end up with the valuable stone.

I cough and sputter my protest, while Justin's eyes bore holes through me. "I'm definitely not the best," I say, "in fact, far from it." *And who told her our names?*

"Being the fastest doesn't mean you're necessarily the best." She grabs a chair and pulls it close to me, then sits.

"Are you going to tell me being the slowest is?" I ask.

"Will you be the carrier of this diamond?"

"I don't—"

Justin points at me in outrage. "She can't. Look at her! She's a muck!"

"Silence." The woman flicks her finger toward him and he seems to freeze in place and shuts right up. Then she turns to me. "Calli, you're here for a reason. You're different from the others, and you're the one who must carry the stone."

"Why not Chris?"

"He's not to be trusted."

"Justin?"

"Same."

"Me? Surely one of the Runners outside would be better."

"No, this task will be carried out by you or no one. I've watched you for some time now, and you are the carrier."

"Then why did you make the offer to Justin first?"

"I wanted you to witness his inner weaknesses, his insecurity and doubt. Remember this moment in the days to follow, and never forget that, yes, he's faster than you, but you're stronger than he is in more ways than one."

"What do you mean you've watched me for some time? Why would a secretary for a gemologist be watching me?"

"I'm not Harold's regular secretary. I'm giving this diamond to you, Calli." She hands me the magnificent diamond. "You'll understand everything in due time," she says with a sly smile. "Take a long look, child. You won't lay eyes on this diamond again until it's delivered."

Cupping my hands around the stone, I reverently study the intense fire of the facets as they reflect the light. A delicious smoky aroma drifts to my nose. The diamond actually has an odor—I'd never thought of a diamond having a smell. On one of the facets, I see a word etched near the bottom: Sanguine.

"What does 'Sanguine' mean?" I ask.

"Don't you sense what it means?" she says, looking deep into my eyes.

I feel so many things racing through my body: hope, optimism, certainty, awareness, strength, and power. I meet her eyes, and my mind unexpectedly opens up and my senses numb as if I'm falling into a dream. A swirl of mist clouds my vision, and then a scene slowly emerges.

I see an expansive clearing or meadow in a forest. Large tents similar to what might be used for a wedding reception are set up near the surrounding tree line. Several hundred people stand near the tents. In the center of the clearing, a mound of stones creates a table. I see myself, Chris, and Justin standing next to the table on one side, and three figures dressed in white robes standing on the other side. My mind recognizes the figures as Death Clan members, even though I've never seen them before. I see myself present the diamond to the three men, and the hostages are brought out from inside the Death Clan's tent. The group of Runners standing near the Runners' tent whisper words that indicate they view me as their leader and that they have absolute respect for me. Another swirl of mist passes by and the vision switches to a scene of destruction. The Death Clan members all wither away, crumbling to nothing. Dead. An enormous glittering circle comes down out of the sky, encircling the clearing and all of the occupants. Outside the giant shining ring, the woman who gave me the diamond speaks strange words and waves her hands high above me. I shake myself and pull out of the trance.

The woman smiles as I blink to refresh my eyes. Unbelievably, I enter her mind and hear her say, *You're protected, Calli. Your mind cannot be entered by anyone, and this vision is now sealed by a circle of light. No other Seer will envision this, nor will they be privy to any additional visions you may have on the subject so long as you never pull the diamond out of this pouch, lest the spells protecting it be broken.*

77

She slips the diamond into a leather pouch and pulls the strings together, sealing it tight. My mind closes and the aroma of the diamond disappears. She chants some words over the small bag and hands it to me.

"Do not let anyone touch this pouch. No one can hold this except you."

I place the bag inside my jacket pocket and close the zipper. This seems a rather precarious place to put something so priceless, but I trust in the protection she's placed upon the stone, upon me.

I don't know how to explain the complete sense of knowledge and trust I now possess. Prior to a couple days ago, if someone had told me I would soon be seeing the future and reading minds, I would have laughed in their face. But after experiencing these events firsthand, I have no doubts whatsoever. The only example I can liken this to would be someone who believes in the existence of a supreme being, versus someone who actually meets and shakes hands with the god in question. It's one thing to have faith and believe. It's entirely different to actually meet the deity.

Is this woman a goddess? No, I don't think so. But in my mind she represents everything I haven't allowed myself to believe in—magic and metaphysical powers.

Even with this firsthand knowledge and full understanding, I still wonder if this is all a dream. Well, it's a pretty good dream, if that's the case.

She says, "You've seen the future as it can become, now make it so. If the diamond is not delivered, your vision will be nullified." She stands and replaces the chair she's been sitting on.

"Wait! What do I do?" Panic races through my body. "I don't know anything about this world."

"You already possess everything you'll need. Follow your leader, follow your instincts, and never tell a soul you carry the Sanguine Diamond. You'll know when the time is right to disclose that it's in your possession."

She walks around the table to Justin, who has been staring at us the whole time with his mouth hanging open. She places her fingertips on his forehead, and says, "You will forget all you've seen and overheard concerning the Sanguine Diamond and Calli." She gently pushes his head back and lets go, walking away as Justin comes back to his senses.

The door to the office opens, and an older gentleman invites the two of us inside. Justin shakes his head and rubs his eyes as he stands. I watch him to see if he shows any signs of recognition of what has just happened, but he appears oblivious.

As I stand to walk into the office, I glance down at my pouch, wondering if the diamond makes a bulge in my skintight jacket. I feel the diamond resting against my stomach, but my jacket doesn't protrude at all. Interesting.

The man introduces himself as Harold Bates, master gem cutter. Then he starts in on his explanation of the task at hand. "One of my gems needs to be delivered to the Death Clan, and I cannot trust this to the standard delivery companies. This particular stone is a diamond and it's the ransom the Death Clan has requested for the release of their hostages."

I glance over at the two guys, wondering if Justin remembers what just happened out in the foyer. I'm also curious about what Mr. Bates and Chris discussed in private.

Harold Bates continues. "The rough diamond was found in the center of a crater formed by an explosion of some kind. Members from all clans died in the blast, and somehow their respective powers collected inside this stone. The diamond was brought to me by a female ambassador to the Death Clan. I was ordered to cut it into a round, brilliant stone. She instructed me to hire the Runners to deliver the finished product using this box." He holds up a small black metal box with a hinged lid. "As I worked with the diamond, I felt an incredible amount of powers racing through my body every time I lowered the stone to the cutting wheel. I normally have no special powers myself, but all sorts of powers surged through me while I handled the diamond. I even experimented with them a bit. I am familiar with the cosmic abilities—I think that's why the Death Clan chose me to cut the stone."

Harold opens the black box. Inside, a diamond identical to the one in my pocket rests on a black velvet cushion.

Why are there two diamonds? One must be a decoy. But which one is real? The one in my pocket, or the one held by the diamond-cutting master?

I already know the answer.

I remember the woman's instructions that I should not tell or show the stone to anyone, so I keep my mouth shut. Justin seems to have no memory of the stone, and it dawns on me at that moment what must have taken place in the waiting room. The woman must be a witch, and she bewitched Justin's mind to make him forget. She'd cast spells on my mind too, both for protection and strength.

I realize I have delved deeper into the woman's mind than I first thought. It's as if I'd been inside her skin. I know her name: Maetha. I know, too, that she is indeed a well-known witch. Clara had warned me about dealing with witches, however I don't feel the vision I saw when I held the diamond was something evil.

Maetha's mind continues to convey messages to me. The experience is like sitting in front of a giant Jumbotron screen, watching her speak to me, while a bunch of other little screens show assorted memories from Maetha's past.

One of those memories is of my mother.

I see Maetha watching my mother when she was a young girl. My mother was once considered for carrying out this mission, but things weren't completely lined for success.

After my birth, Maetha started watching me as well. She did something to me that fateful day at the track meet so I'd be recognized by Clara and be brought to the compound. I'd be fast enough to be spotted, but slow enough to be the weakest member of the team, ensuring I'd meet with Harold Bates, giving Maetha the opportunity to secretly give me the real diamond. It was *Maetha's* voice that had sounded inside my head telling me to leave the track meet. I'm relieved to learn I'm not going crazy.

So, now I know I'm only a human—an enchanted human. What a letdown! Yet not much of a surprise.

I see another memory from Maetha's mind of when she cast spells on my parents' minds. That explains why they hadn't pitched a fit about me going away to Montana. Their minds were being controlled.

"Do you want to see the diamond?" Chris pulls me out of my thoughts, his tone nicer than usual. Apparently they are taking turns holding the black box and examining the simulated diamond, inspecting what they think is a masterpiece.

"Be careful not to touch the diamond," Mr. Bates says. "The Death Clan's ambassador said the cut diamond would be deadly to people with powers. I don't know if that's correct, but I don't think you want to be the first to find out."

81

I take the box from Chris and admire the diamond. To me, nothing feels special about this one. In fact, the stone looks more like cut glass than a real diamond. It has the same dimensions and inscription on the bottom, but it's obviously a fake. I hand the box to Mr. Bates.

He accepts it, closes the lid, and leans forward in his chair. "This delivery mission will be dangerous. This stone is magical and legendary. Not only will you be at risk of being ambushed by those who want to prevent the Death Clan from harnessing the powers within, you'll be sought by those who want the stone for themselves. Through it all, you'll need to keep your trio together. If all three of you are not present when the package is delivered, the Death Clan may suspect you are trying to pass them a counterfeit diamond and the hostages will not be released." His gaze rests on me with this last statement.

Chris asks, "Why would they think we'd be giving them a fake?"

"The Sanguine Diamond possesses unimaginable powers," Mr. Bates replies, "and the idea someone might try to steal the diamond is perfectly plausible. Your clan is respectable and reliable, and your reputation as a whole is clean. Everyone knows this. But this is an assignment like no other, and the Death Clan is aware of the temptation inherent in this delivery."

"So how do we convince them it's not a counterfeit?" Justin asks.

"By simply remaining together as a trio, the three of you are witnesses to this moment. Sometimes, the weakest can be the strongest. Keeping your trio together will help convince them of the diamond's authenticity."

His random inserted statement, "the weakest can be the strongest," causes my heart to pound in my chest. He must be in on the witch's plan. Neither one of them trusts these boys. Should I be suspicious as well? I decide to be careful with my trust account.

Justin asks in his arrogant tone, "Why didn't the Death Clan just come pick the diamond up themselves?"

I can't focus on what Mr. Bates says because my head fills with the real reason extracted from the wealth of information downloaded from Maetha's mind.

A wizard—appropriately named Merlin—brought the uncut diamond to the Death Clan in exchange for their healing services for a dying friend. He told them the diamond held all the powers of the clans, and if extracted correctly they could become the most powerful group on earth.

The Death Clan's Seers revealed that the future showed a round, brilliant-cut stone, cut by Harold Bates. They foresaw an enormous gathering in the forest where members of all the clans would witness the trio of Runners delivering the diamond, and the ensuing transformation of the Death Clan into supreme beings. To ensure the cut stone would be returned in the way the Seers had foreseen, the Death Clan kidnapped members from each clan and are currently holding them hostage in exchange for delivery of the diamond.

I ponder the information swimming around inside my head. The diamond must be delivered to them by a regular human—me—because the Sanguine Diamond is lethal for any person with powers. Because I'm a regular human, I can handle the stone, wear it close to my body, and not die. This would also explain why Maetha was able to hold the diamond in her hands. She's a witch, not a person with powers, and Mr. Bates admitted he was powerless as well. The question is: why did Maetha try to give it to Justin if she knew it would kill him?

We complete our meeting with Mr. Bates and stand to leave. Chris inserts the black box containing the fake diamond into his front pouch and zips the pocket closed.

My thoughts connect with the diamond in my own front pouch, and a wave of warmth radiates through my body. The apprehension and humiliation I'd experienced when leaving the compound has dissipated. Instead, I am filled with a new confidence and feeling of enlightenment. The diamond seems to be causing this metamorphosis.

Leaving Mr. Bates' office, we walk toward the front doors. I'm hoping to see Maetha at the reception desk, but she's gone. We emerge from the building and meet up with the rest of the group.

Chris informs them of our delivery destination. "We are heading to the Death Clan in Canada."

An audible gasp is heard.

"The Death Clan? What's in the package?" Tyler asks.

Chris replies, "You know I can't tell you."

Tyler places his hands on his hips. "No one told me this assignment would involve the Death Clan. I think we should know exactly what we are risking our lives over. What's in the package?"

"Telling you would only put your life in more danger," Chris says. "I will tell you this, though, before we left the compound, Clara told me Dirk, John, and Macey are three of the many hostages being held by the Death Clan to ensure this package is delivered. Their lives are on the line more than yours, Tyler. Let's get moving."

Chris organizes the group to surround the three of us while we run. He says he and Justin will take turns carrying the diamond. I'm left out of the decision-making process, which doesn't sit right with me.

"Hey, I'm part of this trio, too."

Justin laughs. "You'll drop or lose it, muck," he says, focusing only on the package, not on any danger we might be in or whether or not I should have a say about the arrangements.

I start to say something in return, but Chris cuts through the argument. "Back off, Justin. Calli, you can carry the package when your speed increases."

Justin is now staring at me with a devilish grin on his face. "Well, muck, think you'll ever be as fast as me?"

I feel lighter than normal, like the way I felt at the track meet a few days ago, but better. I can still feel the energy of the Sanguine Diamond infusing my body, and for the first time since arriving here I feel amazing. Not sure of how to respond, I look Justin dead in the eye and say, "Yep."

Justin's mouth opens, but nothing comes out for a moment. He shifts on his feet, looks around at the other Runners, then says, "Dream on."

Chris turns to begin the run. He smacks Justin on the shoulder. "Shut up so we can get going."

I plant my feet in place. "Who's holding my hand this time?"

They look at each other, then Chris says, "Justin, it's your turn to help the new member."

"Eww! No! I'm not holding a muck's hand. That's your job."

Chris sighs and rolls his eyes. "If you're going to be a leader here someday, you need to help the mucks."

While the two of them fight over which one will get stuck with me, like I'm some sort of diseased leper, I watch Kayla whisper to Beth. "Trade me spots, okay? I want to be by Chris." They exchange positions without Chris being any the wiser.

I cut the guys off. "Neither one of you is my preferred running mate either, but unless one of your oversized egos gives in and assumes some responsibility, we'll all have to run at my pace, not yours."

Chris steps forward and takes my hand. I feel a tingling in my muscles, and my body feels feather light. He begins running, pulling me along. My legs seem to bounce off the ground with no effort, and my body instinctively knows the best posture, rhythm, and movements. I notice my breathing is fast and light, giving me all the oxygen I need. My body doesn't thirst for water as much, either. I feel like I could run a thousand miles and never have to stop for rest.

Running with Chris's power doesn't seem the same as before. Instead of being dragged alongside him, I run beside him, matching his ability. The speed is wonderful and exhilarating. I wish I could run this fast on my own. I look over at Chris and smile in spite of myself. I feel equal, regardless of how he perceives me.

For once, the expression on his face is blank. Perhaps he can tell I'm not as slow as I have been. Perhaps. He squeezes my hand a little more than before, and I wonder what he's thinking. If only I could read his mind. I read the witch's mind back in the gem cutter's office. Why not his?

Our group streaks north through the Frank Church Wilderness of Idaho. Apparently, the best way for us to remain undetected is to direct our route through uninhabited areas. As evening approaches and the shadows lengthen, we stop near the base of a waterfall to mull over the situation.

Justin pulls out a map and calculates our position. "Nice going, Chris. You've led us into a trap."

"What are you talking about?" Chris says.

"There aren't any nearby towns in any direction we can reach before nightfall!"

"Give me that." Chris grabs the map and I peek over his shoulder.

Beth approaches him. "Chris, you're wasting valuable daylight. We either need to run, or we need to find a cabin or something to hide in. Now!"

Justin turns to Beth and says with a heavy sting in his voice, "This is the protected wilderness, idiot. There are no cabins." He may as well have slapped her in the face. His comment has the same effect and I feel pity for her.

I ask the group, "Can we stay in a cave? The Death Clan hides in caves and the Shadow Demons don't get them." No one speaks for a moment, so I continue, "If we built fires to keep the Shadows at bay, would that work?"

Chris answers, saying, "I think maybe, only . . . where can we find a cave large enough to hold us all?"

I point to the waterfall. "According to the map, this waterfall is called Cave Falls. Maybe there's a cave behind it."

Chris looks at me with confusion in his eyes. Kind of like: *how did you figure this out all on your own and I didn't?* "The three of us will check out the situation," he says. "The rest of you stand guard." He motions for Justin and me to follow him.

I cast a glance at the other Runners, wondering why Chris doesn't have some of them go investigate the waterfall. Isn't that why they're here? To protect us? Instead of second-guessing Chris, I follow him, thinking he isn't handling the stress of the situation very well.

We approach the falls, getting pelted with mist as the water hits the rocks close by. A little way up the side of the hill, I spot an opening in the cliff behind the waterfall. I decide not to point it out to the guys—they hate me enough already. If one of them sees the cave, then they can take credit for the discovery and be the hero. Unfortunately for me, neither one of them recognizes what I'm seeing, so I finally point and ask, "Hey, is that an opening up there?"

"I'll go take a look," Chris says. He runs up the hill and enters the gap.

"You don't have to be like that," Justin says, sizzling with indignation.

"Like what?"

"Little miss know-it-all."

I roll my eyes. "Do you know how long I've been staring at the cave opening waiting for one of you to see it? It's not my fault you're both blind. I only spoke up because we're losing daylight."

"Don't forget your place. You are the lowest on the totem pole, muck."

The muck who just saved your life. If he knew exactly how low on the totem pole I actually am, being a muck would be a step up.

Justin adds, "You are just along for the ride, so shut your mouth and let the men handle this."

I'm about to fire back with both barrels when Chris rejoins us. "Good job, Calli. The cave is big enough for everyone, with plenty of light right now from the large opening behind the water. We'll have to get fires burning right away before it gets any darker, though. Justin, go tell the others to start gathering firewood."

Justin lets out a huff of air and leaves.

"Come check it out," Chris says. Do I detect a smile or some kind of pleasant expression on his face when he looks at me? Unbelievable! He continues. "I'm so relieved you thought of this. Otherwise, we would have been in big trouble," he says.

"Wait, Chris. Can I talk to you for a moment?"

He turns and faces me.

"Would you give Justin the credit for finding the cave instead of me?"

"Justin? Why?"

"Maybe it would . . . well, he doesn't . . ." I struggle to properly express myself. I figure if the credit is given to Justin he may lighten up or, at the very least, be confused. He certainly won't admit he *didn't* find the cave.

As I try to formulate my thoughts, I stare into Chris's bottomless blue eyes. Then it happens—I enter his mind.

Chapter 5 - A Traitor Among Us

I view Chris's mind as if I'm inside his head, looking out through his eyes. I feel what he feels, see what he sees.

Chris's anger toward Justin hangs on the edge of his mind, along with the dissatisfaction of knowing Justin is a faster Runner than he is—a secret only the two of them know. Chris carries a deep level of insecurity and self-loathing on his shoulders. He doesn't feel he deserves to be in the lead position, but continues to hold on to the title as a form of penance for his past mistakes, and to keep Justin from being the leader.

I feel the way Chris's body buzzes when he looks at me, holds my hand, or is close enough to take in what I discover he senses as the flowery aroma of my hair.

Whoa! I wasn't expecting this!

I yank my eyes away from his, my heart races, and I try to recall what we were talking about. I recover and say, "The last thing I want is for everyone else to think I'm trying to step on your toes. You know, me being the new muck and all." I half-laugh in an attempt to relieve the pressure in my chest. "Look, it doesn't matter if you take the credit for finding the cave or if Justin does. I just don't want this on me, all right?"

"I'll figure something out. Go check out the cave." He turns away and runs to the others, and I lose the intimate connection to his mind.

What the heck! I thought he didn't like me. I let out an exasperated huff. Mind reading is *nothing* like I thought it would be. I've always wanted to read minds, constantly wished I could tell if someone was lying or being deceitful, but this . . . this is completely different.

Chris's perception and emotional dilemmas still course through my body and brain as I recount his thoughts like an instant replay of a football game. This is the same type of recounting or download I experienced with Maetha in Mr. Bates's office.

In his head, I'd witnessed the personal race against Justin where Chris lost, but Chris threatened Justin with something in order to keep him quiet and maintain his position in the number two spot. I try to sift through his memories to see what the threat was exactly, but only hit brick walls in that regard.

I'm astounded to discover, however, exactly what Chris sees whenever he looks at me: I glow. I mean literally, because through his eyes, he can detect my iridescent aura. Beth had mentioned something about it on my first day, but I didn't understand her at the time. Seeing my aura with my own eyes through Chris's memory is nothing short of remarkable.

Chris's memories of yesterday morning in Clara's office filter into my mind. He recognized me as the same girl he'd recently seen in a vision, a vision shown to him by a powerful Seer. Apparently, I am to be Chris's future-destined-love . . . and I'm supposed to be a Healer.

I am beside myself! Never in a million years would I have guessed I'd find that in his mind.

When Chris saw me sitting on Clara's couch, with my vibrant aura, he knew in his heart the vision the Seer showed him must be true, and would happen in the future. That explains why he seemed to recognize me. It also explains why he became so distant. The vision the Seer had inserted into his mind had shown an older, beautiful woman who was a Healer—not an underdeveloped teenager, and a Runner to boot.

When Clara told him I was a Runner, his hopes and dreams crumbled in front of him. My presence in Clara's office turned his reality upside down. He had his own paradigm shift at the same time I did.

Of course, I hold no powers or abilities after all, so Chris's vision of me being a Healer is moot. So much for that particular Seer's powers.

Earlier this morning, as I finished last in the time trials, Chris's heart rate increased. He concluded before I did I would be part of the trio on this delivery. He had already intended to bring me along as one of the team so he could keep an eye on me, but finishing last meant he'd have to hold my hand at some point. Doing so was standard procedure. If I'd only been a fellow team member, I would have held hands with someone else, most likely another girl.

Through his memories, I revisit the feeling of my hand in his as we ran through the forest after leaving Harold Bates office, the softness of my skin, and the excitement that rushed through his body when I smiled at him.

I shake my head as if I can empty Chris's memories from my mind. Naturally, I can't. Taking a deep breath, I head to the cave.

As I approach the entrance, some of the other Runners are beginning to arrive with small bundles of tinder to make lighting the fire easier. Our eyes adjust to the dark interior, and we notice the cave opens up into a larger chamber. Ancient cave-dweller drawings are carved onto the walls, and on the ground a couple of rock circles indicates where fires once were. A freshwater spring dribbles water down the back wall and has carved a small stream on the rock floor toward the back of the waterfall.

Beth runs over and catches some of the water in her hand. "Sweet!" She smiles as she splashes the water on her face. She looks good with a smile.

I wander toward the front of the cave to where the back of the waterfall pours down before me in a giant curtain. I stand and let my thoughts fall away like the water in front of me. Ohio and my past life seem so far away. What kind of craziness brought me into this magical world? Maybe I should have answered differently when Clara Winter asked if I still wanted to call my parents.

The echoing voices of teammates bringing firewood into the cave gives me comfort. It seems everyone breathes easier knowing they now have a safe place to sleep.

I twist around to find Chris nearby, watching me. "Oh, Chris, you startled me," I say. *More than you know.* I try not to make eye contact with him because I don't want to be thrown into his mind again. I turn my attention back to the waterfall. "I was just checking this out."

"Thanks again for saving me, Calli," he says in a low voice.

"What are you talking about? I didn't save you. I only pointed out the obvious." I stare straight ahead, wishing he would go back to avoiding me. My brain knows differently now, and I recognize how the quiet and gentle tone of his voice reveals his feelings.

He says, "My thoughts were on . . . other things instead of where we needed to get to tonight. I lost track of how far off course we were and the possible dangers I'd exposed our team to, all because I couldn't control my mind."

"I know the feeling," I say. "You don't need to thank me, though. I'm the muck, remember? I'll go help gather firewood." I turn to walk past him, but he blocks my way and steps close. I can smell his unique masculine scent and feel his body heat. All my senses seem to be on hyper-drive.

"Calli, I'll do a better job of controlling my mind from here on out. That way, you won't become distracted with it too."

Breathlessly, and only halfway meeting his gaze, I ask, "What do you mean?" My heart races even faster because of what he implies.

"Look at me, Calli." He places his hands on my shoulders to command my attention. Hesitantly, I bring my eyes up to his as he says, "Not everyone can tell when their mind is being read, but I can. I also know how to block my thoughts, but I wasn't aware I needed to do that with you."

"I'm sorry." I cast my eyes to the ground as they fill with tears. I don't have the right to invade his privacy. I feel I've been caught committing a crime.

He gently squeezes my shoulders to bring my gaze back up to his and says, almost whispering, "Are you a Runner or a Mind-Reader? 'Cause you can't be both."

I pull away from his grasp and walk over to the falling water. I can't tell him the truth, so I dance around it. "This whole world is new to me, so much so I'm still reeling with confusion." I wipe away my tears. "We're on our way to meet with people who can kill others with their very thoughts, and I'm scared. I looked into your eyes and slipped into your mind on accident. I don't understand why this is happening, Chris. I didn't mean to read your mind."

"Calli, you did more than simply read my thoughts, you delved into my memories. Only a few Mind-Readers can get that far into a brain, and the process usually takes several hours and years of practice on the Mind-Reader's part. I know most of what you saw. Please don't be frightened by what the Seer showed me about you—about us."

"Frightened? Confused would be a better word." I continue to stare at the water.

"I'm confused too. You being a Runner didn't fit into the vision, and you should be older. Calli, please try to understand what I'm feeling here. I've always thought visions of the future couldn't be fabricated, yet here you stand in front of me, a complete contradiction to the vision I was shown. It's as if the vision was a huge lie or something. Try to imagine how I'm feeling now that I know you can also read minds." I hear his footsteps as he moves closer. His voice becomes even quieter as he says, "I cannot have you looking into my thoughts."

I turn around and face him. I look deep into his eyes for understanding, for peace. "Well, I'm looking at you now, and I'm not seeing anything. Maybe that ability went away."

"No, I'm blocking you. You'll learn how to block your mind too. It's not hard, and it comes in handy when you're around Mind-Readers."

I continue to peer up into his eyes, testing his mind barrier, looking for his thoughts. His expression softens, and his head tilts slightly as he gazes into my eyes with the same intensity I had when I looked at him. I observe the reflection of the falling water in his eyes, the length of his lashes, and the thickness of his eyebrows.

My surroundings seem to lighten and I feel like I'm in a dream. The shadows and dancing firelight of the cave disappear and become bright as day. I look around and find the same large clearing or meadow I saw before in Mr. Bates' office. Tents and people are lined up along the edge of the forest, surrounding me.

I look where Chris was standing a moment ago, but he's gone. I am now staring at a slab of stone in front of me and see people in white robes gliding toward us. I look to my left and see myself surrounded by my iridescent aura, facing the stone altar. I realize I am in Chris's mind, observing the scene unfold from his perspective. I see several hundred people standing in front of the tents, organized by clan, and the hooded, ivory silhouettes of the Death Clan as they stand in front of us, awaiting the presentation of the diamond. Chris pulls out his box, opens it, and sets it before the leader, who then examines the stone and becomes angry. The leader launches into a tirade about being tricked, and I watch myself step up to present the real stone. The clan leader is so enraged at the deception he declares someone must die.

Then the vision jumps to an enclosed area, where my entire clan waits for a decision. Through Chris's eyes, I stand with the Death Clan leader, who demands I choose the first person to die. I watch myself choose Chris without any hesitation. I feel everything in Chris's body cease, including his heart. His vision fades to black while his body collapses to the ground.

"No!" I yell, and the darkness of the cave comes back into view.

"What is it?" Chris clutches my shoulders again. I push at his chest and get him to release me, only to stumble backward toward the drop-off. Just as my body leans over the edge, he grabs me and pulls me into his arms.

The strength of his embrace calms me, and I feel my body relax into him. I don't want to move, I don't want to speak, but more than anything, I don't want the future I've seen to *ever come true*. I feel his strong hands caress my back and shoulders in an effort to comfort me and get me to talk.

He says, "What did you see? Did you get into my mind again?"

"I think I just saw a part of your future," I whisper.

"Well," he says, letting go of me and stepping back, admittedly stunned. "Of all the stars above and below, what can't you do? So, what happens to me?" His voice reveals he's amazed, scared, and even more confused than before.

"What does it matter? I'll make sure nothing happens." I wipe my freshly watered eyes.

"Do I die?" he asks.

"The future isn't set. The visions are four weeks out, so I have time to make changes to ensure this doesn't come true, right?" I try to step around him, only to be blocked by his massive, rock-solid frame.

"What did you see? Please, Calli, tell me."

"I'll change things," I say.

"No. That's not allowed. Everyone dies. Don't try to stop it."

He doesn't know what I've seen. He can never know! I try to get around him once again, but when he tries to stop me, I push my hands against his chest with all my effort and yell, "You will not die because of me!"

He steps aside as I rush past him and out where everyone stands, frozen in their shoes, having obviously overheard my last words. I storm out of the cave. I run down the path to the edge of the stream, far away from the waterfall, making a mental note of the position of the sun so I won't be caught off guard by the Shadow Demons. However, I can't help but wonder about the Demons and if they're even interested in me. I am, after all, just a normal human.

The memory of my torn shirt raises some doubts.

I sit down on a rock, take off my shoes, and put my feet in the cool water. I stare into the pool as the water ripples against my ankles and recall the vision I had about Chris's death.

I can't believe how insensitively I acted in my vision. I rub my temples to try to suppress the mess of information circulating through my brain. Why would I choose Chris? And without hesitation? Everything about the vision is wrong, and I vow to fix it. I'm not sure why, but I can sense if the future plays out like the vision, then the world will never be right again. Plus, the Death Clan didn't die in the vision this time. I sense an ominous, heavy reality settling into my mind where the future is concerned, and I don't like it.

What did Maetha say about the proper time to present the diamond? She said I would know. Is this the right time? No, she said not to show anyone, and she was emphatic that I'd know clearly when the time was right. Perhaps I should switch the stones at the last minute so the one Chris presents will be the real one.

That's what I'll do. I'll get him to let me carry the box with the fake stone and I'll exchange the diamonds before the meeting.

"Calli," Chris calls out as he approaches. He sits down beside me, turning halfway in my direction. His close proximity unnerves my heightened senses.

"Can I have a moment to myself, please?" I ask.

"No, night is approaching, and we should all be in the cave soon." His eyes are on mine, gazing deeply as if searching for a hidden video recording of what I've seen.

I'll admit I left him hanging by saying what I did, but I can't tell him that at some point in the future, I'll have to select who dies, and I'll choose him.

"Calli, read my mind."

"I thought you said you could block me."

"I can. But I can also control how much of my thoughts you can access.

I search his eyes and try to read his mind. He thinks, *I don't know much about you, but I can tell you would never do anything to hurt me, Calli. What did you see?*

"Are you able to read my thoughts?" I ask.

"No."

"That's too bad, because it's the only way you'll ever find out."

The breeze shifts and an overwhelmingly delicious aroma hits my nose, intoxicating my senses. The scent is so yummy, my mouth begins to water. I wonder if Chris smells it too. "Do you smell that?"

"What?"

My stomach starts to growl in anticipation of a scrumptious feast. "Do you want some fresh meat for dinner?"

"What?" He sounds intrigued.

"There are a few rabbit holes nearby."

A subtle grin creeps around the corners of his mouth. "Oh, I don't think I'd get very full on rabbit holes."

I can't help but smile at him and he smiles in return. An exhilarating thrill races through my body at the sight of his wonderful smile. Feeling his happiness and my own contentment at the moment warms my soul and shoots lightning bolts to my heart.

"Come on," I say. I jump up and slip my shoes on and take his hand, pulling him in the direction of the mouth-watering scent. The smell! *Oh, splendid, now I'm a Hunter too?* I wonder if Chris is thinking the same thing, so I try to read his mind. He's blocking me. "Chris," I say as we weave between the trees. "How were you able to let me read your thoughts but not allow me to read everything in your mind? That was impressive."

He actually blushes from my compliment. "I can teach you how. I'm guessing it would come easy for you. Apparently everything else does."

I know my mind is safe from the probing of readers because of the spell Maetha placed on me, so I'm not too worried about learning to put up that boundary.

"Shhhh," I whisper as we near the source of the scent. Then I freeze. The smell I pick up on is more than rabbits, it's the tang of seasoned, *cooked* rabbit. I close my eyes to try to picture what has happened.

Chris whispers in my ear, "What's wrong?"

"Someone else is here." A strange stench tickles my nose, teasing my senses with its confusing origins. The stink reminds me of my Uncle Thaddeus, who only showers about once a year, coupled with the memory of being at the firing range with my father and the lingering smell of gunpowder. Gunpowder! "Run!" I spit out.

Chris doesn't hesitate. He turns, grabs my hand, and runs back to the cave in a flash. A few individuals are still outside, and we hurry them inside the cave to safety.

Justin comes over, rudely pushing through the group until he's standing in front of everyone. "What's happening?"

My mind wanders into Justin's, and I see he is familiar with the same stench—the rank smell of Hunters. His mind also divulges he's left markers along the way, some kind of scent, for the Hunters to follow.

So, Justin is a traitor, bent on compromising this assignment!

As I am about to say these words aloud, Justin's mind opens to me, displaying even more appalling revelations. Right up front and center is his past nefarious involvement with the Death Clan. Chris had tried repeatedly to convince Justin not to continue in his ways, insisting working with these individuals will only result in an early death. Then I see Chris speaking with Justin, informing him he will be the third member of the trio because he can't be trusted to be left alone at the compound. But the reason Justin continues to relinquish the fastest position to Chris is information that remains hidden from my view.

"Hunters," I say, still amazed to find these mind-reads only take a few seconds of real time.

"Hunters?" Chris is beside himself. "They've found us already?"

I am a little surprised, but pleased, to see that Chris completely and wholeheartedly believes me.

Justin, however, squirms in his spot. "What is she talking about? She wouldn't know what a Hunter even looks like."

A couple of the others come over and join in.

Shanika panics. "Oh no, how do we get away from them?"

"Are they going to hurt us?" Ricky asks.

Justin says, "Did *you* see them, Chris?"

"No, but Calli did."

"And you believe her?"

I try to add, "Well, I didn't actually—" but Beth interrupts.

"How did they get here so fast?"

My eyes dart to Justin.

Justin states, acting innocent, "Maybe they are only following us, not hunting us."

Will says, "Yeah, right. Since when has a Hunter just followed someone and not killed them?"

Kayla puts in her two cents. "We've got to stop them. How about we climb into the trees and ambush them?"

Chris replies, "No, they would detect your scent on the bark."

Everyone begins discussing among themselves different ways to defeat the Hunters.

I study Justin's eyes again and enter his thoughts. This time, I see he was given a special scent to spray on the trees as we ran, like leaving breadcrumbs for the Hunters to follow. But who gave the scent to him? That particular part of his brain is blocked. I search his mind to see the scent bottle he used. *No way! It was my perfume!*

The image abruptly disappears. *Get out of my mind, muck,* Justin says wordlessly with his thoughts. He stands and storms away from the group.

My gaze flies over to Beth. I wonder if she gave the bottle to Justin, but her mind is blocked. My eyes wander over to Chris, and his thoughts ask me, *Are you able to tell what Justin knows?*

"Yes."

Did he know you were reading his mind?

I nod, wondering how Chris knows what I did.

Is he responsible for the Hunters following us?

I nod again.

How?

I pretend to spray perfume and rub my wrists together, then with my thumb I point to myself.

I'm going to kick his butt!

"No, we need him to talk."

"Well, we're in a dilemma now, aren't we?" Chris says aloud, at last drawing the attention of the group away from their discussion. "The sun is setting and the Shadow Demons are deadly. Hunters have their own ways of avoiding the Demons at night, but the moment dawn breaks tomorrow, the Hunters will be hot on our trail once again."

"Then we'll have to beat them up," I say, then correct myself. "What I mean is we'll have to wake up in the

102

morning before they do and get on our way. We can all wash in the waterfall and try to minimize our scents, making it harder to track us. Until then, I guess we're staked down for the night."

He takes my arm and leads me away from the group. Once we are far enough away from everyone he says, "I need to go talk with Justin."

"But you don't know what to ask him. Someone else is orchestrating this. They gave him my perfume for the Hunters, but he closed his mind before I could find out who it was."

"I'll talk to him. Stay with the others and try to figure out a plan."

My eyes follow him as he walks away and over to the far corner where Justin sits alone.

I walk back over to the group and listen as they hash out plan after plan of how to defeat the Hunters. With every idea comes a problem that will have to be resolved . . . and every problem results in our capture or death.

I fully comprehend now why the real Sanguine Diamond is being transported secretly. If the Hunters catch us tomorrow, they'll take the diamond in Chris's pocket, thinking they've accomplished their goal.

I walk over to the fire by the entryway and glance over my shoulder at everyone. No one seems to care that I'm so close to the doorway, so close to the Shadow Demons. I slowly pull my foot out of my shoe, and, using my toes, fling it out of the cave into the dark. Even though I am fairly sure I'm immune to the Shadows, I'm not certain.

My shoe has fallen out of sight, so I pull one of the burning sticks from the fire and toss it out near where I figure my shoe landed. I need to find out if the Demons shredded it. The flaming stick lands almost on top of my untouched shoe. Now I have a bigger problem. My shoe is about to burn!

Clearly, the Demons have no interest in me or the diamond, so I run out of the cave.

"Calli!"

Chris is closer to the entryway than I'd thought. I hadn't realized he was on his way back over to me when I ran out of the cave. The last thing I want is for him to think I'm being devoured by the Demons, so I answer him. "Chris, I'm all right. I'm going to go scout the Hunter's camp."

"How? Come back . . . the Demons . . . you'll die!"

"I'll be fine."

The rest of the Runners crowd around the cave opening, murmuring in amazement, as I slip my shoe back on. My actions are highlighted by the burning stick I threw out. I leave the small flame burning and make my way out into the night and into the midst of the Shadow Demons.

Isn't it interesting, I think to myself, that from a normal human's viewpoint being able to run fast or read minds or to possess any of the other cosmic abilities would be every person's dream? How many times have I wished to see the future or know what others are thinking? Yet, now, at this exact moment my lackluster human-self possesses more abilities than anyone in the cave because I can walk among the Shadow Demons unharmed.

Nothing prepares me for the traumatic images of the actual Demons. Unfortunately, I can see quite well in the dark due to the Hunter's powers within the diamond. I can see the Demons everywhere, floating above the ground, with huge clawed feet and hind dewclaws similar to those of a cat. Their bodies' thin shriveled forms have a dry leathery-looking skin stretched around skeletal frames that sport heads of assorted animals: dogs, cats, bats, alligators, elephants, lions, bears, birds, cows and horses, to name a few. Each hand has three fingers or digits with terribly long claws, and their eye sockets—devoid of eyeballs—glow red.

As I walk among them, they move out of my way, paying me no attention other than to acknowledge my presence. Instead, they focus on the cave opening, waiting, hoping for a meal. As the last flickers of light from the burning stick extinguish, the Demons glide even closer to the cave.

I emerge from the swarm of Demons and stand in the darkened forest. The stars above twinkle, and I hear water trickling in the nearby river. I breathe in a lung full of crisp air, catch the scent of the Hunters, and off I go. I find more floating Demons, moving in the direction of the Hunters. I follow their lead, walking behind their eerie forms.

The Hunters have constructed a tent system made of a material I've never seen before. I figure it must be some type of magical cloth used to ward off Demons. They have a fire going inside, and four individuals' silhouettes dance on the walls of the tent. The smell of bad intentions permeates my entire being, leaving nothing to doubt. These individuals are our enemies, and they mean to kill us.

However, a familiar scent hits my nose. I close my eyes and inhale, realizing two of the four occupants are Runners. Why are Runners and Hunters together? Perhaps the Runners are their legs, the same way Chris was for me. Or maybe they are traitors and work for the Death Clan, like Justin.

I sit down on a fallen tree to mull over the situation. Runners, whether good or evil, can carry the Hunters at the same speed as our group. There will be no outrunning them. They will catch up with us.

An idea enters my head. I'm fast for a human, and I can run most of the night and use the perfume to spray trees to set up a false trail that will lead in the opposite direction. The Hunters would follow the markers well into the morning, giving us time to increase the distance between us.

All I need is the perfume.

I make my way back to the cave, stepping through the even thicker gathering of Demons outside. Upon entering, I'm immediately assaulted by Chris. His arms pull me against his body as he steps back towards the cave wall. Shaking and holding me in his firm embrace, his body slides down the wall. I look into his moist eyes, and he opens his mind to me. I hear his thoughts as though they're my own.

Calli, why? How? You should be dead. I thought you were dead. Don't ever scare me like that again!

"I'm fine, Chris, really. Let me up. We're making a scene." Beyond the fire the clan members stare at us with open mouths.

Justin pushes his way through the crowd once again and stares at me. "What . . . are you?"

I stand and brush the dirt off my legs. "You tell me and we'll both know," I mutter.

"Are you a witch?" Kayla asks. I can sense jealousy in her voice. Not surprising, since she saw me in Chris's embrace.

"No, I'm not."

"How can you go out among the Demons and not be killed?" Will points to the cave opening.

"I don't understand it either. I only know the Shadow Demons aren't interested in me. But more importantly, there are two Hunters and two Runners camped about five-hundred yards downstream."

The questions come at me instantly.

"You can see the Demons?" "What do they look like?" "Why didn't they eat you?" "The Hunters stay in tents?" "How do you know there are four of them?" "What makes you think Runners are with them?" "Who are they?"

My eyes are on Justin. I ask, "Where is it, Justin?"

"What are you talking about?"

"You closed it off from me and then told me to get out of your mind."

The other members quiet down and try to pick through our conversation.

"What difference will it make?" he says, defiantly. "They've already found us."

"But we have at least six hours before they can leave their tent. I can go out and set up a decoy trail, sending them on a wild goose chase tomorrow. Now, Justin, where is it?"

He says nothing.

"Give it to me and perhaps we can make some kind of amends."

Chris steps next to me, "He doesn't have it. He dropped the bottle on a tree trunk. It's broken."

I turn to Justin, "Show me with your memories, Justin."

The others watch our conversation like a tennis match. I stare at Justin, trying to get inside his head, when his memory flies to the forefront of his mind with such intensity it literally pushes my head back a bit.

My perfume was sprayed at arm's length on a tree trunk, and then it slipped out of his hand and shattered on rocks below. I comprehend his dread, almost empathizing with him, until the face of Maetha fills his mind as she hands him my perfume!

What is she doing in his memory?

Chapter 6 – Unwanted Abilities

I need to know how Justin is connected to the witch, Maetha, and why she's involved with both the potential success of the delivery and the potential failure. Perhaps she's actually working *for* the Death Clan, not against them. No, I saw the Death Clan being destroyed in the vision. Still, her motives don't make sense.

I scan the faces of my fellow running mates, taking in their collective thoughts about Justin. Everyone, except Beth, wants to throw Justin to the Demons for being a traitor. I can't let that happen.

"You can't throw Justin to the Demons!" I say to the group. "I'm ashamed of you for even thinking it. Believe me, he'll be properly punished in due time, but not now at the hands of a bunch of vigilantes."

"You read minds?" several of them ask me collectively, almost in reverent unison.

Before I can answer, Jonas asks, "Are you an Immortal?"

"What?" I scrunch my eyes shut. "I don't know."

Jessica shakes her head. "Immortals are myths."

"What about the Death Clan? Aren't they Immortals?" Ricky asks.

Jessica answers, "They're only Healers. Immortals don't exist."

"Then how can Calli do all these things?" Beth points to me.

"Look, I don't know what I am or am not. I can try to answer your questions later. For now, I need some privacy with Justin and Chris. The rest of you should tend to those fires." My natural assumption of authority is accepted by the group and they retreat further into the cave.

Justin walks forward and stands at the entryway.

"I might as well walk right out to the wolves," he says. "You're going to send me there anyway."

"You can if you wish, but if you had any idea what those monsters looked like, you wouldn't stand so close to death." I pause, then say, "Tell me Justin, how long have you worked for the Death Clan?"

"What?" He swiftly rounds on Chris. "You told her?"

"No," Chris defends, then throws a questioning glare my way.

I calm the two guys by saying, "I read your mind, Justin. You're an open book. Tell me why a witch gave you my perfume."

Chris nearly explodes. "You're working with a witch?"

Justin cowers away and moves closer to the fire. He bends down and pushes a couple sticks into the flames. "She told me the Death Clan hired the Hunters to follow us to ensure the package arrived safely and on time. The perfume was supposed to make their job easier. They're only following us."

I move closer to him. "They're here to kill us, Justin. I smelled it on them."

"Yeah, right, like you can smell death."

I press him. "When was the last time you met with the witch?"

"At the compound, before we left on the assignment. Why?"

She'd been at the compound? "You haven't seen her since?" I need to make sure he doesn't remember Maetha giving the real diamond to me.

He stands. "No."

I say, "Without the perfume, the Hunters will have to rely on the smell that still lingers on you. That was expensive stuff you dropped, with high oil content. Your clothing will hold the scent for a while. I can smell it, and if I can, they can too. I suggest you take half the group and run west tomorrow morning. The rest of us will stay in the cave, and hopefully the Hunters will take the bait and follow your trail. When they do, we'll follow them and ambush from behind."

"Or," Justin shoots back, "you could go kill them tonight and rid us of the problem."

"So I have to become a cold-blooded killer because you're a traitor?"

"Go back to their camp and expose them to the Demons," he says. "That would solve everything lickety-split." Justin sounds pretty sure of himself, but he adjusts his tone when I don't play along. "Well, what are you going to do with them after the ambush? Aren't you going to kill them then?"

"No," I say. "They'll become our captives, and we'll turn them over to the authorities."

"This is not the human world. There aren't any authorities. Man, you're such a muck!"

In the blink of an eye, Chris moves and grabs Justin's jacket front, pushing him up against the wall, his nose about an inch from Justin's face. "Don't talk to her like that! You hear me?"

"I'll talk however I want." The defiance in Justin's voice echoes off the walls.

"And I'll pound your face in."

"Maybe—if you can catch me."

Chris pushes Justin a little further into the wall and says, "You threw the race, forcing Dirk to the top, didn't you? You knew Dirk and the rest of the team would be kidnapped. You'd been forewarned, hadn't you? How could you betray your friends?"

"Oh, yeah, and you're one to talk, Chris. You probably don't want me spouting off your dark secrets," Justin hisses.

"I ought to string you up."

"I'll do you one better. I'll leave the group."

"You can't. We all have to be present when the package is handed over, remember?"

"Tell me how that's my problem."

I feel the need to end this stupid clash. I say, "Justin, you'll be with us even if we're forced to take you bound and gagged. We're all stuck here tonight, so we might as well try to get along." I put my hand on Chris's arm. "Let's decide who will be going with Justin's group."

Chris backs away as Justin straightens his jacket and cracks his neck. Justin says, "It doesn't really matter, does it? They have guns and Runners. We can't compete with that."

Chris points his finger in Justin's face. "You'll have to live with the consequences if anyone dies because of your choices."

Justin walks away, holding his head high as if he doesn't care.

I turn to Chris and say, "Can't Runners dodge bullets?"

"I can, and Justin can too, but only if we know we're about to be shot at. If another Runner is at the other end of the barrel, bullets are almost impossible to evade. They know how we move. We'll just have to stop the Runners before they have time to shoot."

Chris fetches a couple of the other team members to decide how to divide the group. They use the same type of groupings Clara spoke of: an equal division of the three different skill levels. There's definitely wisdom in this tactic.

Justin's group will include Beth, Michael, Will, Kayla, Jessica, and Ricky. The rest will be in Chris's group: Lizbeth, Yang, Ashley, Tyler, Shanika, Jonas, and me.

I walk away from the council and go over to the fire. My thoughts are running a mile a minute.

"Well, Calli, this is certainly a shocker," Beth says as she sits beside me.

"Yes. Isn't life interesting, Beth?"

"What do the Shadow Demons look like?" She speaks with a hushed voice, but others hear her. I figure of all the people in the whole world, Beth is probably the one most genuinely curious about the Demons' abominable appearance.

Everyone else starts to gather around us to listen.

"Well, they're large and scary, with animal heads, huge claws on their hands and feet, and long teeth as sharp as daggers."

"Why are you able to walk among them and not be torn to shreds like the rest of us?" Beth asks.

I shake my head. "I don't know."

"Why are you able to see them and we can't?"

I shrug my shoulders.

Jessica asks, "So, you can read minds too? Can you read mine?"

"I don't really want to. It just happens," I say, entering her mind effortlessly. I feel right away she has a serious crush on Justin, but her friendship with Beth keeps her from pursuing it. "I will say, I think you're right in not acting on your crush."

Her eyes open wide. "Uh, how did you . . . please don't say anything."

"Can I ask you a question?" I say. "What do you feel when I'm in your mind?"

"The top of my head feels ticklish and kind of itches."

Everyone agrees with her.

Ashley catches my attention and asks me to read her mind. I want to roll my eyes, want to point out there are plenty of more important things to worry about than this silly parlor game. But then Ashley's past opens up to me, revealing she spent time in a juvenile detention center for burglary just before her running ability surfaced. The irony of it makes me laugh out loud. She would've been uncatchable as a thief.

"What's so funny?" she asks.

"If only you could do then what you can now, maybe you wouldn't have been caught. Then again, it was best you were reformed before your abilities surfaced." I remember Ashley is only thirteen. She's had a rough life to have already spent time in a detention center.

An amazed expression crosses her face. Then she smiles. "Who says I'm reformed? This is incredible! That wasn't even on the top of my mind. Did someone tell you about my past?"

"No," I say. She obviously thinks I'm some type of shyster, because she jumps to the conclusion someone must have told me about her past instead of believing I'm actually reading her mind.

My eyes wander over to the other fire where Chris is talking to Will. They are both facing me, but whispering to each other, so I do what comes naturally. I read their lips.

"How does she do it?" Will asks Chris.

"Beats me."

"She possesses every single power. It's amazing."

"Not every power," Chris replies.

In order to read their lips, I need to keep a constant eye on their faces. Usually people don't catch on to the fact I'm reading their conversations, but this time both of them are staring right at me while I do what they don't know I can do. I have to look away. It's not every day I have two "tens" staring me down, trying to figure me out, and one of them thinks I'm his soulmate because of some faulty future vision.

The others around me talk excitedly, and my attention is pulled back to them. Jonas, asks me to check out his mind.

"Am I going to find any x-rated stuff?" Everyone laughs, while I see into his past and witness his father beating him, his older brother chasing him, his mother crying at a funeral. A hard lump forms in my throat, and I choose my words carefully. "Who died?"

"My brother," Jonas answers, obviously surprised with my question. His memory displays the horrific event. His father beat his brother to death while Jonas hid in the closet. This happened before his running ability kicked in.

"You couldn't have done anything to stop him." The crowd is quiet as they listen. A quick glance around tells me they are already aware of his story.

Jonas says, "I wish you were a Seer, because you'd be able to tell me if he'll ever pay for what he's done." Further searching of Jonas's mind reveals his father sits on death row, and the appeals are dragging out the inevitable. I bore deeper into his eyes, struggling to see his future, but I see nothing. Strange. Everyone has a future, don't they? Unless . . . unless he doesn't. Why? What's going to happen to him?

I try again to discover his future, but there's nothing there. I turn to Shanika, who sits next to Jonas, and foresee her hugging her parents with her graduation cap on. Tyler's future involves marriage and holding a position in a city government. Beth's future holds prison—not so good. Turning back to Jonas, I still see nothing.

Then slowly it comes to me. My mind passes throughout his body, feeling for a cause or disease. I scan him until I can see what it is that's responsible for his non-existent future. The answer comes in an unwelcome whoosh: cancer. I search his mind to find out if he's already aware of the disease. He isn't.

My stomach twists into a horrible knot. This boy will be dead in less than four weeks, and he has no clue. Should I tell him? No, it isn't my place. I can't do anything to help him anyway, because I'm not a Healer. I put my hands to my head and wish everyone and everything would just go away. Why do I have to see these things?

"She does have future sight," Chris says as he walks over to the crowd.

Thanks, Chris!

Jonas stares at me in earnest, clearly hoping for a reading.

I have to shut him down. "Look, these powers are all new to me, and I haven't quite figured out how everything works. I've seen parts of the future, but they're so far out, they will most likely never happen. I can't summon up a particular event in the future. I can't look for your father's future because he's not here."

"But what do you see about him in my future?" Jonas leans forward, perhaps thinking I'll reveal his father's upcoming death.

"Everything will work out for you in the end." I watch as everyone reacts to the vague answer, but I can't bring myself to tell them the truth—Jonas will die soon.

Beth says with reverent awe, "Do you even have a clue how powerful you are? No clan member holds all the cosmic abilities. Not one! How come you do?"

"Why would a slow muck like me be so powerful, you mean?"

Chris jumps in with calm, reassuring words. "No one here will call you a muck again, Calli. What Beth said is true, though. No one person has held multiple abilities the way you do. This is truly amazing. You seem to wield most of the cosmic powers and also maintain your human guise. It explains the Shadow Demons' behavior."

"Can you cast spells too?" Beth asks.

I shake my head. If the questioning follows this trajectory, I worry that they will soon start to wonder if I've been enchanted. I need to change the subject.

"Chris, do you think you could teach everyone here how to block their minds to prevent mind-reading?"

"Well, yeah, definitely, and you'll be able to test them." He smiles.

"I know how to block," Michael joins in, then several others chime in too.

"Excellent," I answer. "Start teaching the others. I need a moment to think." I get up and walk away from the group. I make myself as comfortable as possible on a rock directly behind the falls and try to reason through the situation. If the team members block their minds, I won't be plagued with their past or present thoughts, and it will help me tremendously. Plus, if the Readers cross our path, they won't be able to determine our mission. Probably the most important thing is my abilities will be kept secret longer. If I am the only one who can do all these things, I will be in danger.

I can imagine the other clans wanting to get their hands on me to discover my secret. And what would they find? They'd find I'm a fraud, no better than the psychics on television, acting like they speak with dead people. There's nothing special about me. Well, that isn't entirely true. I can read lips and I can walk unharmed among Shadow Demons. Clara said the demons are dead Healers. *Oh great!* I can see dead people. I guess *I am* like the television psychics.

I think about the current situations and problems we face. Hunters are camped-out just over the ridge because of Justin's betrayal. How does Maetha fit into all this? Mr. Bates clearly knew she'd given the stone to me but didn't tell either of the two guys. Yet she gave Justin the perfume so the Hunters could track us easily. Are Maetha and Mr. Bates working for the Death Clan? If so, what would be the purpose of having us tracked down and killed?

"You all right, Calli?" Chris sits down next to me.

"Define 'all right.'"

"You're in deep thought over here. Can I help with anything?"

"I don't even understand this myself. How can you possibly help me?" I don't mean to sound rude, but it comes out that way.

"Well, I know a lot about the powers and how they work since I'm good friends with the hired individuals working at the compound."

"I bet you don't employ a Death Clan member."

"No, but we do have a Healer."

"A Healer?" Chris must be anxious to find out if that power will also emerge in me. "Chris, can a Healer cure cancer?"

"I suppose so, but they probably wouldn't."

"Why?"

"We really don't have time to go into that, Calli."

"Well, Jonas has cancer, and the sooner we can get him to a Healer, the better. He doesn't have much time." My eyes water from the emotional exhaustion.

"What? How do you know he has cancer? Did he tell you?"

"I sensed it in him when I tried to see his future."

Chris's eyes widen and his lips part. "How . . . how much time do you think he has?"

"If I can't see his future now, then he will be dead inside four weeks." I wipe my eyes.

"Does he know?"

I shake my head and admire the dancing firelight on Chris's face. He searches my eyes. His gaze falls to my mouth and then slowly rises back up to my eyes.

I realize I'm holding my breath.

He stands, clears his throat, and steps away. "Let's keep this to ourselves," he says. "There's no point in alarming him, especially when we can't do anything about it. We need to focus on everyone learning how to block their minds and how to get away from the Hunters tomorrow."

Kayla approaches and coughs to interrupt us. "Some of us are ready to be tested, Chris."

Chris doesn't even seem fazed by Kayla's presence, so I respond with, "We'll be right there."

Late into the night we work on blocking minds. I learn much more about the clan because of their inability to block effectively. They also learn what it feels like when a Reader is in their mind.

Finally, we stop the exercise and find places to lie down and sleep.

Justin sits on the other side of the cave, staring me down. The defiant expression on his face tells me his feelings won't be changing anytime soon. His mind opens to me. I don't want to enter his thoughts, but I do. *You think you're so high and mighty with all your so-called powers. You think anyone here gives a damn about you? No, they only care to be around someone with more power than—*

I don't want to hear any more of what he has to say, so I turn away to break the link.

Chris comes over and sits beside me. "Did you eat your energy ration yet?"

I shake my head.

"Here, take one of mine. You're going to need all your strength tomorrow."

"Will we arrive at the destination by nightfall?"

"No. We'll have to find lodging again. That's assuming we're able to capture the Hunters in a timely fashion."

"What time do the Demons leave? At sunrise or before?" I ask him.

"I'm not sure. Once the sun is up, it's safe."

"As soon as the sky starts to lighten, wake me, please. I'll watch for the exact moment they disappear, and then we'll begin our plan of attack."

"Good."

"Good," I repeat, mainly because I can't think of anything else to say.

"Well, try to get some sleep," he says, staring at me. His eyes haven't left mine yet. Why not, I wonder? Oh splendid! Now I wish I could read his thoughts. What's wrong with me? I need to decide whether or not I want to be able to read minds. Chris speaks in a low, sultry tone, "Calli, did you get past my walls?"

"No."

"Good." He stands and walks away, leaving me to wonder what he thought about.

Now he leaves me hanging?

I marvel at how handsome he is, particularly now that he doesn't have to keep his vision a secret from me. I think I've lifted a burden from his shoulders. I try to find a comfortable position to sleep in, but with the hard rocks, lack of bedding, and the orange-sized diamond in my pocket, no such luck.

Chapter 7 – The One He Missed

At some point, I must have drifted into a dreamless sleep. For that, I'm thankful, because I was exhausted. I awake to Chris shaking my shoulder.

"Calli, wake up."

My eyes try to adjust to the darkness of the cave. The fires have nearly died out, but the faint light of dawn illuminates the waterfall at the front of the cave. I sit up, stretch my arms, and take Chris's offered hand.

"What time is it?" I ask.

"Five-thirty. Can you come tell us if the Demons are gone yet?"

Justin sits right near the edge of the cave opening and he moves out of my way as I stumble toward the entrance.

I don't need to look. I can tell they are gone because the air smells peaceful. "They're gone now. You can wake the others."

Everyone is ready to go in less than two minutes. I remember I haven't spoken to Chris yet about giving the diamond to Justin. I also haven't noticed if the fake diamond has an odor like the real one. I don't remember detecting a smell when we received the diamond from Mr. Bates—not like the scent of the real diamond anyway.

"Chris, will you come here for a second?"

He leaves the others and comes over to me. I focus on the diamond in his pocket. Even before he gets to me, the intriguing odor hits my nose-buds with an enthralling, invigorating, icy smell. I can't determine if the odor is from the diamond or the metal box, but it doesn't matter which.

What matters is Justin needs to carry the package to attract the Hunters in his direction.

"Chris, the package has a scent. I can smell it, and if I can, I'm sure the Hunters can too. I think—"

"—Justin should carry the package," he finishes for me.

I nod.

He hesitates a moment before he leaves me to give Justin the stone. Justin tries to refuse, but Chris's lips tell him he's responsible for the mess we are all in and he should man up and try to help us out.

Justin takes the small box and puts it in his pocket, zipping it shut. He scowls in my direction. *Happy now, muck?*

Yes, as a matter of fact, I am.

Justin leads his half of the group out of the cave and down the trail, backtracking a little before cutting off to the right and running into the dense forest.

The plan is that the rest of us will stay in the cave and wait for the Hunters to start following Justin's group. They will run for twenty minutes and then turn back. Hopefully by then we'll be coming up on the rear of the Hunters, and Justin's group will be coming back to close them in. I hope the Hunters will simply give up and not try to fight. That would be the easiest way to resolve the problem.

Chris sits down next to me near the cave's opening. We both make sure our bodies and heads are hidden as we keep our eyes peeled for the Hunters.

I ask, "Do you think they might explore the cave before following the scent on Justin?"

"I hope not." The fear in his voice does not go unnoticed.

"I don't think I should watch for them." I begin to move away from the opening.

"What? Why not?"

"My mind-reading ability kicks in whether I want it to or not. If I accidentally go into one of their minds and they sense it, it might alert them to our presence. I'll sit over here, and you can communicate with me through your mind." I move over to the wall of the cave and sit down. "Can you tell me more about Justin?"

"What do you want to know?"

"He's faster than you are, yet he lets you win? Why?"

"Going right for the big questions, huh?" he mutters, then answers with his thoughts. *I've been the fastest for a while now, until recently when Justin challenged me to a private race. Before that happened, I discovered he'd been associating with the Death Clan. When he beat me in the race, I threatened to expose him, but he begged me not to. So I ordered him to tell everyone I won. He did.*

"Why is it so important to be the fastest?" I know Chris isn't telling me everything, but I decide not to press the issue.

He speaks his answer this time. "At my age, once I fall behind, I become washed up. I'm the oldest of the group."

"So, at what point do you accept others are faster than you?"

"When I'm ready to move on, or someone decides to make a scene."

"What will you move on to?"

"Well, there are things I want to do. I'd like to settle down somewhere and get a job. Eventually I'd like to get married and have a family." He looks at me.

I don't want to hurt his feelings. I can't even wrap my mind around his emotions. How do I begin to tell him his vision of us won't come true? "Chris, I'm only sixteen and—"

"Who said anything about marrying you?" He smiles and turns his head away, then tenses. His mind hits me with, *There they are.*

I turn to the group of Runners huddled in the far corner of the cave and put my finger to my lips. They are already quiet, but this is the signal the Hunters are near. I focus back on Chris, and he opens his mind to me.

I find that by looking into his head I can see the present as it unfolds through his eyes. Incredible! I see our pursuers walking around the spot where Justin took his group into the forest, looking for footprints and sniffing the air. One Hunter has a long rifle with a scope over his shoulder and enough ammunition around his belt to take down a pack of wolves. The other Hunter holds a handgun at the ready.

The two Runner slaves are recognizable due to their typical body structure and good looks. One looks like a lean, muscular Viking, the other looks like an African marathon runner. The two Hunters, on the other hand, look like they haven't shaved . . . ever . . . or taken a bath. I can smell their putrid aroma. They both have a lot of what looks like dried mud in their overgrown beards. Gross. Bushy mustaches cover their mouths, and large, protruding noses identify them—as if the other physical attributes didn't—as Hunters.

One of the Hunters must have picked up on our scent because he looks up toward the cave. He takes a step toward us, then another. He sniffs the air and takes yet another step.

The other Hunter calls him, "What is it, Lachlan?"

Lachlan smells the air again. "The scent is stronger this way." He points in our direction.

As I watch the Hunter through Chris's eyes my lungs seem to freeze with fear. I can't breathe.

Lachlan inhales our scent again.

"Come on," the other Hunter says, motioning with his hand. "They've already gone."

Lachlan turns away and takes a step in the other direction, then stops abruptly. He peers over his shoulder in the direction of the cave for a moment before he grabs the hand of the Viking Runner and disappears into the trees.

Chris and I exhale simultaneously.

"That was close!" I say.

"Too close."

"Chris, I experienced the whole scene through your eyes. You didn't even need to tell me what was going on, but I didn't know how to tell you without making a sound."

Chris stares at me in amazement, then turns and motions for the others to come over. "Let's go," he says. "Stick with the plan. Lizbeth and Tyler, you two are the contingencies."

They nod.

I catch Chris's attention. "What's a contingency?"

With his mind, he tells me, *If anything happens to either Justin or me, Lizbeth and/or Tyler are to take our places and deliver the package.*

"What about me?"

You'll be kept safe if a battle breaks out. You're too valuable. Let's go.

"But the three of us have to be together for the delivery to be successful."

"Hey, I don't plan on dying today." He takes my hand, and we lead the others out of the cave.

I consider the fact that no one ever plans on dying. It just happens. But then I realize that isn't entirely true either.

I immediately pick up on the Hunter's scent, and we begin our pursuit. As we run through the trees and thick underbrush, I feel the warmth emanating from Chris's hand. I'm tempted to try to view his future or extract more from his memories about what he saw in the vision about me, but I hold back. We need to get through the present situation first.

We run for about five minutes until the scent of the Hunters intensifies, letting us know they are close by. I detect movement up ahead in the trees, and put my hand up to warn my group to slow down. A loud pop of gunfire causes a flock of birds near us to scatter and our team to hit the ground.

I crawl a couple of feet to get a better vantage point of the gully we've entered. Justin's group is positioned on the south slope, each Runner stands perfectly straight behind one of the narrow tree trunks in an effort to avoid being hit with a bullet. Which means the Hunters are somewhere to the north. I can't locate them. The bigger question is whether or not the Hunters have figured out we are pursuing them.

Another shot splits the air. An agonizing scream from one of the female teammates lets us know someone has been hit.

I cast a concerned glance at Chris and whisper, "Come on, let's go."

"No, you stay here. Tyler, Jonas, Yang, and I will take care of this. We'll double back, circle around, and try to come up behind them."

"No! They may discover you coming and turn on you. The wind is working against you. They'll smell you coming."

"We'll run faster than our scent travels. Besides, Hunters don't have eyes in the back of their heads." He winks and takes off with the three other boys and speeds down the trail the way we've come.

I watch helplessly as more shots ring out in the woods. Another yelp of pain hits my ears, this time from a boy. I need to get closer to the Hunters. I have a bad hunch about how this could all turn out. If only I can get some information from them before the situation turns sour. I start to crawl north.

"Stay here," Lizbeth says. She has a hand on my ankle.

"I have to try to read their minds," I say. "I won't get too close."

Surprisingly, she lets go.

I crawl forward, staying in the bushes as much as possible, until I find a clear view. I try looking into the mind of the Hunter closest to me. Nothing. I try for the other one. Nothing. I try for the Runner's mind, who looks to be African, and enter immediately.

On the immediate edge of his mind I sense fear and entrapment. His name is Azeel, and he's originally from Nigeria. His family had moved to New York right before his running ability surfaced. The day his power emerged, four men arrived to take him away. The highly emotional moment viewed through Azeel's memories humbles me. I witness the death threats, the pleading, and the tears as he is ushered away and forced to be a slave. Definitely a stark contrast to what I experienced when my pseudo-running powers emerged. The Hunters control his rebellion with the threat his family will be hurt if he doesn't obey. His memories fill my mind, showing a council meeting of several Hunters planning this particular hunt, planning to go after the Sanguine Diamond to harness its powers.

I pull out of his head and enter the mind of the other Runner. His thoughts tell me his name is Stefan and he's from Sweden. His family was murdered by the Hunters when his power surfaced. He'd been taken captive as well, and forced to be their slave. He's been beaten horribly for attempting escape. I experience the hatred in his heart for the Hunters, especially the ones right in front of him.

Another shot rings out, and chaos ensues.

Chris and his group assault the Hunters from behind. Chris leads the charge with a running punch to the back of a Hunter's head, knocking him out and sending his rifle flying. One Hunter drops his handgun, but quickly retrieves a knife from his ankle. Chris effortlessly ducks and dodges the Hunter's attempts to maim or harm. Jonas and Yang fight with the last Hunter, while Tyler joins Chris.

No one is aware Stefan has picked up the handgun, except me, because I experience it in his mind. I feel his intent to kill, and the exact moment his finger begins to squeeze the trigger of the gun.

The Hunter Chris and Tyler are fighting takes a bullet to the head and drops to the ground. The second Hunter that Jonas and Yang are fighting falls just as fast from a dead-on shot to the chest. Then, I become aware Stefan is raising the gun to his own temple.

"No! Stop him!" I yell too late. As the bullet enters his head, it seems to enter mine too.

I must have blacked out.

My senses begin to return to my body one by one, making me aware of how much pain is coursing through my head. I can't open my eyes for some reason. In fact, I can't move or speak. Panic begins to spread like wildfire through my body. I hear Chris's anguished voice chastising Lizbeth.

"Why didn't you protect her? Why did you let her get so close? How did she get shot?"

"I don't think she was shot, Chris. She must have passed out and hit her head. She's still breathing. "

"She shouldn't have been standing while all that gunfire was flying around."

"She wasn't. She was lying on the ground, looking through the brush. She yelled something and passed out. Just give her some time. She'll come to."

When I can finally open my eyes, I see Chris bent over me. His eyes reveal his worry. I reach up and grasp his hand.

"How are you?" he asks.

"Better. Help me sit up, please."

He does so, and I look around at everyone. Some of their mind-blocking abilities need work because I can read their concern about blood dripping out of my ear. I touch my ear and my hand comes away with clotted blood, causing a flashback about the firecracker exploding in middle school and leaving me without my hearing.

However, I can hear just fine at the moment, so I put that fear aside.

Kayla and Ricky are sitting near me on the ground. They have both sustained injuries from the gunshots: Kayla in the calf and Ricky in the shoulder. Both have other teammates applying pressure to the bleeding wounds with their hands. I want so much for them to be whole again, for them to be healed. Their agony and pain pull at my heart, and I wish very much to help them.

Somewhere behind me, I hear Justin arguing with Chris about whether to return to the cave for safety or to try to make it to a town with injured Runners. My focus is still on Kayla and Ricky. I examine Kayla's leg wound and instinctively reach out toward her. The heat of her wound radiates against my hand, and the lead in her flesh almost calls out to me. Chris and Justin hurry over after Kayla shrieks. Chris kneels down by us. Kayla grabs Chris's arm and wraps her arm around his while I will the bullet out of her calf muscle with my thoughts. Astonishingly, the dull gray color of the lead becomes visible as it emerges from the wound and falls on the ground. The wound then silently closes.

The hushed amazement of the others tells me this kind of thing doesn't usually happen. Kayla is still holding onto Chris, but he doesn't seem to be aware. He's distracted, watching me. His eyes are wide and his face beams with a different kind of amazement.

I turn to Ricky and reach forward, placing my hand on his shoulder. Again, I locate the hard piece of lead in his flesh. With Ricky, I'm able to sense broken bone fragments in his shoulder.

"Your shoulder is broken," I tell him.

No one says anything as I work the bullet out of the wound. I place one hand on the back of his shoulder and the other on his collarbone and hold them firmly as the bone knits together under my fingers. I can feel his shoulder heating up between my hands.

"How does it feel?" I ask him.

"A bit like broken glass, except it's hot and crackles a little."

I continue working the flesh and bone between my hands.

"Is there any pain?"

"No. I feel great."

"Good. I think you're done now."

I sit back and watch him test his shoulder. He rotates his arm all the way around, raising and lowering it.

"Thank you, Calli!" he says with a broad grin. "You're better than our Healer."

Why hadn't it occurred to me I'd used the healing ability? Where's Jonas? I have to find him. While searching the crowd, my eyes make contact with Chris's eyes and I see the joy there. I can tell what he's thinking without reading his mind: I'm a Healer. His vision will come true, and our lives will eventually intertwine. No time to deal with his grandiose misinformation. I look beyond him for Jonas.

"Who are you looking for?" Chris asks.

"The person I told you about last night."

"Come with me, Calli." Chris pulls his arm away from Kayla, takes my hand and leads me away from the group.

I keep trying to locate Jonas.

"Calli, look at me." His stern tone catches my attention.

He puts his thoughts to the front of his mind. *You can't expect yourself to be able to heal a cancer patient. Healing those bullet wounds was—simply amazing—but Ricky and Kayla knew they were hurt. Jonas isn't aware he has cancer. What if you tell him and try to heal him and you aren't successful? Then you're left with a distraught boy, and you'll be beating yourself up for not knowing how to help him. We simply don't have the time to waste trying out your newfound power. Besides, if we don't reach a town tonight, there will be no healing anybody, ever.*

"All right. You're right, I mean. Okay."

"But?" he asks.

"No buts. We need to get moving. What about the bodies?"

Chris looks over his shoulder and says, "They'll have to stay here. We can't carry them."

"Shouldn't we at least cover them up?"

"With what?"

"I don't know, leaves maybe? They shouldn't be left like that."

"They just tried to kill us. Do you think they deserve a burial of sorts?"

I shrug my shoulders.

Chris continues. "The prisoner will go with us."

"Prisoner?"

"We'll hand him over to the Mind-Reader's council for an interrogation. They'll perform a read to investigate his intentions."

"I've already done that, Chris. I was in his mind. He's innocent. He was kidnapped and obeyed the Hunters only because they threatened to hurt his family. The other Runner was also an innocent captive. His parents were murdered by the Hunters' Clan. That's why he killed the Hunters and then shot himself." I pause while I review the memory of the Runner's death in my mind. "I'm confused. When he shot himself in the head, I felt the bullet go through my own head, and I passed out. But I don't understand why I had blood . . . " I trail off, "unless the experience of being in someone else's mind is far more of a physical act than I originally thought."

"Well, try not to be inside someone's head when they die."

"I'll make a note of that." I smile at him.

"Release the prisoner," Chris orders as we return to the group.

"What?" Justin struts over. "Let me guess. Calli jumped into his mind and saw something that justifies setting him free?" His tone of voice mocks and pokes fun at me.

"Let him go," Chris reiterates, directing his orders to Will and Michael to set him free. "He's innocent."

"What's your name?" I ask the Runner for the sake of the group.

"Azeel," he says with a rich African accent. He appears to be in his twenties and he stands taller than anyone in the clan.

"Where's your family, Azeel?"

"In New York. The Hunters told me if I didn't do exactly as they ordered, my family would be killed."

"How old were you when you were taken captive?"

"Sixteen. Four years ago, after racing my friends home from school, the men showed up and took me away."

"Then, you were the one I missed," Chris states, dropping his chin to his chest. "I'm so sorry."

All eyes fall on Chris.

"I was given the assignment to pick up a new Runner right after I turned nineteen. Only, when I arrived, I'd missed him. That had to have been you—New York, four years ago."

"Four years ago, yes."

Justin has been in the background, pacing, while we questioned Azeel. "We're burning daylight here," he says, placing his hands on his hips. "What direction are we heading, Chris?"

"West. We can make it to a town by nightfall. Azeel, come with us."

"I must make sure my family is okay."

"We can do that once we reach the next town. We have to find a place to stop for the night."

I stop Chris before he starts to run. "The packs. We need the Hunters' packs. They have enchanted tents and who knows what else that might come in handy."

Chris agrees.

We run over to the three dead bodies. Ricky, Yang, and Chris open the Hunters' packs and take a few objects. I don't pay attention. My eyes and thoughts are on the dead Runner, named Stefan. He was a prisoner, like Azeel. Someone missed picking him up, just like Chris was too late for Azeel.

Chris flips open a thin blanket retrieved from one of the packs and lays it over Stefan. Azeel hurries over to help.

Azeel says, "Thank you. Stefan was a good friend."

Chris nods to Azeel, respectfully, then looks up at me. I wish I could read his mind.

As we reassemble to start running again, I overhear Justin throw another hushed jab at Chris. "You and I both know why you missed Azeel. Hope you can live with *your* consequences of *your* choices."

Chris whirls on Justin and utters harsh words. He's definitely bothered over losing Azeel to the Hunters.

We run faster than the wind over peaks and through valleys, over rivers and lakes, until the sun hangs low in the evening sky with clouds tinged red and orange. My running abilities have improved from the day before, and I don't doubt for a second I am the fastest in the group now.

We arrive at the small Idaho town of Kamiah. We maybe have an hour before the Demons will emerge. Luckily, two motels are located on the outskirts of town. Chris, Justin, and I head to the office of the Moon Glo motel to purchase rooms.

"Good evening," says the female clerk at the front desk.

Chris responds, "Hello, we'd like four rooms, adjoining if possible."

"Oh, I'm sorry, we only have two rooms available tonight."

Chris turns to Justin. "Run over to the other motel and see if they have any rooms."

Justin nods and hustles out the door.

The clerk adds, "The two rooms I have are adjoining though, if that helps."

"We'll take them." Chris unzips his front pocket and pulls out a credit card and slaps it down for the clerk to process the payment. I notice the name on the card is High Altitude Sports, the name of Clara's company.

While the clerk types on her computer, Chris turns to me and says, "Go see if Justin was able to get rooms. If so, divide the group the way we did this morning. Azeel stays with us. Tell Justin I'll be over to pay as soon as I can. If there aren't any rooms at that motel, we'll have to cram into these rooms."

The clerk looks up, having obviously overheard what he said. "Uh, we have an occupancy limit per room, young man."

"I'll pay any extra charges per person."

I leave the office and hurry over to the other motel. Justin is coming out the door as I approach.

"Any luck?" I ask.

"Yeah, they have rooms," he replies with an indignant tone.

I turn on my heel before he says anything else and jog back to the group outside the Moon Glo. "Chris asked me to send everyone who ran with Justin this morning over to the other motel."

Justin reaches us and interrupts me. "What are you doing?"

"Following Chris's orders."

His face tightens and I figure he's about to launch into a rant about how I'm the slowest and lowest. Thankfully, Chris comes out the door and prevents a tirade.

I say to Chris, "He said they have rooms. I already told Justin's group to head over to the other motel."

Chris looks at everyone and raises his shoulders. "Well, what are you waiting for? Go." Chris hands me two keys with numbers. "Take everyone else to the rooms. I'll be right back."

Once we are situated in our adjoining rooms and Chris has returned, I part the curtains and spy the Demons creeping about in the shadows. We cut that to the wire.

Chris stands by me and stares out the window into the darkness.

I say, "You know, the Demons aren't interested in me. If we run into this situation again, how about if I handle the payments so you don't have to risk your neck?"

"That would be a good idea, but your name isn't on the account."

"Oh." I pause a moment, then ask, "Are you worried about Justin?"

"Yeah. I'm worried he's going to turn on us. On everyone."

Going to? He already has. "What makes you think that?"

"He's threatened by you and your powers. Haven't you noticed how he looks at you?"

"Like he wants to crush me under his heel?"

"That's the look." Chris smiles, then his expression falls. "What did you see in my future, Calli? What does the future hold for us?"

"I don't like to look," I say, casting my eyes to the floor. I'm not ready to see if anything has been altered yet. "Seers only have visions that start at four weeks in the future and beyond. They can't see something in the near future at all, so it's possible the handoff will have already happened by then and I won't be able to see the future any longer."

He gently places his hand under my chin and lifts it so my eyes are raised to his.

I can't help myself. I look. The future, as seen through Chris's perspective, rushes into my mind: the meadow with the gathered clans, as before, and the three of us standing in front of a stone table. Chris thrusts his hand forward with the box containing the real Sanguine Diamond I had switched earlier and opens the lid for the Death Clan to see. The moment the diamond is exposed, Chris recognizes an extreme amount of powers radiating from the exposed diamond. He pulls his hand back, refusing to give the box to the Death Clan leader. Chris's body fills with pain as the leader kills him. I come back to the present. *Damn!* Switching the stones is not the answer to saving Chris. I step away from him and move to sit on the edge of the bed.

"What did you see?" Chris kneels in front of me.

I notice everyone from the two rooms has gathered around to hear. I can't possibly tell them what I've seen. I choose my words with care.

"The delivery is not going to go well. One or two people may die."

"What do you mean?" Chris asks.

"I can't say exactly what will happen."

"You can't, or you won't? I die, don't I?"

I look at the curious faces, all full of apprehension, and nod my head. I hear several sharp intakes of air.

Chris responds, straightening his spine, "Then, I'll make sure I've put my things in order before the meeting."

"I'll make sure you don't die, Chris."

"How are you going to do that? Sacrifice yourself?"

I don't answer.

My silence alarms him. "No! I won't have that, Calli. If it's my time to die, then so be it. I won't have you—" Chris breaks off abruptly, then stands and turns his back to me as he stares out the window.

All I can do is guess what kind of thoughts he has racing through his mind at the moment.

Chris takes a deep cleansing breath and lets it out slowly. Then turns back to me and musters up a half-smile. He looks beyond me and says, "Azeel, come with me. Let's get you in contact with your family. The rest of you should get to bed."

I use the opportunity to take a much-needed shower to wash the crusted blood off my neck and ears, after which I crawl into bed and try to relax my mind. I share a bed with Lizbeth, while Shanika and Ashley share the other one. Even though the bed isn't the most comfortable, it still beats sleeping in a cave on rocks.

I awake to some incredibly annoying snoring. Somewhat like a bull moose yodeling in pain. I have to find out who has the loud schnoz, so I get out of bed and walk carefully to the open adjoining doorway and look in on the boys to see if I can identify the culprit. My mind is flooded with images and memories and dreams, a jumble of everything going through their unconscious minds.

Let me just say, teenage boys' dreams are definitely x-rated, and I'll leave it at that.

I notice right away that most of Chris's mental walls are down, making for an unusually easy mind-read. It makes sense that maintaining a mind-block is a conscious action that works best when a person is awake. During the day, when Chris is alert, his mind is impenetrable, and I can't get through no matter how hard I try. What is he hiding? Now that his walls are down, I have a chance to explore. I indulge myself a bit and search his head for his thoughts about me. Honestly, his idea of the two of us in a relationship scares me. For him, the thought is comforting. It keeps him going and helps him deal with the stress of his position in the clan. I guess that gives him something to look forward to.

I look beyond, for the memory of the day he missed Azeel and the frustration of his failure. He almost didn't return to the training compound then, he was so upset. More recent is his heartache when he accepts the harsh reality Azeel only became a prisoner because he had been too slow to retrieve him—because he had made a pit-stop along the way. However, I can't tell what the stop entailed because the thought is buried too deep in Chris's troubled psyche.

I pull out of Chris's mind with mixed feelings.

Another loud snore rumbles through the room and I pinpoint the snorer. Jonas. I delve into his body to find the cancer growing inside him. The extent of abnormal growth is worse than imagined: cancer cells are in his abdomen, lungs, kidneys, and brain. In fact, a tumor in his upper throat restricts his airway and causes him to snore. My eyes water at the thought of his impending death. What should I do? I have to tell him. I should at least try to heal him. We have several hours to go until morning. What can it hurt to try?

I focus on the growth in his throat first, feeling the mass within my own head, reaching my mind around the cancer like tentacles, trying to dissolve or shrink the lump. I press with my mind, but excruciating pain fills my head as if the cancer is my own. My surroundings began to close in as the pain increases.

Chapter 8 – Nature's Will

"Calli! Wake up!"

I hear Chris's voice. The pain in my head lingers: a slow, dull, throbbing. I open my eyes to discover his face near mine, and become aware I'm on the floor in the boys' room. Chris has pulled my upper body into his arms. I untangle myself from his arms and sit up. "What happened?"

Chris stands and I see everyone is awake and staring at me.

"You started screaming and holding your head and fell to the floor," Chris says.

I search the room for Jonas, and when I find his face, I search his body, only to find the tumor intact, unchanged.

Chris figures out straightaway what I had been trying to do. All he has to do is glance in the direction my eyes are looking to see who I'm focused on.

"Get up." He holds out his hand to me. I stand, and he leads me into the bathroom and closes the door behind us.

"Why are we in here?"

"Because I don't want everyone else freaked out by what I'm about to tell you, especially one person in particular." He reaches over and turns on the bathtub faucet. "Background noise." He points to the running water. "Try to avoid saying Jonas's name, all right?"

I nod and sit on the floor with my back against the door and my knees pulled to my chest.

Chris positions himself on the edge of the tub, our knees nearly touching. "You're on dangerous ground here, Calli. One of the first things we learn about at the compound is how to accept death, and why we should when our time comes."

"Well, I never started my training so you can't expect me—"

He cuts me off. "I know. This will be your first lesson about death. You told me you can't see his future. Normally that would mean he doesn't have one and he's going to die. Or it could simply mean you are new to the Seer ability and just need more practice. However, at some point in his life, he's going to die and you can't do anything about it. Tell me, how serious is his cancer? Are you able to determine to what extent he's suffering?"

"It's serious. I think it has spread into different organs. He's not in a ton of pain yet. Whatever pain he has, he brushes it off so he won't sound weak to the rest of us. I think it's fast developing because when I looked into his memories, he seemed healthy." I remember hearing my father talk about a cancer patient who was fine one month and dead the next. My father told me that "sometimes cancer sneaks up and takes us by surprise."

"Calli, consider this. If a doctor discovered his illness, do you think they would even try to fight it, or send him home to die?"

"I'm not a doctor, but I can tell the disease is widespread. If he was my father's patient, he'd probably be set up in a hospice program where he'd be kept as comfortable as possible for the short time he has left."

"Exactly. In the early stages, most kinds of cancer are treatable by both human and Healer alike, but when any illness is far enough advanced, both know when to pull back and let nature take its course."

"But this is different. I'm a Healer. I can heal him."

"Think of yourself as a glorified surgeon. You can heal wounds and broken bones. Basically your powers are limited to what a doctor can do. He or she can shock a heart to make it beat again, but if the heart has damage that will prevent it from beating on its own, the doctor's hands are tied. Think about a patient in a coma. A doctor can't wake them, and if the patient is brain dead . . . do you comprehend the limitations doctors have? They are not all-powerful. Everyone dies. Our bodies give out, and Jonas is going to die. Only, he doesn't know that yet."

"I can remove it. I know I can."

"Do you remember falling in agony a few minutes ago? Clearly, you are trying to do something that may not be possible at this point."

"Will it kill me to try?"

"Now this is where you're on dangerous ground. Thinking you can defy death, cheat death, is bordering on evil. Let's imagine for a moment you did heal him, but in five years he's shot in the head. Oh, but wait, you fix his head and he lives. Then, when he's sixty, he suffers a massive heart attack, but you heal that too. However, at ninety, he develops congestive heart failure, and you fix him. And when he's one hundred and twenty his kidneys give out, but you heal him. Then he's one hundred and fifty—"

"I get your point. When nature takes us, it's game over. But he's so young. He has so much life ahead of him. He shouldn't have to die now."

Chris put his finger up to his lips to remind me to keep my voice down. "Why do you believe his time to die is up to you?"

"I don't, I only—"

"You do. You tread on dangerous ground."

"Why?"

"Anyone who thinks they have the power to decide who lives or dies is going against nature and is in direct opposition to the universal order of things. They put themselves up higher than everyone around them and they all, and I mean all, turn evil. They become power hungry, obsessed with total domination and immortality. The Death Clan are Healers—were Healers. Now they are striving for immortality and ultimate control. They don't answer to anyone. They don't care about anyone, only themselves. Their goal is to gain all the abilities of every other clan and become invincible."

"I'm not like that."

"You already are."

"No!"

"Shhh." He puts his finger to his mouth. "There's a natural order to life, to all forms of life, and it's not our place to try to alter that force. Through the years, certain species have gone extinct. The world's populations have taken drastic hits due to naturally occurring illnesses or disasters. But without those, the population today would be astronomical."

"But—"

"But nothing. No one can live forever, Calli."

"I'm not trying for forever with him, just a few more years."

"In a few more years, he might be married with children, and then when he gets sick, you'll feel his children shouldn't be without their father, and so on. Do you follow? Do you understand the limitations and the need to learn how to accept death? You need to learn this before you wind up in a situation where someone who means a lot to you is dying. What's going to happen when someone you deeply love is mortally wounded? It's important you learn to recognize when nature's taking over. If you don't, you'll be no better than the Death Clan, who at one time were good and kept everyone alive, kind of like you and your desires to keep him alive. But then they took nature into their own hands and began deciding when people would die. Their very existence is against nature."

"What about the other Healers? Are they evil?"

"No, because they understand when to stop healing and let nature take over. Let me tell you a story. Several hundred years ago, a clan of Healers started down this path of overriding nature. They wanted, and discovered, a way to achieve immortality by killing others and absorbing their youth. Nature found a way to intervene, and the entire clan, in their power-hungry state, was obliterated. It's said they became the Shadow Demons. You would know them as vampires."

"They don't look like vampires to me."

"They were never called vampires except by humans. They don't have long incisors like Hollywood would have you believe. They don't bite their victims, and wooden stakes through the heart won't kill them. Nothing can kill them except other members of their clan. Humans couldn't handle the facts, so they came up with their own stories of how to kill vampires to satisfy their fears."

"How did they absorb the youth of other people?"

"No one knows for sure because their methods died with their mortal bodies. The Death Clan hasn't even figured out the secret, to my knowledge. Calli, what you need to accept is the Death Clan, and the ancient vampires, all started out like you, learning to heal and trying to keep people alive."

I consider for a moment that my powers are a limited-time offer and will be removed from me once the diamond is delivered. I simply can't see the harm in doing one good deed while having the ultimate power. It isn't like I'd turn evil. My mind wars with right and wrong. How wrong am I to want to help someone? Chris must sense what I'm thinking because he starts up again.

"For every change in the order of things, there's a repercussion. Wise Healers know when not to heal, when not to help, and when to walk away. Someday you'll be a wise Healer."

I want to tell him, *No, someday I'll be a nobody, again,* but, I can't do that without revealing why.

The bathroom has filled with cool mist from the running water and Chris's skin shimmers with moisture. I figure mine does too, because he moves back a little from me and takes in my appearance. I watch the expression on his face change slightly. He seems to be seeing me with different eyes, the kind that make my stomach flutter with anticipation.

Anticipation of what? Is he about to kiss me? I wish I had more experience around boys and the way they think.

He holds his hand out. I take hold, and he helps me stand. We face each other for several electrically-charged seconds. I say electrically, because the emotion in his eyes has a kind of physical energy that makes my skin prickle.

He drops my hand and shuts off the bathtub water. "Let's get some sleep," he says, ushering me out to my bed.

The clock on the end-table says one-thirty as I lie back down on the bed. My heart still races from being with Chris. He's standing in the doorway between the two rooms, looking my direction with a concentrated intensity. He finally disappears into his room and shuts off the light. I let out my pent-up breath.

"What was that all about?" Lizbeth asks.

"I needed a lesson about death."

"What?"

147

"Never mind. Let's get some sleep."

"Do you and Chris have a thing going?"

"Of course not. He's too old for me." I try to sound convincing, but I fail.

"Could'a fooled me."

"And me," Ashley's voice sounds from the other bed.

Shanika says, "Yeah, he's hot for you, girl! You're all powerful, but you seem to be blind about it." Shanika and Ashley both giggle.

"Hey, I'm not an idiot, and don't forget I can read minds. I know about his feelings for me, and you two as well for that matter." I get them giggling again. Then, in an effort to get them to drop the subject, I say, "Anyway, I hear he's holding out for his special someone."

Shanika answers, "That's true."

Ashley says, "When we get back to Montana, I'm going to have you look in my crush's head to find out if he likes me."

"We already know he doesn't," Shanika answers.

Chris says in a loud voice from the other room, "Go to sleep!"

Lizbeth rolls over and whispers, "Why were you on the floor screaming?"

"I tried one of my powers without knowing what it would do to me."

"Which power?"

"Healing."

"Who's hurt?"

"No one," I say, yawning.

"I don't understand."

"Neither do I. Goodnight." I roll away from her, hoping she won't continue. She doesn't.

Morning comes too fast. We meet up with Justin and find his group didn't have any trouble with their sleeping accommodations, but apparently a good night's rest did nothing for Justin's mood. He still glares at me like he's choking on something nasty.

Azeel says goodbye and leaves our company to begin his journey home to New York. I can't help but wonder how Chris is taking his departure. Justin is visibly upset with the idea someone like Azeel is roaming the countryside with insider information concerning our delivery mission. I know he's only worried about his own neck and not ours.

We run over hilly farmlands and skirt far enough around the edges of towns to not be seen. We stop for a lunch break by a large river and eat more of our dry granola bars.

I stretch back on the grass and rest my mind as best as I can, trying to enjoy the pleasant weather and warm sun. I hear splashing sounds and laughter down by the river. I close my eyelids and can tell every time a cloud passes in front of the sun.

I think about Azeel and hope he will find his family to be okay when he gets home. My mind drifts to Maetha and the day we met at Harold Bates's office. A particularly dark cloud blocks the sunlight, causing me to open my eyes. I become anxious as I realize my companions are not down at the river anymore. I twist around, finding myself totally alone. Where have they gone? And why is the sky so dark? When did the sun go down, and why didn't anyone tell me? Somewhere in my brain, I come to the conclusion this must be a vision or dream of some kind. I stand and climb the small hill, discovering large spotlights set up to illuminate the ground. People are entering and exiting several enormous army-style tents. I walk forward, wondering if this clearing is the one from my vision.

As I near the tent, Maetha comes out to greet me. "Ah, you found me. The diamond is giving you bi-locating abilities."

"Bi-what? Where are we?"

"Canada. Your mind sought out mine and brought you here, and from a considerable distance, too. Impressive."

"I don't remember seeking you in my mind. I only thought of you. Is this where the exchange will happen?"

"No, you've seen the clearing in your vision."

"Why is it dark? It's only noon."

"I'm simulating darkness to test the effectiveness of the floodlights."

I glance into the shadows and see the Demons creeping around. Interesting that they can be present in the middle of the day. I deduce that during a full eclipse of the sun the Demons would also be a threat. I turn my attention back to Maetha. "Maetha, why did you give my perfume to Justin?"

"Because he's not to be trusted."

"He'd been seen talking with the Death Clan," I tell her.

"Yes. He's been exceptionally instrumental."

"This is confusing. Why are you with the Death Clan? Do you work for them?"

"No. I work for no one and everyone."

"Why are you being so vague? What are you not telling me?"

"Plenty. Calli, certain elements must align to ensure the success of this mission. I cannot tell you what or when to do anything."

"But I need to know when to bring out the diamond."

"Follow your instincts and desires. Most of all, follow your heart. You are human after all."

"But—"

She smiles at me. "You need to go back now before you get yourself into trouble."

"Will I lose my powers?" As I ask the question, she fades away. I run toward her, and she moves further away. "Wait!" I call out. I run faster, but it doesn't matter. The sky brightens, and without warning a deluge of ice-cold water covers my face and my body as I'm submerged in water. I panic, kick, and flail for my life, trying to find the surface. I desperately need air, but which way is up? My vision darkens, and my lungs are on fire. Inside the darkness I see Chris swimming toward me. He grabs me under my arms and paddles toward the light. I close my eyes and let my body go.

I wake up coughing. My chest hurts, and my head and gut hurt too. Why do I hurt so much? I have been rolled on my side to allow water to escape my mouth. I wipe my lips with the sleeve of my jacket and become aware of everyone standing around me. How embarrassing. I want to die—maybe I have. I sit up and rub my chest.

"Are you okay?" Chris asks, out of breath and coughing. He sits next to me with his knees drawn up to his chest, his arms wrapped around them. He's dripping wet, but so am I.

"I think so."

Justin lights into me. "Why in the hell did you go running into the river?"

"I didn't . . . did I?" I can't remember.

"You did," Chris says, then coughs violently. From the sound of it, he almost drowned too.

"Why would I run into the river?"

Beth said, "I think you had a vision. You stood and started yelling something about losing your powers and took off across the water. You stopped and sunk like a rock. Good thing Chris is such an excellent swimmer and knows mouth-to-mouth or you'd be dead."

I look over at Chris, who glances at me sideways. "Thanks."

He nods.

Kayla reaches for my zipper. "Let's get you out of your jacket so it can dry."

My hand quickly grazes my pocket to make sure the diamond is still inside. It is. I grab her wrist and make her let go. "I'll keep it on, thanks. I'll dry as I run."

Justin points to Chris. "He's in no condition to run now. He can hardly breathe."

I place my hand on Chris's back and become aware of the water in his lungs—not good. His lips have a blue tinge to them. He's out of the water, but he seems to be drowning.

With my hand on his back, I warm the excessive moisture with my mind, pulling and siphoning it, then I stop. "Is this nature's will?" I ask, trying not to sound like a know-it-all. I certainly am not trying to make a point. I just don't want to be going against nature if this is what nature intends.

"Please, help me," he struggles to say.

His terrified plea touches something deep inside me. Perhaps it's the fact he's just saved my life and I feel I need to repay the debt, even if it is against nature. I continue with my ministrations, easing the water out of his lungs, allowing oxygen into his blood. I lay him back on the ground and straddle his waist, being careful not to put my weight on him. With both of my hands, I instinctively massage his chest and lungs, sliding my hands up his chest to his neck. I watch the moisture vapor leave his body through his mouth.

He reaches up and grasps my wrists, not trying to stop me, but to be a part of what I'm doing to him. I continue to massage his lungs up and out. I think about what it must have been like for him to watch me run out onto the river and sink.

I enter his memories and see myself convulsing. I look absolutely scary, even to myself. In Chris's mind, he understands what's happening to me and that I need to be protected from harming myself. He tries to rein my body under control by pinning me to the ground with his own body. I throw him off with inhuman strength and jump up. "Will I lose my powers?" I yell, and then I run out into the middle of the river and sink.

Chris is right behind me, trying to catch up. The moment I go under he dives into the water, panic-stricken. The swift current has swept my body away, but he doesn't give up. He swims until he finds me, which takes longer than his held air allows. He wraps his arms under my arms, then struggles to swim to the surface. The others wait at the river's edge and help pull me up the riverbank.

At the sight of my unresponsive body, adrenaline shoots through Chris's body, giving him a second wind of energy. Out of desperation, he slaps my cheek to try to wake me. When that fails, he checks for a pulse, then gives me mouth-to-mouth with the little air he can spare. He shakes my shoulders as anguish floods his entire being. He couldn't feel worse if I'd died. At that moment, it appears to him I have. He uses both palms and presses on my chest. He does this repeatedly as tears of pain run down his face. When he gives me several more mouthfuls of air, he does so lovingly. He can barely see through his tears.

I start to cough, and everyone standing by gasps with relief. Hope begins to build as he rolls me over on my side and shrinks away from me, pulling his knees up to his chest and hugging them as complete exhaustion consumes him. His adrenaline rush ends, and the water in his lungs is now extinguishing his life.

That is, until I touch his back.

I sense him, presently, and his affection for me. He opens his eyes, still holding my wrists as I massage his chest. His lungs are back to normal, but his heart rate continues to increase.

"Are you all right, Chris?"

"I think you've fixed me, so you can get off me now."

"Oh, right." I quickly moved off his stomach, and he sits up just as fast.

My mind keeps replaying the images from his head. I ask, "Did we go against nature?"

He doesn't answer, nor does he turn to look at me.

I wonder why he let me into his mind? Why were his defenses down? Did he want me to understand his true feelings? The silence between us is deafening. The group has picked up on the tension because they don't hesitate to leave when Lizbeth ushers everyone away.

"I had a vision," I say.

"I figured as much. I've heard of visionaries doing crazy things, even deadly things, in the course of a vision. I tried to hold you down, but you got away."

"It wasn't exactly a vision, but more like an out-of-body experience. I spoke with a witch."

His head swiftly turns in my direction. "A witch? You're dealing with a witch? Is this why you have multiple powers?"

My happy feeling gone, I stand and brush the grass off my wet suit. "I didn't say I was dealing with a witch. I said I spoke with one in my vision."

His eyes narrow and his voice is cold. "Yes, but you yelled to the wind, 'Am I going to lose my powers?' Were you talking to her? She could be watching us right now." The strictness in his voice tells me this is serious.

"I guess so. It's kind of hazy now. I'll have to think about it and try to recall the whole conversation."

He gets up and says over his shoulder as he briskly walks up the hillside, "We need to get moving so we're not captured like the other team. I'll get the others."

I am flabbergasted. He's left me so abruptly. How can his emotions change like that? I witnessed his innermost feelings, his indescribable love for me, his desperation to save me, and his gratitude. Yet, one mention of talking with a witch in a vision and he's running the other way. I remember he freaked out when I confronted Justin about his dealings with a witch, too. I conclude it is unwise to mention my encounters with Maetha, even if it is only in a vision.

My own body still hurts. Why? Can't I heal myself? Apparently not.

The clan comes down the hill, and I prepare to run with Chris, but he takes off without me. Justin stares at me with a slack jaw for a moment, then he takes my hand and we start running, following Chris and the others.

As our group treks north through Idaho, I think about Chris giving me mouth-to-mouth, how he held my wrists while I healed him, the immense feelings of love he had for me . . . and then how he looked at me like I carried the bubonic plague. A look of complete revulsion. My eyes water, sending tears straight back into my hair.

After two more hours of hard running through thick forests, we approach a town called Coeur d'Alene, situated on the north end of a large lake. We stop at the water's edge to rest while Chris and Justin pour over the map. As dusk draws near, I listen to them argue over the risk of staying in a large town versus searching for a more remote spot. They finally decide to stay the night in Coeur d'Alene at two motels near each other and Chris issues room assignments to the group without looking in my direction. I can't believe it when I hear him order me to room with Justin's group. I'm absolutely stunned. Chris is completely distancing himself.

Fine! Fine! All I can say is FINE! I'm not myself when I'm around him anyway. I can't think straight. I keep having these visions, along with desires I'd rather not have. So if staying with Justin, who couldn't hate me more, will help my situation, I welcome it.

Once we get checked in, I discover I'll be sharing a bed with Beth. No surprise there. I wonder if she'll draw an imaginary line down the middle, indicating "her side." Kayla and Jessica have the other bed. None of them dare talk to me, for fear of ticking Justin off. They only stare in awe. At least they aren't asking me about their futures.

Justin sits in the adjoining room, speaking in a low voice to the guys. I pick up on some of their conversation. "Visions . . . future . . . minds . . . hunts . . . must be a witch for Chris to turn away from her like that."

I lie back on the bed and close my eyes. The girls leave the room and join Justin. I place my hand over the diamond and feel its pulsating power under my palm. This is my true addiction, giving me capabilities beyond imagination, as well as attitude and a new sense of self. Right or wrong? I don't know.

Maetha advised me to follow my desires, to go with my gut, so I get up and walk out of the motel room, closing the door behind me. I move through the Shadow Demons who prowl beyond the edge of light, and make my way down the block to the motel occupied by Chris and the others.

I focus on all my senses and listen at the windows for him. Why am I doing this? He rejected me. Yet I want to listen to his voice or look into his mind to find out why, hoping he regrets being angry and cold with me. I pray I'll discover I misread his reaction on the riverbank. I can't hear or see anything, though. I only detect his scent.

Why is he so repulsed at the thought of me talking with a witch? He didn't get upset when he found out Justin was consorting with a witch—the same witch, although neither Chris nor Justin know. But still? Why would he ditch me over that? More importantly, why am I so upset? It's not like his vision of me will come true anyway.

I walk back to my motel room in a weary state of mind, dragging my feet so much I trip on the uneven sidewalk. Two middle-aged men step out of the shadows. They stand about the same height. Both wear ragged clothes, and neither looks as if they've shaved in several days. One of the stale-beer-stinking men has ratty blond hair and the other has black. Their minds reveal they are not from around the area and are just passing through on their way to the west coast.

"Careful miss, you'll hurt yourself." An evil grin spreads across the blond man's face. He has a jagged scar creasing one cheek. Without delay, I gain access into his mind. What I view appalls me. How can anyone think such horrible thoughts?

The black-haired man places his hand on my shoulder and says, "Young lady, are you lost?" A cigarette dangles from his lips and as he inhales, the orange glow of the tip illuminates his pock-marked face.

To any passerby, these men might appear to be worried about my safety and are just trying to help, but as a Mind-Reader, I deduce I'm the only one concerned for my safety. These men reek with evil intentions.

It's odd, really, the point at which I've found myself. The sixteen-year-old Calli of two weeks ago would never have wandered the streets of an unknown town alone and after dark. I wouldn't have spoken to two strange men, let alone have tried to fight them. Neither Chris nor my teammates can't help me now. The Demons are thick, and there isn't enough light. I'm on my own with two scary-looking men who mean to harm me.

But I'm not the same girl anymore. I've changed and am no longer frightened of them. Instead I feel uneasy because I've never used my powers to hurt anyone. If they don't leave me alone, they will be my first experiment.

"Thank you for your concern, but I'm not lost," I say as if I walk the streets all the time. "I'm on my way back to my motel." I point to the building at the end of the block.

"Little late for a pretty young thing like you to be wanderin' about," Blondie says.

"Yes, I suppose so. Good night." I start to walk away, knowing I won't get far.

They both grab me from behind. Blondie wraps his arms around my chest, holding my arms down, and the other man seizes my ankles. I know they are going to try to abduct me, and with my heightened reflexes, yes, I could have avoided being caught, but I'm angry. I've been unjustly dumped today, and holy hell, these men are about to feel the wrath of a scorned woman—a scorned young woman with amazing powers, that is.

I don't struggle much. I don't even scream. Instead I focus on the black-haired man who holds my feet. Obviously, I don't want to be dropped by attacking the man holding my upper half, so I go after the foot man first. I scope his body with my mind and find he has an old knee injury. I irritate the tendons and he starts limping and grunting, yet the cigarette never slips from between his lips.

"What's wrong?" the blond one growls as they haul me toward the entrance of an alley.

"My bad knee! I must have stepped in a hole." The man drops my feet and falls in agony, his cigarette bouncing on the ground. He now holds his other knee, which I have just blown out with my mind. He lets fly a string of colorful swear-words.

The other man still has me restrained, but not for long. I explore inside him and find a weakness: his heart. I say to him, "You shouldn't be hauling me around with your bad heart, sir. You might get hurt."

"Shut up, kid!" he yells. He tightens his hold on me, but then lets go and clutches his chest, screaming, "Aaagh! What did you do to me?"

I move away from him. "Well sir, I think you're having a heart attack. You'd better sit down and take it easy. I'll run for help." I don't wait for them to protest. I run like a regular human away from the men and straight to my motel room. I have to pound on the door to get the others to open up. I run in and call 911 for an ambulance, telling the dispatcher a man appears to be having a heart attack in the alley near this motel. When the time comes to report my name, I hang up.

Chapter 9 – Protector

I turn around to find Justin standing and blocking me in the corner. He puts his hands on his hips and says, "So, you think you can just waltz out of here and do whatever you like without telling anybody? You put us all at risk when you did that. What if the lights had gone out and a Shadow Demon got someone?"

"Leave me alone, Justin." I try to push past him.

He reaches up and pushes my shoulders back, making me bump into the end stand, knocking the phone to the floor. His face moves close to mine. "You can't tell me what to do, muck."

"Don't call me a muck," I threaten, my heart still pounding from the encounter with the men.

"I'll call you whatever I want, and you can't stop me." He sounds like a second-grader out on the playground.

I wish he'd move away from me. "Yes, I suppose you can call me whatever you want, but I *can* make you stop."

"What?" His eyes widen as he straightens his back, pulling his face away from mine.

I reach inside of him and irritate his stomach so much he literally has to jump across the bed to make it to the bathroom in time to vomit.

I sit on the bed, shaking. This ability to cause pain or injury astounds me. I will never have to worry about being mugged, kidnapped, or bullied again. I won't have to put up with Justin calling me a muck either. To prove my point, I go to the bathroom door.

"How's it goin' in there, buddy?"

"Leave me alone, muck!"

I twist his stomach again, and he wretches even more. "Justin, I don't want you calling me a muck anymore."

"Shut up, muck!"

More dry heaving.

"Justin, stop calling me that. I'm asking nicely now."

"Muck."

I wrench his gut and hear, along with everyone else in the two rooms, Justin struggle to get his pants off in time to unload the biggest grumbly tummy ever. Nasty.

"Oh God!" he screams in pain and disgust.

"Justin, please don't call me a muck anymore," I say letting my voice rise an octave to sound sweeter. "And before you do it again to spite me, think about the fact you'll dehydrate if you keep it up."

After a small stretch of silence, Justin manages to say, "It's wrong to use your abilities to cause pain, Calli."

"It's equally wrong to bully and tease others, *Justin*. Can we call a truce?" I ask through the door. *Through the door!* I hadn't even realized I'd continued to affect Justin even though he was out of eyesight. Is that a normal practice for Healers? Of course, hurting his stomach isn't something a Healer would probably do—it would be something a Death Clan member would do.

Chris's lecture on the Death Clan and the natural order of things springs to my mind. *Uh oh. Am I turning to the tantalizing evil side of the healing ability?*

"Truce." Justin's muffled voice comes from the other side of the door.

"Thank you." I walk away and sit on my bed.

The phone rings and Jessica answers. She greets Chris on the other end. Justin must have called him to report me missing. Jessica hangs up the phone and throws a concerned glance in my direction, then turns away and goes into the other room. Was Chris worried about me?

When, oh when, will this assignment be over? I can't wait to . . . to what? To meet the Death Clan, lose my powers, and watch Chris die? This new life of mine positively sucks!

Justin comes out of the bathroom, pale and trembling, looking like death warmed over. His eyes shoot daggers through the air at me. Jessica informs him Chris wants him to call back.

I listened as Justin whines and complains to Chris on the phone, claiming I've tortured him, that I used my powers to harm him, and I'm turning evil. But what about *his* bullying? The whole "sticks-n-stones" saying isn't true at all. I wonder if it is absolutely imperative for Justin to be with us when the diamond is delivered. I imagine the possibility, picturing the details in my mind, and now all I have to do is peek into someone's future to see the outcome.

I wait for Justin to come tell me Chris wants to speak with me, but that never happens. I fall asleep and don't wake until morning.

▽ ▽ ▽

A loud knock at the door about six o'clock startles everyone. Kayla opens the door to find two police officers outside. "We're looking for the young lady who made the 911 call last night," one of them says.

Everyone points to me. *Thanks guys.*

"I made the call, officers," I admit. "Is there a problem?"

"You reported the medical emergency in the alley?"

"Yes."

"Well, the man died, but not before he claimed you had hurt him with your mind." The other officer behind him tries to stifle a smile.

"I'm sorry to hear he died, but how could I hurt him with my mind? That's ridiculous. What about the other man? He seemed hurt as well."

"He was transported to the hospital. We need to speak with your parents."

"I'm not with my parents. This is a track-and-field team. We're on our way to Calgary to attend a meet. You can speak with our supervisor, Justin Macintyre."

I sit on the bed, listening as Justin assures the officers I had nothing to do with the man's death. I had gone out for a walk and returned all scared and called 911. He told them I didn't dare stay with the man because I was only sixteen, so I had come back to the room and called for help. The officers seem to buy the story.

I'm amazed at how Justin maturely handles the situation, proving when he wants to, he can behave like a decent guy. I look for the future concerning his presence at the delivery. I see the clearing through his eyes, but the view is from a distance, as if Justin is watching from up on a hillside. Chris and I stand near the stone table. Chris crumples to the ground along with all the hostages. I pull out of Justin's head. He definitely needs to be with us at the meeting to transfer the diamond, or many people will die, including Chris.

Chris and his group arrive at our motel shortly after the officers leave. The night before, all I wanted was to be near him, to try to understand his actions, but this morning as I watch him storm over to me with dark clouds of anger on his face, I'm not so inclined.

The force of his exposed mind hits me hard. *You attacked two poor defenseless men and killed one! How dare you use your powers like that!*

"That's not what happened," I say. I roll my eyes as I try to appear unaffected by his anger and disappointment, but inside, my heart thuds and I feel my cheeks flame.

Why don't you tell me what happened then?

"I didn't kill the guy. He had a bad heart anyway. He and his friend shouldn't have tried to kidnap me. I was only protecting myself."

Protecting yourself means staying put in your room and not venturing out after dark! And what about Justin? What did you do to him?

"Save it, Chris. I don't want to hear this from you, of all people."

"What does that mean?" he asks aloud.

"Whatever you want it to mean. We better hit the pavement if we're going to make it to the clearing tonight." I try to change the subject, but I inadvertently dig my hole deeper.

"What are you talking about? What clearing?" Chris asks in confusion.

"Isn't that where we're headed?" I ask.

Justin jumps in. "I thought we were going to the Death Clan's caves. What's all this about a clearing? Do you have something you need to tell us, Calli? Are you working for the Death Clan?"

"If I was, you'd already know, wouldn't you, Justin?"

"You little bit—" Justin moves toward me with his hands outstretched, as if he wants to squeeze my neck.

Chris jumps in front of Justin before he can get his hands on me. I don't flatter myself one bit by thinking Chris is protecting me. He's merely keeping the peace.

"I've seen the clearing in a vision, complete with floodlights and tents, and all the clans, and the delivery," I say over Chris's shoulder, drawing the attention of everyone.

"And you think we're going to reach this place by tonight? Your visions are four weeks out, Calli, remember?" Justin points out.

I hate to admit it, but he's right.

Shanika jumps in with, "What happens when the package is delivered?"

I respond casually, "Doom, destruction, and the end of the world . . . stuff like that."

"Don't be stupid," Justin scoffs. "Tell us what happens!"

"Aren't you worried my visions are somehow related to a witch? Chris is. Maybe my visions are null and void. Who knows? After all, I'm the new girl. What the hell do I know about your world?"

Chris turns away from me and issues orders over his shoulder for everyone to be ready in a few minutes. He leaves the room and stands outside my window, where he puts his thoughts to the front of his mind. I look away. I don't want to acknowledge him at the moment.

We run all day long and cross over the border into Canada. I convince Justin to let me try running on my own to see if I've gained speed. Naturally, I have, and I'm relieved. Now I won't have to hold hands with anyone as if I'm a little kid. We stop for a short break for lunch. I'm careful not to close my eyes for fear of having a repeat of the day before. We all know how well that went. Chris continues to avoid me, and he finds reasons to leave the area whenever I approach. It's a good thing he doesn't know about the diamond in my pocket or else he'd really be freaked out.

The only thing to lighten my mood is watching Kayla's antics as she continually tries to place herself next to Chris. She thinks for sure he likes her, and if she keeps herself under his nose long enough, he might make a move. Emotions, hormones, and misconceptions are the same whether you have cosmic abilities or not, I observe.

I think more about the fact the heart-attack man actually died. I consider it an act of self-defense, especially because if I was a normal girl, I'd be defiled and dead and dumped in a ditch right now. That's what they'd planned. In fact, I probably prevented future kidnappings and deaths of other girls. So was it so wrong for me to have done what I did? No. My only regret is that the other guy lived.

The mountains grow larger and larger as we run throughout the day. We stop at the edge of the forest near a town in southern Alberta in the late evening. When the wind hits my nose, I smell danger.

"Hunters!" I yell to Justin and Chris. For a moment, I think they don't believe me, but Chris would rather err on the side of right than wrong. He leads us into a thick wooded area where we have more options to hide.

"Where are they?" Justin asks.

I put my thoughts out into the forest and find the two Hunters. I smell their rancid odor as they carefully follow our scents. "They're hot on our trail."

Ashley asks, "Why don't we run to the safety of the town? The Demons will be out soon."

Lizbeth answers, "Then they'll know exactly where we are."

"They already know where we are!"

"Quiet," I command. "Chris, take everyone further into the forest."

"Justin, you take them. I'll stay with her." Chris hands the order down.

"No! I don't want you here. Leave Beth with me."

The decision is made in an instant, and Beth stays. We reposition ourselves a little higher up the hill to provide a better visual advantage.

Beth whispers, "They know we have to stay in that town tonight. I wonder why they didn't wait there for us to return?"

"Beth, use your mind to talk to me. We need to keep quiet."

"Oh, right."

I grab her arm as the Hunters come into view. I scan the closer one's body and find his weakness: an aneurism in his brain, which I rupture, and he collapses to the ground. The remaining Hunter gives his companion a brief glance and continues moving forward, tightening his hold on the rifle in his hands. I feel inside his body and struggle to find anything wrong. His entire body is in excellent condition. I scan him again as he moves out of my sight but still find nothing to irritate or aggravate. He stops and leans against a tree stump, positions himself, and raises the gun, focusing down his gun sights.

What can I do? I wonder what he's aiming at, and with that thought I enter his mind. I see through his eyes, the same way I'd observed the present through Chris's eyes. He has the back of Justin's head in his cross-hairs. He can smell the icy aroma on Justin and he begins to squeeze the trigger. I have to act fast. I break his neck with my mind, feeling the vertebrae and spinal cord crunch and grind. Then I throw up.

Beth grabs me, all excited. "Calli, you did it! What exactly did you do?" Her confusion at what has happened makes me throw up again.

She leaves my side and returns to the others. I'm still nauseous over what I've done. I could feel his vertebrae as if I'd snapped them with my bare hands. As I replay everything in my head, the crunching sound sickens me, and I heave again.

The group returns and Chris scrutinizes me. I think I detect a glimmer of sorrow. But before I can analyze his emotions, the horrible smell of approaching Demons startles me. "Run!" I choke out. "Stay in the light!"

In a flash, the other Runners disappear. I roll over on my back and stare up at the tiny patch of darkening sky above me. What have I become? *I'm a cold-blooded murderer.* Tears fill my eyes, and painful sobs erupt from my mouth. Why was this burden placed on me? Why me?

I lay on the ground, wallowing in my misery for several minutes until I see the Demons float above me on their way to the broken-necked Hunter. I had thought he was dead already. Why would the Demons still be interested in him? I stagger over to his body, which lies in the light. He's still alive. I'd only paralyzed him, so I delve into his mind to find out who sent him. I find that the two Hunters had been hired by the Mind-Readers to find the diamond before the Death Clan could take possession. They had every town directly over the Canadian border staked out with Hunters, not knowing which town we would stop in. The Mind-Readers were doing what they thought would be best. I also discover they did not issue an order for our deaths. The Hunters decided on their own to kill us to get the diamond.

"Please finish me! Don't let the Demons get me!" the dying Hunter pleads.

"I thought I'd already killed you," I say. I walk away, knowing now I hadn't actually murdered him. But I'm not going to help him either. I'll let the Demons take care of him. So I guess I am a murderer after all.

I find the other Hunter's body. I can't enter his mind. The Demons aren't interested in him at all. He's definitely dead.

I walk out of the forest, contemplating what I've done. The Hunters would have killed whoever they needed to kill in order to get the diamond. And I am the only one in my party who can do anything about it. My shoulders aren't big enough to carry this load.

I take an hour to walk the distance to town. I need every second of the hour to get my emotions under control. I come to the conclusion the teammates are like my family and I need to protect them. Just as a parent would protect their loved ones from a burglar, I will protect these friends. I'm the only one who can do so, therefore, it's my responsibility. I smile a little as I realize I'm finally thinking of them as friends.

I make the assumption Chris will choose a motel on the outskirts of town based on the fact the sun had set when they left me. They wouldn't have wasted any time securing rooms. I wander the parking lot until I spot Chris looking out the window on the second floor. I go to his door, which he only opens a crack.

"You're in room number 213," he says, not making eye contact.

I walk away, incredibly sad, and will my tears to stay behind my eyes.

I knock on the door of 213, and Justin pulls back the drapes to confirm it's me. He unlocks and opens the door. Once I get inside, he and the others bombard me with questions.

"What does it feel like to kill someone?" Beth asks right away.

"I don't know."

"What do you mean? You were puking your guts out. It must have felt awfully gross!" Beth's curious eyes search mine.

"You think? I only paralyzed that guy. The Demons finished him off. The other Hunter was on death's door anyway. I opened the door, that's all."

"Well, aren't you just the goody two-shoes," Justin taunts.

"Yeah, that's me. Saving *your* goody two-shoes! You were the one with the package. They were after you and you alone. The rest of us would have been safe. Maybe I shouldn't have stopped them."

Justin stomps away in a huff.

I pick up on the fact the room is crowded and lacks an adjoining door like the other motel rooms we've had. One quick look into an available mind tells me there were only two rooms left in the motel and eight of us would be trying to sleep here.

Well, I will help that situation a bit. I take a pillow and walk to the door as the phone rings.

"Where are you going?" Beth asks.

"Out."

"Why?"

"Because I can." My voice cracks, but I don't care.

I storm out and slam the door. I spotted a truck parked in the lot on my way in, and I intend to sleep in the truck bed. However, I have to walk past Chris's room to get to the stairs. Great. I take my shoe off and throw it at the light hanging outside his door. It crashes into the bulb, sprinkling glass on the ground. Chris won't dare open his door now that his light is off. But that doesn't stop him from staring out the window as I pass by.

Well, stare all you want! Stare at my back as I walk away. I pick up my shoe and keep going. I climb into the bed of the truck and position my pillow. I glance back at the building only to find Chris has a direct line of sight from his second floor window. I roll over, putting my back to him, in an effort to put this all behind me.

Yeah, right.

Chapter 10 – I Don't Want To Die

Morning begins abruptly when the owner of the truck discovers me and shakes my shoulder.

"Missy, if you needed a place to sleep, I had an extra bed in my room." His mind doesn't show any ill intention behind the remark, and he seems friendly enough. I grab my pillow and apologize. As I jump out of the truck, Chris and the gang meet up with me.

Beth says, "Sleep well?" Her smile reveals growing admiration.

"Yes, you?" I answer with a smile on my lips.

We move out of the way so the man can drive his truck out of the parking lot. I notice Chris makes an extra effort to avoid eye contact, but I don't mind. Somehow, it makes it easier to focus on the task at hand. We need to check-out and get moving.

Soon we are running through the thick forest. The group is arranged differently than before. I'm placed up front to protect the group, I assume, with Justin somewhere in the middle of the pack, and Chris bringing up the rear. I suppose Justin is carrying the package because he has the full protection of the group. Ironically, it's the real diamond in my pocket that allows me to protect him.

I lead the team over a hilltop and stop so abruptly a couple of kids crash into my back. I stand rooted to the ground with my mouth hanging open.

Beth comes up behind me. "What's the matter?"

I gulp and say, "This is the clearing I keep seeing in my visions, the place where the package exchange is supposed to take place, only . . . "

Justin overhears and pushes his way to the front. "So, if this is where the exchange will happen, why were we headed to the Death Clan's caves?"

His cantankerous attitude is really getting under my skin.

"I don't know. Everyone should block their minds now. I need to check this out."

I walk around and smell the air, trying to pick up on scents, intentions, clans, but I come up with nothing. I jog down to the clearing with all my senses on high alert, looking for smashed grass or footprints, anything signifying someone has been here already. Still nothing. Along the edge of the trees, I spot an old logging road with deep ruts carved into the forest floor. In the center of the clearing, a mound of stones forms the rude table where the exchange will happen, the place where Chris will die. Seeing the clearing I've seen in my visions, untouched and undefiled, stirs up strong emotions.

I rejoin the group, looking for Chris. He is near the back of the crowd. Clearly he still doesn't want to be around me. He waits like the rest of the team for my assessment of the situation.

"Three of you need to work on your mind-blocking abilities," I say. "I'm not going to single you out, but you're probably aware I'm in your head. This is definitely the clearing from my vision where the delivery will take place. Chris, where are we headed?" I figure if I bring him into the conversation, he'll have to answer me.

He looks over his map for a couple of seconds and announces, "There's a town not far from here to the east."

I turn to Justin and say, "We'll follow you."

"Me? Why me?"

"You're second in command, right?"

"Well, yes, but you're the one with all the powers." He leans in close to my ear and whispers, "Even Chris has stepped aside to let you take the lead. Why shouldn't I do the same?"

"You want to give up the lead?" I ask.

"Chris did."

"Oh, so you do everything Chris does?" In the back of my mind, I can hear my mother saying the same thing to me when I was younger about my friends jumping off a bridge.

"No, I just follow the leader like I'm supposed to, and right now that leader is you."

I lean even closer to him and whisper, "But, we all know the rightful leader is you, isn't it?"

He pulls away from me as if my breath is a sharp knife cutting into his flesh.

I take in all the faces in the crowd, not seeing Chris's, and realize they respect me as their leader, but I know it's only because I have these powers. This very clearing where we presently stand will be where everything ends. This is where they will discover the truth about me.

An idea pops into my head that might allow me to preserve the illusion of my powers. What if I present the diamond to the Death Clan all by myself? I know where the clearing is now, and if Chris isn't present he can't be killed. In fact, why would anyone else need to be here at all? I can meet personally with the Death Clan and hand over the magical stone on my own. Why haven't I thought of this before?

Now, I only need to peek into Chris's future to find out if this change will be a good one.

I catch a glimpse of him, and that's all it takes for me to view his future. I find this alteration is by far the worst to date. The future through Chris's perspective reveals that handing the stone over myself without the others present doesn't destroy the Death Clan. Instead, they become even more empowered, propelling forward their ambition to rule the world by killing all other clans and humans who stand in their way. Not only would Chris die, but *millions* of other people would die.

When Harold Bates and Maetha said all three of us must be present at the delivery, they were absolutely right. Maybe it's impossible to find a solution that will result in the Death Clan being obliterated, leaving everyone else unharmed. Perhaps these attempts to save Chris from imminent death are pointless. I feel as if nature is speaking directly to me, informing me someone will have to die for the mission to be a success—a sacrifice of sorts. I look over my team. I don't want them to become alarmed by trying to second-guess what's going on in my head, so I say, "Let's get going."

I take off running, leading the clan east, in the direction Chris had pointed. We can't move as fast as usual because of the density of the forest undergrowth and the fallen trees. The deeper we go into the trees, the darker it becomes, and the more panicky the fading light makes everyone feel. Two different times I'm stopped and asked if Demons are in the shadows. I assure them the shadows are only that, shadows.

As we near the little Canadian town Chris targeted for our next stop, I halt the group to investigate. After clearing the area, we secure motel rooms with two sets of adjoining rooms. I let others make those arrangements and am not shook up at all to discover Chris makes sure we don't end up together.

♢ ♢ ♢

Justin sits in the adjoining room, talking on the phone with Chris. He calls me in and hands me the receiver without looking me in the eye.

"Yes?" I say into the phone.

Chris clears his throat and delivers the message. "Calli, I spoke with Clara, and she informed me we need to stay here at the motel until she reaches us. I told her . . . I told her about you and your abilities."

"She's coming here?"

"Yes, and she's bringing most of the Runners. In fact, all the clans are on their way here. The Death Clan is demanding a large gathering of representatives from each clan be in attendance for the handoff." I remember seeing that information inside Maetha's mind at Harold Bates' office. Chris continues, "She recommended I continue to steer clear of you, considering the circumstances."

"So she thinks I'm a target as much as the diamond is?"

"No, that's not why she told me to continue to avoid you."

"She thinks I'm working with a witch. Am I right? You must have told her about my vision."

"No," he says with hesitation in his voice.

Why won't he just come out and tell me why? "Are you sure? The moment I said the word 'witch' you high-tailed it away from me."

"Clara knows things about my situation. That's why she's advising me to keep my distance from you and your mind-reading ability."

"Well, I figure we have about four weeks of wait-time here at this podunk motel in the middle of nowhere. I hope Clara's credit card will be able to support our bill."

Chris pauses before saying, "Calli, the meeting is taking place in two days."

"What?" My breath escapes my chest with a whoosh.

"I told her about the clearing and that you'd already seen it in a vision. She said arrangements will be made for the hand-off to take place at that location. She figures it will take about forty-eight hours for everyone to arrive." He pauses, then says, "Would you look for my future again?"

"I don't . . . forty-eight hours? I won't be able to see exactly what happens. It's too soon." My mind still struggles to grasp the news.

"You could look to see if I have a future, or if my future looks like Jonas's."

His request unnerves me quite a bit. What does he want me to tell him? *Nope, sorry dude, you're still gonna die.* Or, *Wow, hey, looks like you're going to live.* He clearly doesn't understand what he's asking of me. It's one thing for me to look and see if I can change the future, it's another to have to tell someone their life is about to end. I'm actually happy I didn't immediately tell Jonas of his terminal illness—and upset with myself for ever revealing to Chris his own future isn't so bright.

"Let me get this straight," I snap back at him. "You lecture me on nature's will, then you beg me to go against nature and pull you back from the edge of death by the river, after which you freak out and abandon me. Now, you want to know if you're going to die at the delivery. Why not roll with Mother Nature's punches, Chris?"

His reply is soft-spoken. "After nearly drowning, I've changed my mind. If you saw me in person, could you do a reading?"

"Yes," I say as I exhale. Maybe it will get him off my back.

"Would you only search for my future, though, and not delve into my memories like last time?"

"What do you mean?"

"By the river, you broke through my blocking defenses. So can you please only look for my future and not go deeper?"

I broke through his walls? "Okay."

"I'll step outside my door, and you step out yours. Don't come toward me, or I'll go back in my room," he threatens.

"Am I that dangerous?"

"Calli, you waltzed right through defenses put in place by a Spellcaster. They were supposed to be unbreakable, and no other Mind-Reader has broken through them, but you blew me away with how easily you did it."

"You didn't want me to know how you felt about me, did you?"

"My feelings are not the issue. If a witch is watching both you and Justin, then I can't have you sifting through my head and discovering—um, it would put everyone in danger."

"All right. Step outside your door in two minutes."

Well, that was the biggest temptation of my life! He may as well have dangled a chocolate-covered carrot in front of me. It makes sense to hear he's distressed about the fact that I've broken through his defenses. That is the reason he's distanced himself. He isn't necessarily disgusted with me, he's protecting the group.

I spend the next couple of minutes contemplating what I have decided to change for the future, what I know needs to be altered, and the fact that he won't approve. But I've come to believe this is the way the delivery was meant to happen from the inception. I don't know why I feel this way, but I do.

Ready to delve into Chris's mind and see what I can discover, I step outside my door to find Chris standing across the way, looking like a lost puppy, sad eyes and all. My heart clenches. I focus on searching for his future. Before I can see what's in store, his outermost feelings of disappointment and sorrow fill my mind. He hates himself for hurting me, but there was no other way to protect the team than to distance himself.

The diamond in my pocket warms up as the vision of the future fills my head. I'm bowled over to realize I must be viewing the near future, knowing the delivery is slated to take place in two days. I see the clearing, tents, floodlights, the stone table, the three of us meeting the Death Clan. Chris presents the fake stone, which is immediately detected as a counterfeit. Our clan is sequestered in a tent until a decision can be made. I *refuse* to surrender the diamond. They tie my hands together and place me on the stone table in a sacrificial position with the diamond resting on my chest. Chris is with the rest of the clan, trying to comprehend what's happening and basically freaking out, but he is alive. The Death Clan begins the ritual, then an explosion rocks the forest. The Death Clan dies . . . then so do I. The entire scene plays out through Chris's eyes, meaning he will live through my death and the end of the Death Clan.

I have figured out the solution: keep the diamond, and Chris lives, and the Death Clan will be annihilated.

The diamond cools as soon as the vision is over, leaving me to believe the Seer power held in the diamond is stronger than that of regular Seers. I must have been viewing the near future the entire time whenever I'd seen visions of the delivery over the last few days.

I turn and walk back into the room and sit down in a chair by the table. Others mingle amongst themselves and talk about trivial matters, unaware I have just seen my own death. I feel sick. The phone rings, most likely Chris calling, but I don't want to talk to him, not yet.

"Calli." Jessica extends her arm with the receiver in hand.

"Tell him he lives," I reply without even looking at her.

"What?"

"Just . . . tell him he lives." I choke out the order on my way to the bathroom. I hear Jessica repeat what I said and then she tells Chris I don't want to talk to him. I'm sure that goes over quite well. I don't care. I figured out how to save Chris and bring about the fall of the Death Clan, but doing so requires my own death. I'm at peace with this new scenario. Sick to my stomach, but at ease.

I sit on the bathroom floor waiting, expecting Chris to come and talk everything out, but he never does. I try to go to Maetha with my thoughts, but that doesn't happen either. After a while, I pull myself up off the floor and decide to take a walk because the sun has gone down and no one can follow.

While I walk the sidewalks of the peaceful town, I contemplate my death, and a question arises in my mind. I'm a human with powers derived from a magical stone. Maetha cast spells of protection over me, so how can Death people kill me? I can't ask anyone or they might wonder why I would ask such a question. One thing's for sure: I watched my life end through Chris's eyes.

I return to the room and settle into bed. No one speaks to me or asks me any questions.

The next morning I awake to the delightful aroma of breakfast delivered by room service. I sit up and am amazed at the mess of food setting at the foot of the bed. Is that burned toast I smell? What kind of restaurant burns their toast? The stack of golden-brown bread confuses me further. It isn't burned at all.

Wait. I smell poison!

"Stop eating, it's poisoned," I shout and bolt out the door for Chris's room. I pound on the door. Jonas opens it and I quickly push him aside, my eyes searching the room.

"Did they bring you food?"

"Who?" Jonas asks.

"Anyone? Did they bring you breakfast?"

"No."

"Don't eat anything brought to your room!" I run back to my room and find three Runners on the floor, writhing in pain. Justin is one of them. Michael and Jessica are the other two.

I panic and yell to the nearest person, Shanika, "Call 911!"

She doesn't move. She only exchanges helpless glances with the others.

"Hurry!" I insist.

Beth speaks up. She has tears in her eyes. "Calli, we don't do that. It's probably magical poison anyway. Only a Healer can help now."

The door opens and Chris's group enters the room.

I kneel over Justin because Michael and Jessica are clearly already dead. I examine his body with an MRI kind of vision and find the poison on its way to his heart and brain like an evil serpent. I stop the progression and will it backward against the flow of blood, back to his stomach, forcing re-entry. I pull the toxin up his throat, causing it to exit his mouth as a dime-sized puddle of clear liquid. It floats into the air above him and then falls on the carpet.

Will and Kayla collapse as I work on Justin. I hurry over and do the same procedure on them simultaneously, with one hand on each of their stomachs. Then I check Beth and Ricky to make sure their bodies are clean of the poison. Apparently they didn't eat any toast.

I go back to Justin and press my hand against his stomach to determine whether or not the poison is still present.

"It's gone now. You'll live."

I stand to leave, but Justin catches my wrist. My peripheral vision takes in Chris from the doorway as my mind enters Justin's. His humility and thankfulness compound exponentially by the second. His eyes express deep gratitude that could be mistaken for love or attraction by Chris. Is Justin attracted to me? No. He views me as an attractive girl, but he has no romantic feelings. What I *do* sense within his mind are feelings of desire, but not for me—for power, an insatiable lust for the incredible superpower I hold.

I pull my wrist away and look over for Chris. He's left the room. I run out the door, but he's already out of sight.

I don't know how to handle the all-consuming turmoil that comes next. Two dead friends, sobbing girls, and somber boys—what is the protocol for this type of situation? With calling 911 out of the question, what needs to happen next? I have to find Chris and ask him. I go down to his room and find him sitting on his bed with his head in his hands.

"Chris, what do we do?" I ask, barely able to talk.

He doesn't make eye contact. "I called Clara," he says. I sense his anguish. "She's taking care of everything. Your group will be moved to another room, and some people will be by to pick up . . . "

I feel he needs comfort, so I go over and sit beside him on the bed. The moment my butt hits the covers, he vaults up and crosses the room. I guess I'm still pretty scary to him.

"Calli, please go back with the others. I'll be over in a second. I think it's time everyone learns exactly what we are delivering and why our two friends died."

"Okay."

I leave his room and walk back to mine, dragging my feet. What a horrible thing to have happen. The remorse I feel for not being able to help the two fallen friends eats at me.

Before I reach my door, I hear two car doors slam shut and tires squeal as an expensive sports car speeds out of the parking lot. I make eye contact with the female passenger. I enter her mind with ease and discover she's responsible for the poisoned food, but that she considers the mission a failure because the trio lived. Interestingly enough, the woman is not a person with powers. I look for the vehicle's plates, only to find nothing. For a brief moment I consider chasing after the car. I decide against it. My friends need me.

I enter the silent room where my fellow teammates sit with their heads hung low. Beth sits by Jessica's body, gently smoothing Jessica's red curls with her fingers. Sniffles are heard throughout the room. I squeeze between Jonas and Yang and grab hold of the breakfast cart. They move out of the way as I wheel the cart out the door and leave it on the sidewalk. I take the platter of toast and dump it in the trashcan just inside the door to the room. I don't want to take any chances that some unsuspecting soul may eat a piece. I study the remaining foods on the cart, sniffing for any other tainted items, but I find nothing. I move back into the room and stand by the door.

Justin sits at the other end of the room with his back to the wall by the bathroom, gazing at me in admiration. I almost prefer his seething glares to this. At least I could tell what was going through his head when his expressions gave him away.

To keep my mind and hands busy, I pull the blanket and sheet off the nearest bed and gently cover Michael's body with the blanket. Then I hand the sheet to Beth and help her cover Jessica.

Chris enters the room and walks straight to Justin. Justin stands as Chris approaches. Some of the Runners near me are talking so I can't zero in on Chris and Justin's conversation with my intensive hearing. I can't read Chris's lips because his back is to me. I pick up on half of the conversation by reading Justin's lips, which is easy to do because he's still looking directly at me. Our eyes meet, but his mind is blocked tight. Chris must be frustrated with Justin's lack of attention because he turns his head and follows Justin's unbreakable gaze. As Chris's eyes meet mine, he whips his head back to Justin and then to me again. Chris has a confused expression I can't read. He turns his back again and speaks harsh words, pulling Justin's eyes off me by saying something stern enough to irritate Justin.

Justin thunders back, loud enough for everyone to hear, "You can't tell me what to do!"

Chris continues dressing him down, to which Justin replies in an irritated voice, "Whatever."

Chris turns to find the entire group glued to their conversation. He clears his throat and removes the box from his pocket. "Losing our friends is the hardest thing we've had to deal with on this journey so far. This room was targeted, I believe, because two of the trio members were here. Without Calli's healing ability, five of our delivery team would have died, including one of the trio."

A few of the team members talk to one another. Chris looks at me and I sense he's putting thoughts out for me to read. I enter his mind. *Late last night, Beth reported that Justin had called someone and told them he had the package. I felt I should take the diamond from him. He was reluctant to hand it over, but finally did. He's responsible for Michael and Jessica's deaths. I will make sure he pays for what he's done.*

Chris continues to address the group. "The three of us have agreed to show you what it is we are transporting. You will find out soon enough anyway, but with all the clans coming, and with the many powers that will be floating around this small town, it's vitally important to control your thoughts, avoid other people, and not accept gifts of free food or mysterious packages."

He holds the black box out in front of him and lifts the lid.

"This is what the Death Clan wants in exchange for the release of the hostages. This diamond is what Michael and Jessica died over, but if we can be successful in its delivery, then they won't have died in vain. Two men are on their way here to take Michael and Jessica and it's absolutely important for us to block our minds and keep our mouths shut. We can't fail now when we're so close to completion."

"Who's coming?" Will asks.

"I'm not sure, but other than Hunters, this will be the first time on this journey we deal with people who have powers. We won't know what their intentions might be."

I say, "I'll be able to tell. When the men arrive, I will give a signal of either a smile or a frown depending what I pick up. They'll know we're a delivery team even if they don't know anything else. We must all use caution with what we say and we should be ready to run on a moment's notice, just in case.

A white windowless van with the words: Physical Therapy—At Home Care, backs into the parking spot in front of our room and two middle-aged men get out and approach our door. I watch them through the window and determine they are Healers and not a danger to us.

I nod and smile at Chris, who opens the door after they knock. The older man says, "I'm Andrew Stuart and this is Robert Yates. Clara asked us to come."

The two Healers enter the room and assess the situation. Andrew explains the complications that will arise if the police are involved. Andrew tells us that our only safe option is for he and Robert to discreetly move the bodies into the van so they can be transported to a secure location where final arrangements can be made.

As difficult as all this feels, we're all in agreement.

Andrew and Robert carry the two Runners in a way that makes them look like they are alive, but unable to walk, and place them in the back of the van. If any motel guest happens to catch the activity in the parking lot, they won't suspect anything out of the ordinary.

The Healers come back into our room and talk with us before leaving. I sit on the bed, excluding myself from the conversation. They ask the others what happened and check them over for traces of poison, including everyone from Chris's room. I'm relieved, knowing Jonas will finally get the care he needs for his raging cancer. However, they look him over and move on to the next Runner. I jump up off the bed and approach the one named Andrew. Chris eyes me from across the room and tells me with his mind to stop.

"Excuse me sir, may I speak with you a moment?" I say to Andrew.

"Certainly."

We step outside and, before the door closes, I catch Chris's stormy expression.

"The last boy you checked snores all night long. Is something blocking his airway?" I try to sound innocent.

"I didn't pick up on anything."

"He holds his head a lot as if he's in pain," I lie.

"Does he complain about discomfort?"

"No."

"There's probably nothing to worry about."

I nod, realizing this Healer most likely doesn't possess exceptional healing skills. I will search out a better one when the clans converge in the clearing.

After the men leave and the motel manager moves Justin's group into our new rooms, we all sit quietly in heavy contemplation. Chris calls on the phone and asks for me.

His voice sounds exhausted. "Why did you ask about the sick one earlier?"

I figure Jonas must be nearby, and Chris doesn't want to say his name. I answer Chris's question saying, "I couldn't believe they missed the problem. I asked a couple questions and got nowhere. I'll find a more experienced Healer to help."

"Calli, would you please tell me about your vision?"

"I've already told you, you'll live."

"Why the change? The last time you looked at my future, I was going to die."

"I guess I figured out the magic formula that keeps you alive."

"What did you change? Why will I survive?"

"I'm tired and I'm going to bed. Bye." I hang up the phone before he can respond.

Chapter 11 – Questions Without Answers

The next day starts early with a lot of commotion out in the parking lot as the only two motels in the one-stoplight town begin to fill to capacity. Vehicles and buses arrive throughout the day, as do other Runners from our compound. Our instructions are to remain in our rooms until Clara arrives later in the morning.

Clara pulls in shortly after ten and takes charge. Clara's job is damage control and she's definitely good in that role. Family members of the deceased will be flying in to pick up the bodies later in the day, she tells us. She tells the news reporters that hover nearby, intrigued by the influx of people to their small town, we are all part of a family reunion, and more of us will be arriving.

I distance myself from the whole ordeal as much as possible, which is not an easy task. Clara assigns two female bodyguards to shadow me. Chris and Justin have male guards following them around for safety too.

I need some fresh air, so I convince my guards to escort me to the observation deck on the roof. They stay at a distance, but not out of sight. From the elevated vantage point, I can see the parking lot, swimming pool, and a flurry of assorted people with powers in the near vicinity. The canyon we will be running through to get to the clearing looms ominously in the distance. An uneasy flutter in my stomach makes me nauseous and I walk to one of the tables with umbrellas and sit down.

I hear my bodyguards talking and glance over to see Beth asking them to let her come talk to me. I nod to my bodyguards and Beth walks over and sits at my table.

"Everyone's wondering where you went," she says. "I thought to myself, if I wanted to get away from the world, but couldn't leave, where would I go? I was right. What's up?"

"Just trying to listen to the wind," I say.

"Does it bother you to have two escorts following you around everywhere?"

"It's annoying, but no more so than having to sleep in Clara's room tonight. It's like I'm grounded or something."

"Well, you do kind of take off at night like it's nobody's business."

"Hey, whose side are you on?"

"Yours, of course," she grins. "I envy your freedom."

Her comment makes me remember the vision I saw at Cave Falls of Beth in prison. I can't help but wonder. "Beth, what do you plan to do with your life?"

"I don't know." She scratches at her chipped black nail polish.

"You don't have a plan?"

"Like what?"

"Like something not involving incarceration."

"What? Do I go to jail?"

The astounded expression on her face amazes me. "Do you mind if I look?"

"Didn't you already?"

"Sometimes things change."

She closes her eyes, letting me take over her brain. I find what I'm searching for and withdraw from her mind.

She opens her eyes. "What's the verdict?"

"Can I ask you a couple of questions first?"

She nods.

"Can you tell when I'm in your mind?"

"Yes."

"Do you see the future at the same time I do?"

"No, I was wondering what you were finding."

"Would you block me from your mind so I can test something?"

"Sure."

Her walls go up, and I focus my attention away from Beth and to the parking lot to reorganize my thoughts. I see Chris talking with Jonas and Tyler. They seem to have lost something. Tyler nudges Chris's shoulder and points up to me. I don't want to analyze him at the moment. I turn my head back to Beth. I find her future the same as when she let me into her mind. I try to break through her walls to read what she's presently thinking, but can't, until . . . until I think about specific things, such as her relationship with Justin. Then I get right through. She opens her eyes in astonishment.

"You busted in. I need to practice harder on my blocking."

"Beth, I'm going to tell you something I'm sure you won't like. Justin is trouble. If you follow him you might end up in prison. That was the future I saw for you at Cave Falls. It's different now, though."

"Different? How?" Her eyes light up.

"You'll be on some type of committee, one that seeks out and annihilates evil amongst the clans. No prison."

"I broke up with Justin. He's a jerk."

"I agree. I'm glad you came to that conclusion."

"Why did you save him when you could have saved the others . . . when you could have saved Jessica," she adds, her voice lowering.

"Justin is part of the leadership trio and must be present when the diamond is presented to the Death Clan.

191

If he's absent . . . well, he simply can't be absent. Jessica and Michael were already gone, and I couldn't help them."

Beth stares toward the distant mountains. She clears her throat and says, "What will happen tomorrow?"

"What do you mean?"

"Is the meeting going to go wrong?"

"Define 'wrong.'"

She looks at me, one eyebrow raised.

"Things will go as they need to go, as nature intends them to go," I say, trying to reassure her.

"Oh." She studies her fingernails, then looks in the direction of the parking lot. "Chris is watching you from the lot. He cares for you. *A lot.*"

"I'm aware."

"Of course you would be. You can read his mind. Is it cool to be able to read other people's minds?"

"Well, not too long ago I thought it would be cool to be able to read minds, especially a guy's mind. But not anymore. I always thought it would be awesome to predict the future, but I can tell you: no, it's not. The only cosmic power I like using is the healing power. I only wish I would have been able to save our friends."

A silence falls between us for a few seconds.

"Does your future hold anything with Chris?"

"I can't view my own future." Which isn't true. I visualize my future through the future of others.

"When the two of you saved each other on the riverbank, I cried at the passion of it. I was confused when he pushed you aside afterward. What happened?"

"I don't know for sure."

"He's still watching you, you know. I don't mean, like, from the parking lot. I mean from his room. He asks us to watch you and report. He calls on the phone because apparently you can't read his mind through the phone lines. He keeps tabs, like he's doing now. He loves you."

"That's not love, Beth. He loves the fact I possess all these powers. I'm handy to keep around . . . at arm's length, at least," I try to jest. Beth doesn't know about the crazy future-vision Chris clings to.

"Whatever, girl. I see it differently, and I'm pretty sure you do too."

Talking with Beth feels so natural, so much so that I find it hard to believe she ever hated me. The other Runners have changed their opinions of me as well. It's only been a couple days since I arrived at the compound and was the slowest Runner. Now, everyone wants to be around me. I consider that what everyone is drawn to is my artificial self. The diamond I carry in my pocket makes me someone I'm not—someone with powers. Those powers make me seem more mature than I really am, but the whole thing's a lie. I'm a fraud, a swindler they follow as if I have all the knowledge and solutions. Maybe I do, for now, but only because of a magical stone.

I look down at Chris and enter his mind immediately, almost as if he opened the door and let me in. I feel his amazement that I've gained entry yet again, but he continues to remain in my eyesight when he could walk away.

At the forefront is his shame for being a hypocrite on the bank of the river. He didn't want to die, and he didn't want to lose me. So he pleaded with me to help. After that, his guilt set in. He fully comprehends he encouraged me to go against nature. He believes I have ventured down the evil path because of him and feels responsible for the heart-attack guy and my torturing of Justin. Misusing my healing powers is his fault . . . or at least that's what he thinks.

I also experience his dilemma about the age difference between us, mainly my younger age, which has him tied up in knots. Apparently I am older in the vision he'd had, and he essentially understands now is not the time for us to be together.

Some of his own personal demons continue to haunt him, including dishonor and deception. He can't figure out how to relinquish his position of fastest without Justin rising to the top and revealing his sensitive information— this is the damaging info that he feels puts all of us at risk.

I look for Chris's intentions. I get the message loud and clear: he needs to fix certain things in his life and find his own happiness before trying to make anyone else happy. He wants me to experience my youth and he knows I can't do that if he's in my life. He desperately clings to the romantic vision he's been given, believing one day we will meet again. All because I currently possess the healing ability I had in his vision. For now, he wants to distance himself from me for my own good.

At least he figures it's for my own good.

I wish with my entire being to be able to speak to his mind. If I could, I'd tell him to move on with his life, that I don't hold any power, and certainly not the healing power. His vision is wrong. I'm nothing!

An all too familiar swirl of mist swims around my body. Chris, the parking lot, and the entire surrounding area is replaced with four walls and a desk. I'm looking through Chris's eyes at a man seated on the other side of the desk. His name plate says General Stanley Harding. I recognize him as Chris's father. On the desktop calendar, I see the month is July of the same year.

Chris says, "I'm done. I'm resigning."

"From what?" his father responds. "There is no such thing as resigning, Chris. This is who you are,"

"Not anymore."

"I'll march troops in and wipe out your little compound if you quit."

Chris doesn't say anything. In his mind he's sweating bullets.

"I'll hunt you down and charge you with abandoning your post."

He replies as calmly as possible, "I never signed up for this. I volunteered, so good luck with that."

"Maybe not, but you are signing death warrants for all your friends by quitting."

"I can't protect them forever. Do what you must, but I'm done being your spy."

Daylight floods in, crowding out the vision of Chris's future.

Chris is a spy?

Chris walks toward the motel and disappears from sight.

I ponder the new information I've gathered. Justin knows Chris is a spy for the government, Chris knows Justin works for the Death Clan. Their mutual agreement to keep each other's secrets is dependent on Justin continuing to allow Chris to hold the fastest position. How long the agreement has been in place remains unknown to me. Clara Winter obviously knows about Chris's spying, but does Justin know Chris is a double agent? So many questions with no answers . . . yet. The knowledge of Chris having a future solidifies in my mind the diamond delivery will be successful. This brings tears to my eyes.

Beth still sits next to me. She asks, "So, what's going on?"

I have to let my throat relax before I can speak. "I don't understand a lot of what I've seen. I need to think for a little while."

"Do you want me to kick his ass?"

I laugh and wipe my eyes. "No, I just can't figure out why he feels the way he does."

"Well, if you ever need some advice or experienced female help, come and find me." She smiles and I smile back.

"Beth, you've become a good friend. I'm glad we've reached this level."

"Me too."

"Promise me you won't be upset with me after the exchange?"

"What does that mean?"

"I only hope you will still be my friend afterward."

"Girl, you're not making any sense."

"I guess not." I smile at her again.

She gets up and leaves me alone on the roof. I think about what I've seen in Chris's mind and the fact that after the diamond exchange I will be dead. Chris's intention to distance himself after the delivery will be for naught. He will be devastated because his "destined Healer" dies, no doubt. But with time he'll recover.

Later, when I come in off the roof, Clara sits down with me and we have a private chat.

"Well, Calli," she says, "I'm impressed with everything you've accomplished this far."

I suspect Clara hasn't had a hand in the diamond plot. I can't help but check. Her mind reveals I'm correct. "You heard about my many powers from Chris?"

"Yes. I must say, I wondered about your ability as a Runner when I first picked you up. You weren't as fast as the others, but I couldn't tell you that. Also, and I'm not sure if you paid any attention, but the Shadow Demons didn't tear your shirt the same way they shredded mine. The biggest difference though is your physical frame is not that of a typical Runner."

"I noticed."

"After what happened with your heart monitor, I certainly wondered about you."

"Wait, what about the heart monitor?"

"Runners and all other people with abilities have quiet heart beats. You don't. You have a regular human heartbeat. Yet you aren't fully human anymore. When did your additional powers first emerge?"

Not fully human? Ha! "In the late afternoon of the first day, at Cave Falls. They emerged one by one within a few hours."

"You're the very first one to possess all these powers, Calli. It's quite astonishing."

"Well, now you're just embarrassing me." I know the powers will be gone soon enough.

"You're young, Calli. Maybe that's why nature gave them to you, because of your age and inability to grasp what you've got."

"I don't know about that. I do have a lot of questions, though."

"I'll answer as many as I can for you. But, I would like to ask *you* a question first. What will be the outcome of the delivery tomorrow?"

"The hostages will be freed, and the Death Clan's progress will be halted. However, some people will die."

"I don't suppose you will tell me who will die."

"No. Telling you might change the outcome."

"Of course. I apologize. I don't know how you're able to see the near future, but I'm happy you can."

I change the subject. "Clara, I don't understand why this clearing was chosen as the location of the delivery."

"Well, because you told Chris the clearing was the one from your vision."

"No, that's not what I mean. I foresaw the delivery happening a few days ago before I located the clearing. I thought we were heading up to the Death Clan's caves to do the transaction, somewhere in Canada."

"Originally, yes, the caves of the Death Clan were where you were headed—that is, until you found the clearing. It's an ideal location for all the clans to meet, because it's near a town, but far enough away to be secluded."

"But the clearing was not the original planned destination?"

"There was no *planned* destination. Once your team reached the Death Clan's caves, a location would have been selected at that point. The caves were not the destination, they were a scheduled stop. Remember when I told you our Seer couldn't determine the future because it was too foggy? It's still foggy to all Seers. Well," she amends, "except for you. Yet, therein lies the beauty of everything: because you selected the clearing, we can be assured the site is safe and hasn't been booby-trapped."

"You're telling me I envisioned a location that I would eventually choose to be the location? That's deep."

"What's deep is you hold all these powers for a reason none of us can grasp."

I say nothing for a moment, then change the subject. "Are we going to have a memorial or candlelight vigil for the dead?"

"Yes, we'll gather tonight and remember our friends. Tomorrow this delivery will be behind us and we can begin to heal."

She is more right than she could ever know.

After a tear-filled memorial for our friends that evening, there's a phone call for me.

"Ms. Courtnae, my name is Charles Rhondell," the voice on the other end of the line says. "I'm Head Reader in my clan and I've obtained some information you might be interested in, concerning the safety of your team."

I politely reply, "Then I think maybe you should be speaking with Chris, the fastest Runner in my group."

"No, you're the one I need to speak with, Ms. Courtnae."

I scan the room looking for Justin. "Me? I'm the weakest. What about Justin?" *Justin must have told the Readers about my multiple abilities . . . of all the selfish, arrogant, mindless . . . I will wring his neck!*

"I will only share this information with you, Ms. Courtnae."

"Let me guess: you've hired more Hunters." *If Justin didn't have to be at the delivery, I'd . . . ugh.*

"What makes you think we hired Hunters?"

"One told me . . . right before the Shadows got him."

"You mean you read his mind, don't you?"

"Interpret how you wish."

"I'm told you can walk amongst the Demons. If this is true, then you should come to my motel right now so I can give you this information."

"Why don't you tell me over the phone?"

"I don't trust the line. Anyone can tap these days."

"Good point. I'll meet you in the lobby in a few minutes."

"Oh, and Calli, leave the diamond behind."

"What?" My heart pounds in my chest. *He knows! Somehow he knows I'm carrying the real diamond. But how? Maetha said the stone would be protected as long as I kept it in the pouch, which I have.*

"Leave the diamond, Calli. My purpose in calling you is not to get hold of the stone. If the Hunters weren't able to capture it, then we certainly don't have a chance either. But you're not the only one who can walk among the Demons. Don't give anyone the opportunity to swoop in and take the magical stone."

"Okay. Look for me in a few minutes." Relief sweeps over me as I end the phone call. He must have assumed because I possess multiple powers, I must be the leader of the Runners' Clan now. It would make sense in his mind that I would be the one carrying the diamond.

Clara asks, "Where are you going?"

"I've got to talk to Justin."

"It's dark. Can't this wait?"

"Nope."

My blood is boiling. I leave the room and head straight to Chris's room, hoping Justin is there. With all the readjustments in sleeping arrangements, I'm not sure where Justin is staying. I pound on the door. Jonas opens it a crack.

"Calli. What's up?"

I can see Justin standing by the far wall. "I need to come in."

Jonas opens the door and I storm across the room. Conversations come to a halt. My overly-attuned senses locate Chris off to my right. I don't even need to look with my eyes to confirm. I can smell his scent. Justin realizes I'm here for him and he changes his stance to a defensive posture. I grab him by his jacket front, shove him up against the wall, and press my body against his large frame.

He is dumbfounded by my actions—along with everyone else in the room—and doesn't fight back. I hiss through gritted teeth, "You just can't keep your mouth shut, can you? Are you carrying a cell phone?" I slide my left hand down across his belly and over the zipped pocket in an attempt to locate a phone. Nothing. "How do you do it? How do you tell people?"

"Tell what?" he whimpers, belligerence for once has drained away.

I push him harder. "My abilities! You told the Mind-Readers didn't you?"

"They would've found out soon enough anyway. I don't know why you're all upset."

I let go of him. "Why would I be upset? Sheez, Justin, you were the one with the Hunter's target on your head—Hunters sent by the Mind-Readers. Now you sidle up with them and give away vital information?" I turn to leave the room, but before exiting I say, "If I only had half a brain I'd have twice as much as you! *You* are the muck, Justin!"

Chris follows me out the door. "Where are you going?"

I stop and turn to face him. "I'm on my way to meet with the leaders of the Mind-Readers, thanks to him." I point in Justin's direction.

"They might be dangerous," Chris says. His eyebrows draw together.

"No more than I am."

"Be careful," Chris adds before I walk away. I can tell he's worried and wishes he could go with me.

As I walk in the direction of the other motel, I think about Chris and the fact someone other than my parents and my cheek-squeezing grandma is concerned about my safety.

The cool night air does wonders to calm my anger. I inhale deeply and try to gain control of my emotions. I need to be on alert, not caught up with the stupidity of others.

I can see the motel and three men wearing jewel-toned robes standing near the glass doors. As I near them, one opens the door. I remember what Maetha told me about the protection she cast around the diamond pouch. The spells will protect my mind from being probed about its presence. I'm confident no one will be able to tell it's the source of all my powers.

"Hello, Calli, I'm Charles Rhondell," says the tall, kind-looking figure in the middle. I shake his hand and immediately view his future. Charles's wife is one of the hostages being held by the Death Clan. They will be reunited after the exchange. Experiencing their joy brings tears to my eyes.

"Are you all right?" Charles asks.

"Yes, I am."

The other two men, Grant Winbush and Steven Zufelt, shake my hand, introducing themselves as images flash through my mind of their futures. Grant will relocate near the east coast and assist the leaders of our country with his abilities, and Steven will get married to a woman he's been dating. For once, I'm encouraged to see happy futures. No death, no destruction, only peace, joy, and contentment.

They lead me to couches in the lobby.

"Your walls are extremely strong, Ms. Courtnae," Charles tells me with admiration.

"You can sense my walls?"

"Yes, and I must say, they are unlike any I've encountered. Blocking takes training and time to achieve. You've accomplished this in a matter of days. Who instructed you?"

In truth, no one. But I can't tell them Maetha placed the walls within my head. I decide to give the credit to Chris. "Chris Harding instructed me."

"He's the topic of our discussion, Calli," Charles says, his eyes widening.

Grant joins in, keeping his voice low. "He's been feeding information to the enemy."

"What? I thought Justin was the spy."

"Justin is an afterthought. His intentions are self-serving. Chris, on the other hand, is dangerous. His connections go much higher than Justin's."

I know exactly what they're talking about, but I pretend I don't. If it wasn't for the fact that I envisioned Chris's future and the positive outcome for him, I might be worried.

I say to the three men, "So, the important information you couldn't tell me over the phone is that Chris is more dangerous than Justin?"

"Yes."

"That's it?"

They look at one another and shrug their shoulders. Charles says, "Calli, you obviously don't understand the severity of the situation."

"Maybe not, but I've been inside both Chris's and Justin's minds, and believe me, Justin is the one to be worried about, not Chris."

"None of us were able to break into Chris's mind. How did you?" Steven asks.

"I don't know, I just looked in."

"His defenses, like yours, are impenetrable. Clearly you possess a much stronger ability to break through tough mental walls than we do. Perhaps it's because you are the first multi-powered individual."

Grant asks with complete sincerity, "What can you extract from my mind, Calli? I'd like you to test my walls."

His mind is blocked. However, knowing his future as a political aid, I use the knowledge and enter his mind—a trick I learned from my experiments with Beth. "You wish to work with the President," I say. "You've been fascinated with politics since childhood, and you've spent countless hours researching the world's governments."

"Amazing! I felt you enter that part of my mind. It's been years since anyone was in my head. Absolutely incredible! How did you access my childhood dreams?"

"I honestly don't understand my abilities or why I can do what other learned Readers can't," I say, trying to sound as calm as possible. I'd hoped these men would be able to shed some light on why my powers are stronger than theirs.

Charles says, "Will you test my walls?"

I look at Charles and enter his memories about his wife. "Your wife is beautiful, and I'm sorry for your pain. You two have had many happy years together."

Charles bows his head.

I turn to Steven and say, "I hope someday you can marry her." His eyes widen, bewildered at how easily I can enter his mind and find memories about his love.

None of them can comprehend how I've gotten into their minds, and a little nagging voice in the back of my mind says to keep this a secret. Let them continue to think I'm all powerful.

Charles says, "Do you understand how many years of training a Reader goes through to develop the ability to see memories?"

I shake my head.

"Years of training, years of learning. In fact it took me five years to learn how to retrieve someone's recent memories. But, here you sit, mere days of mind-reading under your belt, and you can pull up Grant's childhood with no effort. That's incredible!"

I say nothing.

"Calli, you broke through our walls. We three are the strongest of our clan, but we still can't read each other."

Grant asks, "How do you do it?" His mind reveals he suspects I'm an Immortal.

I say, "I was kind of hoping *you* could help *me* understand my ability."

Charles informs me of what I already know. "You are an anomaly, Calli. You tell *us* what it's like."

"It's a burden." That is the truth. "I witness and experience the insecurities, pain, anger, fear, depression, and anxiety of everyone around me. I don't—"

"You feel? You actually *experience* other people's emotions?" Grant is astonished.

"You *don't* feel emotions when you enter other people's minds?" I ask the three of them. I watch their heads shake in unison. I look to the floor. Great! Another ability unique to me.

"How do you walk amongst the Shadow Demons?" Steven asks.

I shrug my shoulders.

Charles leans forward. "I've searched the archives of prophesy and found nothing that tells of a girl with the multiple powers of running and intense mind-reading."

They must not be aware of my other abilities, and frankly, I'm a little shocked Justin didn't tell them everything. I decide I will always be careful about what I volunteer up to anyone until I figure out what they know about me.

"I should get going now." I stand and they follow suit.

"Are you a witch?" Steven asks in an unexpected rush. "That would explain how you can do these things, why the Demons ignore you. Are you?"

"I don't think so. A few days ago, I was a less-than-popular girl in high school trying to fit in, and now I'm a freak living among freaks in a world I didn't even know existed. Does a witch gain abilities, or does she learn how to enchant herself with them?"

Charles intervened, "She's not a witch, Steven. She's simply a girl with a destiny. The Seers foresaw her running ability surfacing, but nothing more."

"I don't know what I am, or if this is my destiny. I've always wanted to be able to read minds, but I now despise that skill. I wish the ability would go away. I don't want these powers, and I haven't enchanted myself with them. Frankly, I'm at my wit's end." I can tell my frustrations are evident in my tone of voice.

Charles extends his hand, and I shake it. "It was a pleasure to meet you, Calli. I wish you the best with the meeting tomorrow."

"Thank you. Goodbye." I turn and leave the building and don't look back once.

As I walk back to my motel, I think about the fact a group of Mind-Readers would be able to communicate with each other non-verbally by dropping their walls and placing their thoughts at the front of their mind, definitely a handy advantage in a situation such as the upcoming gathering. Being able to project their thoughts into others' minds would be better, but to my knowledge, that power doesn't exist.

I turn the corner and enter the motel parking lot. Almost every window in the motel is illuminated from within and the lot is completely filled with vehicles. As I walk past the lobby, I glance at the manager, who's speaking on the phone while writing something on a pad of paper. A quick mind-read reveals he is stressed out by the guest-load verses employee ratio. He has a running list of supply requests such as extra towels and blankets for numerous rooms, and complaints of broken items or dirty rooms. Poor guy. He probably hasn't had so many guests at one time, or if he has, he at least had advance notice if there'd been something like a scheduled concert or event.

I climb the stairs and walk past Chris's window on the way to my room. I pause and peek through the narrow opening in the curtain. The mirror on the wall is angled just right, reflecting Chris sitting in a chair against the opposite wall. He's unaware I'm watching him, and I try to enter his mind. It doesn't work. I try thinking of a specific detail to gain entry but am unsuccessful. I deduce a mind cannot be read unless the subject can be seen in person, the same way I can't "read" a photograph of Chris.

However, I *had* continued to harm Justin through the bathroom door even after I couldn't see him. An idea comes to me and I reposition myself so I can see Justin's reflection through the mirror. I try to upset his stomach, but nothing happens. I'm not surprised. The night I "tortured" Justin, I had eye contact with him in the beginning. The connection to his body's energy remained even after he placed a barrier between us.

Looking at his reflection right now, I feel no connection.

I continue walking to my room and enter to find Clara pacing the floor. My incompetent bodyguards stand directly behind her with grimaces on their faces, knowing it's pointless to think they can guard or protect me in the dark.

"Calli, how did it go?" Clara tries to sound calm.

"Like I expected, they were full of questions, but I had no answers for them. I'm tired. I'm going to bed."

Everyone moves aside and lets me lie down. I close my eyes so I can't see their minds, and I try to channel Maetha. If I could speak with her, ask her some questions, it would help out a lot. No such luck. I think about calling my parents, but dismiss the idea because it's late, and even later in Ohio. I miss them. I decide I'll call in the morning.

I lie in bed with a million thoughts running through my head. I wonder if there's another solution where Chris can be saved, besides not giving the diamond to the Death Clan. Perhaps there is another scenario I haven't explored.

Chapter 12 – The Clearing and The Clans

The morning starts early and with a lot of disorder all around. Everyone is on edge and trying to figure out how to be useful. I try to call my parents, but the motel's phone won't allow me to make a collect call out of the country. If I could speak to them, I'd tell them I love them, that I'm happy—and a little scared—and that I'm traveling the road before me to see where it leads . . . just as they recommended.

We leave the motel as soon as the Shadow Demons are gone and run through the forest to the delivery location. Tents need to be set up, floodlights erected, and generators assembled. As more and more people arrive, the small tent city grows in proportion around the edges of the clearing, escalating the level of my nervousness to near suffocation.

Each clan has anywhere from fifty to a hundred representatives present. Clara tells me about the Death Clan's demands to have a specific amount of "ambassadors" in attendance in order to free the hostages. I already know this information, but I figure the Death Clan is only trying to best match what their Seers foretold. They are struggling to make sure every aspect is in place to allow their proper transformation into immortals . . . or so they think.

I'm not any different than them. I've struggled to make sure I have found the proper formula to ensure success.

I stare at the stone table in the center of it all. My heart beats mercilessly in my chest with the knowledge these are my final hours of life. I look at the place where I'm doomed to die. While wallowing in my thoughts, the Sanguine Diamond warms up against my body, almost as if it's trying to comfort me.

Like an eerie dream, the crowded clearing becomes completely silent as the Death Clan arrives in three large military-type trucks. The rutted logging road causes the vehicles to bounce and sway as they turn off and park near the clan's designated tent. I can only imagine what it must be like to ride in the back of the cavernous vehicles and be tossed around.

The twenty or so Death Clan members unload from the trucks first. White robes shroud their bodies; the small amount of their exposed alabaster skin seems to glow. They are the embodiment of pure evil, and even the insects and birds of the forest seem to freeze in fear. Several of the robed figures look directly at me, causing my skin to prickle.

The hostages spill out of the back of one of the trucks and are escorted to the tent. I read their collective minds and find their spirits succumbing to the expected dismal end. They all believe death is imminent. Once the Death Clan and their captives have disappeared inside their tent, the commotion picks back up in the clearing as everyone resumes their tasks. I sit down on the matted grass and contemplate my decision to keep the diamond. My bodyguards remain nearby. Have I exhausted all the avenues? Is there no other way to end this?

I don't know how long I've stared at the stone table imagining myself lying upon it, waiting to die before Clara brings me back to reality. "Calli, come inside," she says. "You're too exposed out here."

Everyone inside our tent stops what they are doing and falls silent when we enter. My eyes search the large crowd of Runners, spotting the members of the delivery team, realizing once again we are minus two. I don't recognize a lot of the faces in the crowd. I didn't have much time at the compound to learn any names before being launched out into the world of powers.

Clara addresses everyone. "The meeting is scheduled for this afternoon at three o'clock. Give Chris, Justin, and Calli their space until then."

We are ushered inside a curtained-off private cubicle within the tent. I can tell right away the cubicle must have some kind of enchantment surrounding it because the noise of the Runners outside is muted when the curtains close. Three folding chairs are positioned in a triangular arrangement in the center of the small room, and I sit down on one of them. The two guys sit as well. I have to stop and think of when the last time was that the three of us were together like this: it was in Harold Bates's office. Our journey here with our accompanying entourage and the practice of dividing us up among the motel rooms has made it so the three of us were never alone.

So much has changed since the beginning of the journey. I climbed the rank ladder having begun at the level of muck and ending up as the most important member of the clan. Justin's traitorous nature surfaced, along with his insatiable desire for complete and utter power. Chris, who appeared like he had everything together when we began our journey, now looks to be falling apart at the seams. The two of them watched as every ability and power surfaced in me. Chris is intrigued, yet guarded, while Justin is intimidated and jealous. I don't feel a need to probe their minds at this point. Instead, I relax into the chair and accept the reality that the last few hours of my life will be spent in the presence of one boy who inexplicably loves me, and one who hates me. The two opposites create an odd sort of balance to the situation.

Chris pulls the box out of his pocket and opens the lid. He examines the beauty of the diamond. He looks closely at the fake stone, angling the box in the light to examine the many facets. He comments reflectively, "The word 'Sanguine' is an adjective meaning 'positive, hopeful, and optimistic.' It's a word representing the intended outcome of this meeting. This diamond is meant to obtain the release of the prisoners and to render the Death Clan powerless, securing an optimistic future for all of us."

Justin glares at Chris, a disgusted expression on his face. Then, true to form, he says, "Thanks for sharing, Chris. Like we didn't know that already. But, don't forget 'sanguine' originally meant 'bloody,' as in 'nourished by powerful blood.' So, in this particular context it could just as well refer to an eagerness for bloodshed and violence. Bet you didn't know *that*, Chris." Justin's smug gaze shifts to me. "What will happen at the meeting, Calli?"

"Success. The outcome will be good for all the clans."

"Don't you see details?" Justin presses.

Chris comes to my defense, or so he thinks. "Of course she does, Justin."

I keep my voice steady. "Sometimes those are better left unknown."

"Will anything bad happen?" Justin asks.

My eyes meet Chris's. "Nothing that nature doesn't intend."

I turn my body away from Justin to signal I'm done with this conversation, but he grabs my shoulders to try to force me to turn around and face him. His fingers grip me firmly, causing pain. I realize this physical contact creates a link into his mind I couldn't access any other way. His past and present open to me, bombarding me with images I'd rather not have in my head. His future flows in, along with the dark, foreboding intentions of his heart. I already understood this about him, but not in as much detail. I now see he will lead a group of people on a quest for ultimate domination and will not be above kidnapping and murdering in order to gain power. With the Death Clan wiped out, Justin will rise to the top and become the next evil force to be reckoned with.

I pull out of his mind, crashing onto the ground. Justin's hands are still on my shoulders and Chris is trying to separate the two of us—but, so is Justin. His hands are stuck to my body. My mind holds his hands on me. I mentally let go, and his arms fly back. He scoots away, terrified.

Chris stands over me. He doesn't appear to want to touch me, so I get up on my own power. He moves back and we both sit down in the chairs facing each other . . . once again.

Justin whispers in a raspy voice, "What was that? My hands were glued to you!"

Chris's eyes project the same question.

How do you answer a question to which you have no idea what the answer is? Instead of admitting my own confusion, I choose to issue an empty warning to Justin.

"Physical contact with the intent of harm is no good on me. Don't touch me again."

"I won't! After this meeting, I'm going to petition your removal. You're becoming too dangerous to remain in the clan."

"Oh no you're not, Justin!" Chris jumps in.

"She's evil, Chris! She's probably a witch or something. We can't keep her around."

"She saved your life."

"She had to!"

I stare at the two of them as they fight back and forth, then I interrupt, "You won't need to forcefully remove me from your clan. I'll leave on my own. I've had enough of this life and this world of powers, and I don't want to stay. Besides, I suspect my abilities will be gone once the diamond is out of my presence."

"Why?" they both say in unison.

"I didn't get my additional powers until I was around the diamond."

"Why didn't *we* get any other powers then?" Justin sounds as if he doesn't believe me.

I shrug my shoulders.

Chris opens his mind so I can sense his thoughts. *Please don't leave the clan, Calli.*

"I may not have a choice," I say to Chris, which angers Justin when he becomes aware we're having our own semi-private conversation.

"Oh, so now you two are carrying on a conversation without me?"

What do you mean? Chris asks, ignoring Justin.

I repeat my answer. "I may not have a choice."

Clara enters the cubicle, interrupting our conversation. "Calli, you have visitors." Two older men follow her into our already cramped area. "This is Arthur Stiles and Curtis Shultz from the Seers Clan. They would like to talk to you." She motions to Chris and Justin and asks me, "Do you want these two to step out while you talk to the Seers?"

Before I can answer, Justin jumps forward. "I'm not going anywhere. I insist on being present for all meetings with Calli."

I want to say, *why, so you can spy?* But Chris speaks first. "I think the trio should stay together, being that we're so close to the delivery time."

The older man, who Clara called Arthur Stiles, nods and says, "Yes, they should stay. Calli we represent the Seers. We would like to ask you some questions about your multiple abilities."

I glare at Justin. "Is there anyone who doesn't know what I can do?"

He only shrugs his shoulders.

"We're wondering why we can't view your future." Arthur angles his head and narrows his eyes.

"I can't see yours either," I respond before Chris has enough time to surmise I have no future, just like Jonas.

"You can't see our future because we're blocking you," Arthur replies.

"Runners and Mind-Readers try to block me, but I can still observe their futures," I challenge.

"Seers are different," Arthur says, raising his chin in superiority.

"Well, then you've just answered your own question," I say, feeling confident.

"Perhaps."

Curtis Shultz speaks up, "We never saw this clearing as the meeting place. Why and how did you change the location?"

"I recognized the clearing when we came upon it because of a series of visions I had. Then the plans were put into motion to relocate the exchange here."

"Yes, but we never envisioned this location."

My thoughts revisit my earlier questions about Seers. The men in front of me evidently had not seen the same future as The Death Clan's Seers. The Runners' Seer only saw a mysterious fog concerning the future of the clan. The

215

results are all over the board with little similarity. All I can figure is the Seers got the butt-end of the cosmic superpowers. I certainly hope my use of the Seer power works out as planned. I ask Curtis, "Well, what do you envision now for the future after the delivery?"

"It's too near, and anything beyond is foggy."

I say, "Will you unblock your mind and let me try to read the future?" Not that I need them to remove their mind-blocks. I ask them to do so to avoid appearing exceptionally abnormal—again.

They hesitate, but Curtis reluctantly agrees. His walls come down, and I clearly envision him addressing a large group of some kind, discussing the happenings at the clearing and the destruction of the Death Clan. I pull out of his mind and say, "Your future involves teaching others about the fall of the Death Clan."

"So, they will fall?" Curtis asks.

"Yes."

Justin lets out a grunt and folds his arms across his chest. I assume he doesn't believe me. I hope that's the case, otherwise he might pass along the foreseen outcome of the gathering as he has apparently passed everything else along.

Arthur says, "Why can't we visualize that?"

Justin speaks out of turn. "This girl is surrounded with mystery. She can't be trusted."

"Shut up, Justin," Chris commands.

I ask the Seers, ignoring Justin, "Can a Seer learn how to have visions closer than four weeks?"

"What are you talking about?" Arthur asks.

"Is it possible to have visions of the near future, of things that will happen within days or hours, or maybe a week ahead?"

"No," Arthur replies. "Seers foresee changes in the far future, not the immediate or near future."

I'm curious about this process. I have to know how my visionary abilities differ from theirs. I think carefully and ask, "When you look for someone's future, what do you usually see?"

"It depends." Curtis answers this time. "We often see what a person's general emotional state will be—their happiness or sadness or fear or anxiety—but we can also see the consequences of their actions and major changes in their life on a grand scale."

"Yes, basically general things related to the individual," Arthur adds.

I ask, "Can someone train their mind to identify details about an individual's future?"

"In theory, perhaps," Arthur replies, "but no one's done so to my knowledge. Our visions are big-picture, not fine-grained."

Chris's expression falls as if all the wind has been let out of his sails. "That *can't* be true," he says. His eyes meet mine and I effortlessly slip inside his mind to find he's confused about the detailed, fine-grained vision he saw of me.

"*She* can," Justin says, causing me to pull my mind out of Chris's.

"She can, what?" Curtis asks.

"She can view somebody's future in great detail, and she sees things that will happen very soon, just days out, not weeks."

All eyes are on me again. I look at Justin and wish I had the bat Clara had talked about.

"If you do possess that ability, Calli, tell us what will happen today at the meeting," Curtis demands.

"I already did. I told you it goes well."

Justin rolls his eyes and inhales sharply through his nose. "More detail please," he insists.

"It goes *very* well," I answer, leaning back in my seat.

Justin throws his hands in the air. "See what I mean?"

"Will the Death Clan be stopped?" Arthur asks.

"I already told you they will be."

"Will anyone die?"

"Yes."

"Who?"

"I'm not going to answer that. Telling you might change the future. Right now all you need to know is our main goal will be accomplished. The Death Clan's rise to ultimate power will be stopped. For good."

Arthur nods. "It's logical you don't want those who have mere hours to live to panic, but please help us understand how you're able to view the immediate future. Why should we believe you?"

My patience wanes, and the tension in my voice grows. "I don't know why, all right? I don't know!"

Chris stands and steps between me and the Seers. "Leave her alone. She can't answer any more of your questions."

The men look at each other, then walk out of the cubicle.

Chris turns around and sits down in front of me.

I meet his gaze and say, "Thank you."

"The burden on your shoulders is too much." He looks deep into my eyes. I sense his overwhelming compassion for my situation and it melts my heart. He continues. "I don't know how you're holding up under so much pressure. I wish I could do something to help."

I nod my head. "Well, the delivery will take place soon, and everything will be over."

Chris scrunches his eyebrows together. I figure he's trying to decipher my comment.

Justin states with his usual overconfidence, "You're wrong. The Death Clan won't be stopped."

We are served lunch, but I'm not hungry. Chris doesn't eat much. He keeps his eyes on me. Justin, on the other hand, seems pleased he has the fruit and nuts all to himself. We each leave the cubicle for bathroom breaks. I muse to myself, *even super-powered people have to tend to their bodily functions.*

After lunch, Clara announces two visitors: Hunters. Alarm bells go off in my head. We've been running from Hunters since the moment we left Harold Bates' office. The last thing I want is to be forced to end another life in the attempt to preserve the trio.

Justin is the first to speak. "Why do Hunters want to meet with us?" I pick up on the nervousness in his voice. Naturally, he would be worried about being outed to the entire Runners' Clan as helping the Hunters track us. His predicament is his own doing.

Clara says, "These Hunters are good. They follow nature's law."

"How do you know?" Justin squeaks as he talks.

"I know the good Hunters very well, Justin. Trust me." Clara looks to me and waits for my approval before allowing the two men to enter the cubicle.

These men look completely different than the Hunters we've encountered. They are in their mid-thirties, well dressed, and they look and smell clean. I'm amazed, however, at the size of their noses. I deduce they were probably made fun of as children.

The first extends his hand toward me, inviting a handshake.

Justin lunges forward. "I wouldn't touch her if I were you."

I don't reach forward. The man lowers his hand and says, "My name is Dominic. This is Fred. May we speak with you?"

"Yes," I answer.

Fred sniffs the air and says, "You don't have a scent. Why?"

I look over to Chris and exchange glances. "It's nice to know I don't stink. I don't know why you can't smell me. I can smell you."

Dominic scratches his chin. "Yes, that is why we're here. You hold many powers, yet you have no scent. Tell us about these powers."

"Why should I tell you anything? We've been hunted by your clan since we started this delivery."

Fred raises a hand to stop me. "Those Hunters were mercenaries. Their actions don't represent our clan."

Dominic adds to Fred's statement. "Some Hunters work independently, and some don't act according to nature's will. The rest of us, who chose to follow nature and support the other clans, live in a community with our leader."

"Your leader?" I ask.

"Yes. She chose not to attend, but is curious about your multiple powers. What should we tell her in our report?"

"That I'm just a girl, following my gut instincts." Dominic and Fred exchange glances. I continue. "I don't have any answers to give you. Tell your leader whatever you want." I look to the floor and squeeze my eyes shut.

The two Hunters speak with Chris and Justin momentarily and turn and leave. I don't pay attention their conversation. My mind is preoccupied with their earlier statement: "You don't have a scent."

Soon after the Hunters leave, Clara announces the Healers' leaders have arrived to see me. I'm tired and just want to be left alone. Then my mind pictures Jonas and his illness and I become energized. Finally, Jonas will have access to the most powerful Healers.

Clara says, "Calli, this is Andrew Stuart and Robert Yates. You probably recognize them from the hotel."

Recognize them? Yes! Am I let down? Absolutely! Andrew couldn't detect the cancer then, and I have no reason to believe he'll detect it now.

Andrew says, "We're in awe, Ms. Courtnae."

Robert nods his head.

"Call me Calli, please."

"Is it true," Robert asks, "you caused a heart attack in someone and also killed two Hunters?"

I know Justin had everything to do with leaking the information and I struggle to keep my mouth shut. Instead, I say, "The heart attack guy was trying to abduct me, so I protected myself. Besides, he was a walking time bomb anyway. His heart was ready to fail. The Hunters were trying to kill my team. I had to protect them."

"You can feel weaknesses in the body?" Andrew asks.

"Yes."

"Death Clan members learned how to sense weaknesses. To identify physical impairments they need to sense healthy tissue and organs, and that's how they are able to kill: they go after the heart and stop the electrical impulses."

"Are you likening me to a Death Clan member?"

"Not at all. I'm only amazed you learned so quickly how to scan inside the body for weaknesses."

"Well, pardon my candidness, but what's the use of being a Healer if you can't sense imminent illness or disease?"

Robert Yates, speaks up. "We heal injury and sickness when they make themselves known, similar to what you did with your clan members when they were shot in the forest."

"What about cancer?" I ask. "At what point can you detect a tumor, and when do you attempt to heal it?"

"We can detect tumors when they become painful, but only because the individual comes to us with pain. Usually by that time the person has advanced cancer and not much can be done."

"I know someone who has cancer. Will you help him?"

"Who?" they both ask together.

Justin also wants to know, and I realize Chris hasn't said anything to anyone. He and Justin are so different.

I move to the opening in the curtain and point to Jonas who's on the other side of the large tent, talking with a group of boys. "That boy has cancer."

"I'm sorry, but I don't sense anything in him," Robert says.

"I do. It's so obvious to me." My voice rises as my frustration peaks.

Andrew clears his throat and closes the curtain. I take my seat and he says, "Try to imagine for a moment how we view cancer. Cancer presents itself in its early stages as regular cells. Therefore we can't detect them until they are mutated and extensive, and, as I said before, it's too late to help the patient at that point."

"This isn't early-stage cancer, it's nearing end-stage," I explain. "Why can't you sense it?"

"Well, how did you discover his illness? What tipped you off?"

"I couldn't read his future. He didn't seem to have one, so I searched inside his body and found the mass. I could feel the way its tendrils had spread from organ to organ."

"Do you realize you used your future-seeing ability to detect the problem? We don't have that ability. You are a rarity, Calli."

"So, can I heal Jonas? Or can you?"

"Well, here we get into sticky water. If nature—"

I cut him off before he can go any further with all the nature crap. "I don't care about that in this case. I can feel his tumor. I know it's there. If I'm able to, after the delivery I'll try to heal him. He's too young to suffer and die of an illness I can do something about."

Chris looks to the floor. I can't tell what he's feeling, but I can guess.

"We will assist you if we can."

"Thank you."

I know I won't live past the delivery and Jonas will therefore probably die. I made the promise to help Jonas mainly so Chris will think everything will be okay after the delivery.

The Healers leave the cubicle, and once again Justin and Chris stare at me in silence.

I turn my back to them so I don't accidentally connect with their minds. I certainly don't want to hear Chris lecture me on nature's will again, not that he actually would after the way he reacted on the bank of the river.

We are brought fresh running clothes before the meeting. I step out while Chris and Justin change, then they step out for me. I pull the pouch out of my pocket and hold it in my hands for a moment, appreciating the diamond's weight and heat. Without putting it down, I change my clothing and place the invaluable treasure in the front pocket of my clean jacket and zip the pocket shut.

I stand alone in the cubicle, thinking about my parents and the fact I didn't get to say goodbye. I haven't even spoken with them since I left home. I guess once I learned Maetha had manipulated their minds, I haven't been concerned that they will worry about me. It would have been wonderful to hear their voices one more time, though. I think about Suz and how much I miss her, too. I think about myself, only to realize my fear and sadness is for everyone else, not for myself.

I recall once in my English class we debated whether or not it would be good to know when you were going to die. The class had been pretty much divided equally. Half argued that if you were aware of the exact date and time, you could say your goodbyes and have all your affairs in order. The others argued that if you knew exactly when you were going to die, you wouldn't be able to live and enjoy life. You'd be focused on your impending death. I remember I sided on the "I don't want to know when I'm going to die" side. But, look at me now. I know I'm about to die, yet I don't get to put things in order and say goodbye. I got the bad end of the deal all the way around.

I think foolishly, not for the first time, *now would be a good time to wake up*. However, I know this is not a dream. This situation is very real. For a moment, I wonder what would have happened if I'd decided to call my parents and have them come pick me up at the compound. Who would have carried the diamond then? Would they have had the guts to do what is necessary to save my friends and companions?

Chapter 13 – Sacrifice

The time comes to walk out to the stone table. As we make our way to the center of the clearing, I glance around at the many hundreds of anxious people staring at us, awaiting the unknown. More tents line the perimeter at the tree line, and the floodlights are already turned on, illuminating the area. Clearly, no one wants to take any chances with the Shadow Demons, even though they won't be out for several hours.

I sense Chris's and Justin's apprehension. "Don't worry," I assure them. "Everything will work out. You'll see."

We stop and stand on the north side of the rock altar.

Chris catches my eye and opens his mind. *Calli, let nature decide. Please.*

I say out loud for Justin's sake. "Everything that's about to happen will be in the best interest of all the clans."

Justin turns to me and blurts, "You really annoy me. Do you know that?"

I think to myself as I focus on Chris, *not for much longer.*

Chris's eyes widen with alarm. For a moment, I wonder if he's heard my thoughts, but the whoosh of murmurs throughout the crowd moves my attention to the tent of the Death Clan.

We all stare across the meadow and watch as several individuals wearing white robes emerge from the tent. They are ghastly in every way. I believe it is the Death Clan's intention to appear unnerving with their sinister beauty: long, silvery-white hair; flawless white skin that never sees sunlight; perfect facial proportions; and eyes black as obsidian anchored in their eye sockets—probably modified to see in the darkness of caves. None of them look old, but none of them look human either. The self-given title of Immortals seems appropriate. Three hooded men emerge from the thirty or so clan members and approach the table.

Chris addresses the figure in front. "We have the package," he says. "Where is yours?"

The man ignores Chris and turns to me. He pulls his hood down to show his face, the mere sight of which sends a chill down my spine. His skin is so thin I can see the shape of his skull, which makes me realize the whiteness is due to the bones beneath it. Up close, I can see Death Clan members' eyes are totally black, lacking a distinct iris or having any white around the eye. I shiver, despite trying to remain calm. He speaks with a high-pitched, smooth voice. "You are Calli Courtnae?"

I nod. In the man's mind I find his name is Markus.

"The dynamics of this group has changed," Markus announces. "You are the true leader of this trio, Miss Courtnae, and I will only address you."

I *had not* foreseen this happening in my visions. My panic-infused heart beats rapidly. I step forward and address the eerie leader. "We have our package. Where's yours?"

He turns and nods to the guards near the tent, who then begin to bring out the hostages. I hear murmurs throughout the circling crowd. The captives' hands are bound, and they appear pale and weak. Dirk, John, and Macey are easy to spot since they are wearing green running suits. They are all young, like me.

"Now, Miss Courtnae, mysterious member of all clans, Runner, Seer, Healer, Hunter, Mind-Reader, Thought-Extractor—Witch—present the package."

227

Thought-Extractor must be the newest power, the one that had held Justin's hands on my shoulders while I sucked out his memories and future by force. Justin sure hasn't wasted any time informing the enemy of my new talent. I realize he must have contacted someone during his bathroom break. I'm not sure why Markus referred to me as a witch, though. I look at Chris as he pulls out the box with the diamond. Markus doesn't even acknowledge Chris, so Chris hands me the box—again, something I never saw in my visions.

I feel his thoughts as I take the box from him. *Don't you dare offer yourself up as a sacrifice to save me!*

I direct my gaze down to my hands. Have I been too obvious with my words and actions, causing Chris to draw the conclusion I might sacrifice myself? I glance up at Markus and probe his body, trying to detect any weakness, only to find none. I try for his future. Of course he doesn't have one, and I have no reason to read his mind, so I hand him the box. I make sure our skin doesn't touch. I don't want to accidently extract his thoughts, like I did with Justin. I can only imagine what kind of mass hysteria that might cause.

The ghastly leader hesitantly takes the box. No doubt he fears the diamond's power. He slowly opens the hinged lid and the other two members of his trio step forward. He examines the diamond closely and then confers quietly with the other two men. Markus then turns to the tent and waves his hand, and the hostages are ushered back inside.

Markus's high voice roars out across the field, echoing against the mountains surrounding us, "You have betrayed us, Calli Courtnae! Where is the real stone?"

Chris's and Justin's eyes appear like they might burst from their sockets. Both of their mouths hang open. Sweat beads on my forehead. I know I need to speak truthfully, but misleadingly. "This is the diamond the gem cutter gave us," I begin. "We are delivering the stone he personally handed us in his private office. The three of us were all present and are all present now at this delivery. We can all testify that is the diamond the gem cutter gave us."

Markus states: "The Sanguine Diamond radiates intense power. This stone contains nothing. The diamond is so powerful it cannot be handled with bare skin." He grabs the fake diamond out of the box and holds it out to prove his point. "This one is counterfeit. Where is the real stone, Miss Courtnae?"

I simply stare at him.

The three men turn away and huddle together.

"What's happening?" Chris worries aloud.

Justin whispers, "We've been duped by Harold Bates. He's sent us on a suicide mission." Then Justin's head whips in my direction. "Wait. He told us 'sometimes the weakest can be the strongest.' What did he mean by that, Calli?"

Before Justin can continue, the three Death Clan members turn back, and Markus says, "We will have retribution for this grand deception. All Runners will be held until the diamond is found. If anyone tries to flee, they will be killed. Runners, to your tent!"

The immense power and control the Death Clan leader has over all the clan members stuns me. Everyone fears for their lives, knowing the nightmarish men can kill them instantly. The Runners head into our tent. Our trio is the last to enter, followed by twenty or so Death Clan members.

Clara tries to talk with Markus but is ignored. Markus ushers me into the partitioned cubicle. Neither Justin nor Chris tries to accompany me this time.

How inconceivably odd it is to be alone with an alien-looking, two-hundred-year-old man.

"Care to explain the *real* situation, Miss Courtnae?"

"Believe me, if I knew why the master cutter would deceive both you and me, I would tell you."

"Our witch tells me you know where the diamond is."

"Your witch? May I talk to her?"

"She doesn't wish to speak to you."

"Do you believe her?"

"Why should we not?"

"Well, I'm new to this world of cosmic abilities, but one of the things I've learned is witches are not to be trusted. I find it rather amazing wise men of several hundred years of age would put any stock in what a potentially evil Spellcaster has to say."

"Only someone with something to hide would say such things."

"Perhaps she has cast a spell on you to make you believe her."

"Tell me where the stone is!"

"We have given you the stone the master cutter gave us. That's the only answer I can give you."

"Fine. We'll handle this matter a different way."

Markus orders me to exit the cubicle and to go stand next to Chris and Justin. Markus then addresses all the Runners in the tent. "Until the real stone is presented to us, one member of your clan will die every day, starting right now." A huge gasp drifts through the tent, and heads swivel back and forth. "Miss Courtnae will choose the first to die, for this trickery must be punished."

I yell, "We have not tricked you! We gave you the diamond Mr. Bates gave us. Surely you could give us one day to try to get an answer from him?"

The leader glares at me with soulless eyes. "The number of Runners in this tent is the same as the number of days you have to find us the stone before your clan is wiped from the face of the earth. Make your choice, Miss Courtnae."

I'm on thin ice. I glance around the room, not in order to decide who will be first to die, but to take in the faces of my clan. I find trust, fear, respect, and angst permeating their thoughts and feelings. I hold one of their lives in my hands—at least that's what they think. My eyes rest on Jonas, and my mind pauses for a second, knowing he is fated to die soon anyway. What would be the harm in offering him a quick, painless way out, a way that will satisfy the Death Clan leader at the same time? My stomach flips over at the horrific thought. No! I will never sacrifice anyone but myself. I look away from Jonas and scan the crowd. At length my eyes rest on Chris. I have foreseen this moment many times over. As if on cue, his mind tells me to choose him.

"Make your decision," Markus thunders.

"I can't. I cannot sentence a friend to death."

"Very well. We shall hold a lottery. Numbers will be issued to all Runners."

Time seems to move forward in slow motion as members of the Death Clan write numbers on pieces of paper. I get the idea the Death Clan makes a lot of their decisions this way: luck of the draw. They add insult to the impending injury by using the metal box Harold Bates gave us to hold the pieces of paper.

I glance around the crowd. Some of their minds reveal they are considering escape options, but hold back because of knowing how quickly the Death Clan can kill with their thoughts.

Two Death Clan members take the box around the tent, allowing each Runner to choose a number. This was not in my vision, but I know no matter what, I will not give up the stone willingly. It's the only way to prevent them from becoming all powerful, and to also save Chris's life.

"Now, you shall pull a number out of your head between one and one hundred, Miss Courtnae. You have ten seconds to do so."

"You think you can make me condemn one of my friends to death? Forget it."

"Unless you produce the stone, you'll be condemning all your friends to death."

I totally hadn't foreseen this in my vision. I wonder if keeping the stone is the right decision, but I remember the vision with Chris. He will live because I will die.

"The number, Calli."

"I cannot."

Markus's piercing stare burns into my eyes. "Then I'll choose for you. The first to die is the Runner with number twenty—" He is interrupted by a disturbance spreading through the other Death Clan members. He looks over his shoulder and steps aside.

I cast a quick glance over at Chris. He turns his hand, showing me his number: twenty. He has sweat rolling down his forehead as he points his thumb to his chest.

The door to the tent pulls aside, and a small, withered, cadaverous old man steps inside and walks slowly to stand beside Markus. His face is creased with many centuries of decay, and his eyes glow with a cold, red flame. I quickly deduce this bent-over man is in fact the real leader of the Death Clan because all Death Clan members move back a couple of steps and bow their heads.

His voice rattles and quivers in a raspy whisper. He says to Markus, "Why are you going to kill to expose the diamond? The Runners have done nothing but try to appease us. They have risked much and have lost a great deal in journeying here to make the delivery. They are ambassadors for their clan, a clan we have need of and will need again in the future. Are you so willing to wipe them out, all because you are too weak to realize the truth?"

"My apologies, Great One, but realize what? What truth?"

"The Sanguine Diamond is right in front of you, in this very tent."

"Master?"

"You do not sense its power? Its strength?"

"My apologies, Master. I do not."

"Then it is your own folly."

This shriveled up old man knows I have the diamond. He can sense it.

"The air is alive with its presence, and a peculiar energy emanates from its bearer. For you not to acknowledge this means you are weak and not fit to make decisions for the clan."

"Master, I beg you—"

"You beg? Further verification you are not fit to lead. The counterfeit diamond was a decoy given as a means to attract those who would steal it before it could arrive here. Attempts were made, albeit unsuccessful. The genuine diamond was brought here through a different means. Everyone needed to be fooled, including the delivery-team members. And they were. Now, one of *us* will die to demonstrate our clan's trustworthiness."

"Master—"

"You will die because of your intention to harm the Runners simply because you are too pathetic to be a proper leader."

"But Mast—" Markus's eyes roll back in his head, and he drops to the ground, clutching his chest before finishing the word. His body convulses a few times before it stops moving.

The other Death Clan members bow their heads even lower out of respect for their ancient leader . . . or more likely because they don't want to be next. The dead man named Markus must have terrified and terrorized many people over the past two hundred years, and yet in an instant it is all over for him.

I watch as the old man brings his eyes to mine, and wait for my death.

He straightens his posture, becoming taller and more intimidating. "How does an entire clan become fooled by one of their own?" His voice sounds different now, almost like he needed time to warm up his decrepit vocal chords. He speaks with a deep, rumbling, authoritative intonation. "By the least likely individual possible, the slowest. As time went on, she became your fastest. Every ability and power emerged in her, setting a precedent. But why? How? You must have asked yourselves this many times, yet no one thought to investigate further."

My name travels through the crowd on whispers and gasps. I don't look at anyone. I keep my eyes on the ancient leader.

He turns his head back to me. "Bring forth the diamond, Calli Courtnae." His direct order almost pushes me backwards.

My vision into Chris's future shows him living because I don't give up the diamond. Do I give it now? Do I force them to kill me? I don't know. I walk away from Chris and toward the little old man, trying to descry his future . . . but naturally he has none. That's a good sign, I figure.

He stares at me, angling his head to the side, studying me, waiting for me to produce the stone. His eyes travel over my body, looking for the unmistakable bulge, but not finding anything.

I move to stand directly in front of him. "I will not give you the diamond."

"You are afraid?"

"No, I'm not afraid to die."

"Yet," he points to Markus's dead body, "you know that is what will happen to you."

"Yes," I say with confidence.

"Why? You could hand the stone over and live. You don't have to die."

Behind me, Chris whispers, "No, Calli. Give him the diamond if you have it."

How can I even begin to explain this is the way it has to be in order to save the most amount of lives, including Chris's?

"I won't give you the diamond." A monumental realization hits me: if I hand the pouch to this man, he will die. That wouldn't be so bad, would it? I don't have time to look to the future to see if the results will be better than if I keep the stone. I decide not to change anything. The vision of keeping the stone had the best results in the overall sense.

His anger shoots through me. He opens his mind, and once I enter he blasts me with his thoughts. *Stubborn girl. I don't want to kill you, but you are making this impossible. Hand it over!*

"It will kill you."

He smiles, turns around and motions for one of his clansmen to give him something. When he faces me again, he holds a basket with a handle.

"Place it in the basket."

"No. If you want it, you'll have to remove it from my pocket yourself."

His eyes move to my pocket, then back up to my eyes. He puts his thoughts forward. *I suppose you think you're safe because you're human. Yes, that's right. I know about you. You've probably been told our clan only kills people with power. Well, Miss Courtnae, that's not true. We can kill humans too. Is that what you want?*

"I'm not afraid." In truth, I'm scared to death.

His eyes narrow, and his jaw clenches. He places his hand on his forehead and closes his eyes for a moment. Then he glares at me and I read his thoughts. *Clearly, you have a protection enchantment. My powers don't work on you. We will kill you the old-fashioned way after we absorb the powers of the diamond.*

I am speechless. He just tried to end my life . . . and failed!

His voice thunders through the tent. "Usher her to the altar. She will die for her insubordination after we extract the powers of the stone."

Shouts of protest arise from everyone, but the one voice that matters most to me cuts to the absolute center of my soul. I hear Chris cry out, "No, Calli!" He shouts at the leader, "Me, take me!"

Several Death Clan members lead me to the center of the clearing and bind my hands behind my back. Then they lift me and lay me down on my back on the rock altar, which is especially uncomfortable with my hands beneath me.

The withered old leader speaks to his other clansmen. "Bring two slaves."

Two emaciated individuals in shackles are delivered to the leader. They have the scent of Runners.

"Unzip her pocket and remove the diamond," he says to the first slave.

"No. Don't do it. You'll die," I plead with the Runner.

His mind reveals he knows he'll be killed if he doesn't follow orders. He opens my pocket and pulls out the leather pouch. It slips out of his hand and lands on my stomach. I realize too late he's dropped the diamond due to his heart stopping. I wanted to try to heal him. Now I can't feel anything in his body. The slave crumples to the ground, dead.

The second captive is ordered to slide the diamond out of the pouch onto my chest without touching it. I try to warn him, too. He's hesitant to pick up the pouch, and I can't blame him, after seeing its deadly effects on the first person. Instead, he carefully unties the strings, trying not to touch the pouch. I delve into his body and monitor his heart while he performs his duty. He quickly tips the pouch upside down, sliding the diamond out into the late afternoon sunlight and onto my chest. The Sanguine Diamond catches the light and its radiant brilliance reflects everywhere. The gasps from the onlookers float through the air. Just as I begin to think the second slave might survive, he collapses to the ground. Dead.

My eyes water and my throat constricts. I thought by keeping the diamond, I'd be the only one who died. Now two innocent men are dead because of my decision to keep the stone.

The withered leader addresses the clans. "Today, you will all witness ultimate powers bestowed upon our clan, and you will discover the fate of all who stand in our way."

He and the other Death Clan members form a wide circle around the stone table and begin chanting unrecognizable words. Their arms are raised and their hands shake. I look to my left, then to my right, and find Chris standing in front of everyone with a terrified expression. He opens his mind.

Why didn't you tell me, Calli? Why didn't you confide in me that you had the real stone all along? Why didn't you let them kill me? Clearly nature wanted that to happen. I had the number he called. But now I'll be saved, only to live without you.

Oh, how I wish I could communicate with my mind. I would tell him everything. I would tell him the witch told me—no, ordered me—to keep this absolutely secret, not to remove the stone from the pouch, not to tell anyone and not show anyone, to keep it safe. She informed me I was nothing more than a regular human, enchanted to appear as a Runner. She did not tell me the stone would give me all the powers, including Healing. She did not say that so much about me would change. She left out the part about how I would become selfish and greedy with my newfound powers and how I would do anything to make sure Chris didn't die in the end. I would tell Chris he clings to a misguided vision about someone else, not me, and he should move forward in life and find the girl of his dreams: his Healer. I'm only a human, the Sanguine Diamond deliverer, being used to do what people with powers cannot.

Then Chris says to me with his mind, *I don't care that you're human. You are the girl in my vision. I wish you would have trusted me. I would have been your support through the hard times. There is nothing selfish and greedy about you. You* are *my Healer.*

I spoke with my mind! And he answered! I reply back, *Chris, I'm just a regular human. Am I defying nature, or am I completing what nature intended all along?*

Our eye contact is blocked as the Death Clan members tighten their circle around me. I wish they would move so I could continue talking to Chris.

The language the Death Clan chants sounds like gibberish. My mind wanders to the cave by the falls, to the day I first discovered my powers, the day I learned Chris had feelings for me. I remember how I felt inside and how my heart warmed.

The stone on my chest heats up, and a new awareness fills my senses. The exposed diamond, unhampered by the pouch barrier, infuses even greater powers into my body. The present blurs away as a new scene comes into focus. I stand on well-trimmed grass before the headstone of a grave. Several children run toward me shouting, "Grandma, Grandma!" I kneel down and open my arms, embracing them. Together, we lay flowers on the grave of Chris Harding, loving husband, father, and grandfather. My mind, body, and soul fill with an intense love that takes years to develop, the kind that will grow over the years needed to reach the point in the future where this vision will take place. I experience love for the little ones in my arms and love for the man we are there honoring, and who is and will always be the love of my life. The vision switches to a gathering of ten or so middle-aged people, including myself and Maetha, where the decision is being made to harvest another diamond. I pull out of my vision due to the searing pain on my chest.

The stone becomes hotter and hotter, and I cry out as it feels like it will burn a hole right through me. Why can't they kill me and get it over with? No, they have to put me through agony first. But wait, I've just viewed my own future which means I'm not going to die after all. The thought buoys my spirits, yet the diamond is becoming dangerously hot and it begins to vibrate. My breathing does nothing to knock the stone off my chest. The sheer weight of the diamond holds it in place, even though my chest is rapidly rising and falling with my breathing. Some of the Death clan collapse, and I can see Chris again. He's being held back by several guys, including Justin. His face glistens with tears.

I send my thoughts to comfort him. *Everything will be fine, Chris.*

He's too distraught to reply.

The pain intensifies, and I can't stand it any longer. It feels as if a hot sword has been stabbed right through my heart. I arch my back and scream in agony as a bright explosion rocks the clearing all around me.

Then everything goes black.

Chapter 14 – Unaltered

I hurt. I always thought when you die you go to a better place, one where you feel great. I don't believe in heaven or hell, but instead in more of a higher plane of existence or perhaps a different dimension—*one that doesn't include pain.* Then again, maybe I was wrong and this is hell. That would explain the throbbing in my chest.

I figure I'm still alive. My chest burns where the diamond had been placed and I feel extremely weak, too weak to open my eyes. Someone has placed me on a cot or makeshift bed with my arms beside me, no longer tied behind my back. I hear voices far away but can't tell what they are saying. I drift back to unconsciousness.

I open my eyes and see the inside of a tent above me. My chest still hurts but in a different way than before. This time it hurts with every heartbeat. I turn my head to the right, hoping to find Chris, but no.

"She's awake," a female voice sounds from my left. Slowly I turn my head to the other side. Several Healers come toward me, including Andrew Stuart.

"How do you feel?" he asks.

"My chest hurts. Did the diamond burn me?"

Mr. Stuart exchanges uncomfortable glances with other Healers. No one wants to answer my question. I try to sit up, but their hands hold me down.

Clara comes in and pushes her way to the front. "Calli, you made it! You had us so worried! I had no idea that when you said some people would die, you meant you." Her face reflects genuine caring.

"Where's Chris? Is he okay?"

"He's fine. He's helping repair the tents and floodlights."

"I need to talk to him and explain everything."

"Calli, please don't move around right now, or you might hurt yourself further. A piece of the diamond is still in you, and no one's sure what to do."

"What do you mean a piece is still in me?"

"The diamond exploded and killed all of the Death Clan. However, one shard entered your heart. If it's removed, you'll bleed to death before they can heal you."

"The Death Clan is dead?"

"Yes."

I look into her eyes and slip past her walls with the thought, *What happened when the diamond exploded?* Of course, I highly doubt I'll be able to gain entry into her mind now. With the whole diamond gone, my powers should be gone too.

Amazingly, her memory opens up to me. The small piece in my heart must be strong enough to give me this power.

Through her eyes, I watch the Death Clan's bodies alter in strange ways. Their skin seems to fall off and regenerate at an alarming rate. Some of them fall to the ground and writhe in agony, while others literally crust over into a statue-like form. A bloodcurdling scream reverberates throughout the air, and it takes me a moment to recognize my own scream. The bright supernova explosion disintegrates the remaining Death members into dust. Chris runs to me. Clara looks at the remains of the

Death Clan, if dust piles qualify as remains, and then at Chris, who is lifting my limp, bloody body off the table. He has his arms under my knees and behind my shoulders and has pulled me close to his chest. Distraught, he slides down the side of the stone edifice until he sits on the ground. He catches Clara's eye and yells for her to get the Healers. She scans the area. All around is pandemonium. People run crazily in mass hysteria because the explosion has blown out the floodlights and shredded many of the tents. The one individual I'd hoped she'd locate stands across the way . . . Maetha. Clara makes eye contact with her briefly and turns her head to find the Healers. All along, Chris's despondent cries intermingle with the chaos, pleading, "Come back, Calli! Don't die—come back to me, please!" The Healers run over and take my broken body from him. Clara pulls him into a warm embrace, trying to comfort him. He sobs against her shoulder saying angry, unintelligible words.

I pull out of Clara's mind and look her in the eye. "Would you tell Chris I need to talk to him?"

"Yes."

Andrew places his hand on my shoulder and says, "Calli, we were able to mend the walls of your heart around the diamond piece to stop the bleeding, but other than that, I don't think we can help you."

I hold his hand on my shoulder with my mind and forcefully extract his thoughts. I need to see what else happened and see Chris again. Mr. Stuart was the first one to reach Chris in the clearing. Chris didn't want to let go of me but eventually did. My lifeless body was moved to this tent, where they worked quickly to stop my blood loss. My heart was not beating, yet the blood flowed like that of an animal being bled out. After mending the holes, taking care to avoid touching the diamond piece, my heart started beating again. Mr. Stuart told someone to "go get him," and soon Chris entered the tent, still covered in my blood. He told Chris I was alive, but only barely. Chris walked over to my side and placed his shaking hand carefully on my head. "I'm so sorry," he whispered as he bent forward and kissed my forehead. He turned and walked out of the tent.

When I pull out of Mr. Stuart's mind, I find three different people trying to pull his hand off of my shoulder. No one else touches me, but they have hold of Andrew's body in different places, pulling and yanking to break the connection. I release the hold with my mind and apologize.

"What kind of power physically holds me to you like a magnet?" his startled voice cracks.

"Thought-Extraction, I think," I say.

"I would like a word with the girl, alone," says an authoritative female voice. I recognize the voice as Maetha's, speaking from behind the crowd and causing the group to part. After the tent empties, Maetha walks in a circle around me, chanting some sort of spell. When she's done, she stands by me and says, "Calli, I'm so pleased you are all right. I've isolated our conversation so no one will be able to eavesdrop on us." She sits down by me. "You are the Sanguine Diamond Bearer. You successfully carried, protected, and delivered the stone, bringing about the fall of the Death Clan, as was intended by nature. Now, you bear a piece of the diamond within you."

"But, why am I alive? In my previous vision at the motel, I died," I say, with limited strength.

"Future sight is a tricky thing and can be difficult to perceive and accept. You did die, but we brought you back."

"Before the diamond exploded, I saw another vision— a time in the distant future. I realized I would survive."

"Again, let me say, future sight is a tricky thing. Let's focus on the here and now. The Death Clan is eliminated and the delivery was a success on all levels."

"I just wanted to make sure Chris didn't die, and I kept altering the future until I found the formula for saving his life."

"And you did."

"What's going to happen to me now?"

"You will keep the shard in your heart . . . let's just say for safe-keeping. You will mend over time."

"What about my powers?"

"You will possess your powers permanently because of the shard embedded in your heart. I would recommend you focus on one of the abilities in particular."

"Healer. I want to be a Healer." *The first person I'll use my healing ability on will be Jonas.*

"Excellent choice."

"I witnessed the Death people dying through Clara's memory, but I don't understand what happened."

"They were originally Healers, so when they tried to extract the powers contained within the diamond, the power of healing began to infuse their bodies. You see, normally Healers cannot heal themselves, but the Sanguine Diamond gives the ability to heal oneself."

I interrupt her. "Wait, I couldn't heal my own injuries earlier."

"Because the diamond was in the pouch, making it difficult for you to access the power. With enough time, you would have been able to heal yourself. You already figured out how to extract thoughts while the diamond was still in the pouch. As I was saying, the Death Clan began to access the other powers, which gave them the ability to heal themselves, and at the same time compounded their ability to kill. Kill the girl, absorb the powers. But you're an

Unaltered, and they couldn't kill you. So they tried harder. Their killing power was increased ten-fold, and the diamond reflected it back on them. They were then destroying their own bodies, but also healing themselves. The rapid decay and regeneration created a kind of super cancer in which the accelerated cell growth mutated all their organs, tissues, and bones. They didn't know that would happen. They didn't understand the reason this occurred was because they chose to pair the absorption of their powers with the attempt to kill you. That's the true beauty of it all. They didn't know you're an Unaltered human, nor did they fathom the significance.

"Calli," she continues, "I chose you to carry the Sanguine Diamond long ago because not only were you an Unaltered, you displayed the necessary traits of behavior needed for a successful delivery."

"Long ago? I'm only sixteen!"

She ignores my outburst. "You are selfishly unselfish. Because of this trait, you developed the need to make sure Chris lived, and that helped you discover the proper formula for success."

"What does 'Unaltered' mean?"

"You are an Unaltered human. No cosmic energy waves have changed or altered you in any way. You are a physically pure human girl. This makes you very rare."

"What?"

"Calli, you belong to a bloodline of purity. I've followed this bloodline through many centuries, both male and female, watching the effects of being an Unaltered human. I have learned an Unaltered is more powerful than any other individual on the planet and is superior to all others. I know you're already aware of the differences between you and others your age, but there's more to being an Unaltered. Mind-Readers cannot enter your mind, and your future cannot be seen. Death Clan members could not kill you, Healers cannot heal you, and Hunters cannot smell you. You, and others like you, hold the greatest potential to be powerful. This is the reason I selected you, as with others in your bloodline in the past. In fact, a few hundred years ago, one of your ancestors aided me in the destruction of the Vampire Clan."

"So, the Death Clan didn't actually kill me?"

"No. The splintering of the diamond and the force of the shard entering your heart is what caused it to stop beating."

I place my hand over the sore wound on my chest. I take a slow, deep breath, "How were the Healers able to fix my injuries? You said they can't heal an Unaltered."

"I healed you. I let them think I helped them."

"How did you cast spells on me at the gem cutter's office if I'm so immune?"

"I didn't need to protect you. You're an Unaltered. I cast protection spells on the diamond."

"What about at the track meet? Didn't you enchant me to run fast?"

"The method I used to help you run faster wasn't magic. Don't waste your energy trying to figure this out. You will learn what I'm talking about soon enough."

I nod, feeling let down that she isn't going to answer all my questions. However, I have a pressing question in mind. "Why didn't *you* take the diamond to the Death Clan from the get-go?"

"They would have thought I was attempting to wipe them out like I did with the last clan who sought ultimate power. Besides, their deaths needed to be brought about through the selfless sacrifice of an Unaltered—you. I had to alert the Grand Master to the presence of the stone on one of the Runners in the trio. He put two and two together and came up with you. Because you stood your ground and didn't hand over the diamond, they ended up killing themselves with the diamond's power."

"The Grand Master didn't know I had the diamond?"

"No, dear. I spoke to Markus's mind and told him you knew where it was after he realized the first stone was a fake, but he became determined to eliminate the entire clan, so I alerted the Grand Master."

"Why did he trust you? You're a witch."

"I've earned the reputation as a witch among the clans, which is useful when dealing with shady characters. Over the course of several decades, I've infiltrated the Death Clan's inner circle, giving them reasons to trust me—some of which I'm not proud of. Everything was done with this exact moment in mind. There's more to this, Calli, but this isn't the time or place to tell you."

Instead of pressing for more information, I decide to ask some other questions. "Why are my powers so much greater than anyone else's?"

"Thousands of years ago when the Sanguine Diamond was created, it absorbed the most common powers of the day. The powers were stronger then and there were more varieties. Some powers have died out entirely since the creation of the diamond, while others have weakened. In today's day and age, the cosmic energy waves collide with so much pollution and space debris before reaching the embryo that the intensity is diminished."

"Mr. Bates said the diamond was found after an explosion of some kind. Was that true?"

"It was a half truth. I will explain the origins of the diamond at a later time."

"Oh, okay. Is it my mother's or father's side that's Unaltered?"

"Your mother's, from her father, and he inherited from his mother. It's a bloodline trait. You will pass the same purity on to your child someday. Something about the structure of your DNA is immune to the cosmic energy waves."

"So are there other Unaltereds?"

"Yes, a few, but they are unaware of their potential."

"How can you tell who is and who isn't?"

"Your family is easy because I have followed them throughout history. Others stand out due to their unique auras. Harold Bates is an Unaltered also. I'm sure you already figured that out."

"Right, because he could hold the stone. Beth spotted my aura on the first day. She even referred to it as a sign of a human. Chris was drawn to my aura right off the bat. Can I learn to visualize auras?"

"Yes, I'll train you how at a later date. Chris didn't comprehend what he saw, only that you were very special. Beth, on the other hand, is extraordinary. Not many individuals can detect an Unaltered's aura. I'm guessing she has seen other Unaltered humans in her lifetime."

"Chris views me as his 'one and only.' He had a vision."

"I gave him that vision so he would play his role in helping fulfill the diamond's destiny."

"You did? So, he and I aren't—"

She cuts me off. "Visions of the future are not manufactured, Calli. They are windows into what can be. Certain aspects of the future can be altered, but not by much. In your case, you were only able to do what you did because you carried the diamond. Regular Seers do not possess the ability to alter so many possible outcomes in so short a time."

"Is the future between Chris and me any different now because I altered the delivery?"

"Calli, your mind and ability to comprehend isn't ready to hear the answer yet. I will say this: the future I foresaw before you received the diamond is now."

"You knew I'd end up with a shard in my heart? Couldn't you have prevented that?"

"Yes, I knew how this would end, and no, I would not have prevented it. Everything has to play out as nature intends."

"Unless I alter it."

Her tone of voice deepens in a serious manner. "The destiny of the diamond cannot be altered. The process will complete itself all on its own. This is why I took great care in selecting you, making sure everything was in line before you were given the diamond. Your mother was a candidate at one time, but all the pieces were not in place to use her effectively. Now, Calli, I will give you a stern warning about looking for your own future through others' minds: don't. Can you imagine what you would have thought if you'd known from the outset you'd have to sacrifice yourself in the end? By not knowing the end at the beginning, you were able to come to the proper conclusion of self-sacrifice, which was the only ending for this journey. Do not search for your own future, and remember, no one can alter the destiny of the diamond once the splintering has taken place. Not even me."

"You're right. I'm not ready for this yet. You said you'll train me later. When?"

"I will come to you in the near future and teach you more about your powers, the history of the diamond, and how to visualize auras. I don't know exactly when. I've asked Ms. Winter to send you back home."

"That's fine. I don't belong at the compound."

"Calli, I want you to understand something. I explained to the clans what happened today and why the Death Clan was destroyed. However, the details I told you and what I told them are two different things. I would recommend you keep most of what I've told you to yourself, especially the part about having a shard in your heart and being an Unaltered. Only a small handful of people know about the shard. "

"I'll do my best."

"Oh, and Calli, I'm going to block your Thought-Extraction ability. As you've probably noticed, that ability no longer exists in the world. Back when it did, it was seen as an evil force and viewed as devilry. All humans who possessed the power were hunted down and killed. Eventually, the power vanished altogether. Some of your other abilities may lessen significantly or disappear, but don't be alarmed if that happens."

I shake my head, trying to get the overload of information to settle into order. "Maetha, how long have you been alive?"

"Many thousands of years. I was once like you, an Un-altered."

My thoughts spin in confusion. "You were an Unaltered and then became a witch?"

"I'm not a witch. I let people think I am. It's easier that way."

"Then where did you get your powers?"

"That's a story I will tell when I come to visit."

"Wait. Doesn't it go against nature for you to live so long?"

Maetha stares at me with a pleasant smile on her face. She isn't going to answer my question. "Do you have any other questions before I go?"

"Not a question, but a request. I want to try to heal Jonas. He has cancer."

"Calli, I want you to understand something about healing. Your ability to heal life-threatening conditions comes with two responsibilities. The first is the decision whether you should or shouldn't heal someone. Contrary to what you've been told, the balance of nature won't be thrown off by saving one person or a whole family of persons within the normal age range, and it's all right to do so, but use discretion wisely. By the way, saving Chris's life by the river was not against nature. Chris doesn't have a full understanding of the balance of nature. He only taught you what he'd been taught. You did nothing wrong by saving his life, in fact, you were acting in the best interests of nature's will."

I smile and say, "Well, that's a relief. You should let Chris know so he'll stop beating himself up over it."

"He'll learn for himself soon enough. The second responsibility when choosing to heal someone with a fatal disease or injury is that you need to ask the permission of the individual you wish to heal. After all, shouldn't it be Jonas's decision whether or not he's healed?"

I hadn't even thought about Jonas's wishes. I simply wanted to heal him.

"Calli, the power to heal cases like Jonas's comes at a high cost. The physical toll on your own body is enormous—not fatal, but debilitating. You are not in any condition at this time to attempt to heal him. However, if Jonas wants to be cured, I will do it."

"Well, let's ask Jonas then."

Maetha steps outside and sends someone to find Jonas. I'm filled with overwhelming excitement to finally be able to help him. It doesn't matter that I won't be the one healing him. I only want to know he'll be fine. While she's outside, I think about what she said about being an Unaltered. So many things make sense in my head now.

After a few minutes, Jonas enters the tent with Maetha. He rushes over to me and grabs my hand. "Calli, wow!" he says. "I had no idea you were carrying the diamond. No one did. This is so cool! I'm happy you lived." He can barely contain his happiness.

Maetha sits down on a chair nearby and says, "Jonas, we have something to discuss with you." She motions toward an empty chair by her, and he sits. "Calli would like to tell you something."

Jonas's puzzled gaze shifts over to me. I say, "Jonas, the reason I couldn't tell you the future of your father's fate while we were at Cave Falls was because I couldn't detect your future."

He stares at me for a second. "What?" he asks with a slight laugh, his smile still in place.

I continue. "Once I detected you didn't have a future, I felt inside your body and found you . . . you have cancer, Jonas . . . and it will end your life . . . probably soon."

His smile begins to wane. "What are you talking about? I feel fine."

"For now you do, but soon you won't. I'm asking your permission to heal you."

"My permission? Calli, I don't . . . I'm confused. I'm not sick."

"I tried to heal the tumor in your throat a few nights ago in the motel room."

A flash of recognition comes over his face. "Is that why you were on the floor screaming in pain? You were trying to heal me? Why would you do that to yourself?" His excitement disappears completely and is replaced with seriousness. He seems more worried about my well-being than his own.

"Because," I say, "you should have your whole life ahead of you, and I want to make it possible for you to live."

"What does my future hold now?" His question is almost inaudible.

"You don't have one, but you can if you want to. Maetha can heal you, Jonas."

Jonas glances over at Maetha, who gives him an encouraging smile. Then he looks back at me. "Calli," he says, "you haven't been with the clan very long. There are things the clan teaches us to guide our beliefs and actions, and one of the most important is the will of nature. If nature wants something to happen, we can't interfere. We have to let nature take its course. It's something that, once you understand, you respect entirely and wholeheartedly. I don't want you to think I'm disrespecting you because you're willing to go against nature in this case, but if my time is up, then so be it. I can't change that, and I can't let anyone else change it. I'm as grateful as I can be that you tried to heal me, but obviously it wasn't meant to be, and I have to accept that. Calli, if it's my fate to die of cancer, then I'll die of cancer, and I'll do so willingly. I'm sorry. I can't accept your offer."

"But Jonas—" I try to protest, but he cuts me off.

"I'm honored I was able to go on this assignment with you and be a part of such a fantastic mission. It was amazing to be with you and watch you discover all your abilities. That was a once-in-a-lifetime experience. Thank you for thinking of me, Calli, but I don't want to be healed."

Astonished, I look at Maetha only to see a similar expression on her face. I get the impression she has been in this same kind of situation many times over, and each time the person she has offered to help has accepted her healing. I listen as Jonas asks her if he'll be able to go home to his mother to live out the rest of his days. Maetha nods and escorts him out of the tent.

For the life of me, I cannot understand why someone would decline help in a situation like his, but that's exactly what's happened. He didn't freak out or melt into a puddle of tears. He simply handled the biggest bombshell of his life with complete maturity and acceptance. I'll never forget the look on Maetha's face when he asked her if he could go home. I'm guessing she has never run across someone like Jonas Flemming in her whole long life.

Chapter 15 - New Beginnings

Clara maneuvers the car onto the highway and says, "Calli, I want you to know I won't tell anyone about the diamond piece in your heart. I figure you won't be telling anyone either,"

"Thanks, Clara. Maetha told me to keep it secret."

"Are you able to tell me if you still have all the powers?"

"Yes . . . and yes. However, I'll be trying to keep them a secret as well."

"That's why we're driving instead of running back to the compound. Hopefully this will encourage the belief that your powers are gone. We will have to get a little creative when we get to the border because you don't have your passport with you. I'm sure we'll think of something." She smiles.

I don't know how to respond, but I feel the need to tell her something else. I say, "I know about Chris and his dual life. I read his mind and saw his future. Justin's too."

She nods her head. "I sense a big change is coming for the Runners' Clan. But we'll get through it. We always do."

We continue talking about the happenings at the clearing as we make our way toward the border checkpoint to get back into the U.S. I can't believe it has been only a handful of days since I was spotted at a track meet and whisked away to Montana with Olympic dreams. My parents will be told I was involved in an automobile accident sustaining injuries that prevent me from being able to compete. They won't be told anything about the diamond or the delivery.

Clara tells me that after the Death Clan died, Maetha talked to the clans about nature's will. Her explanation was simple and basic, leaving out many of the points she told me in private. Her main focus, according to Clara, was to address rogue clans or individuals who seek after ultimate power. Maetha said, "Nature always finds a way to eliminate this type of bullish thinking."

I respect Maetha's decisions, even though I don't fully understand them, and I don't tell Clara anything I'm not supposed to, but I can't ignore the double-standard with Maetha.

When we are a couple miles from the border checkpoint, Clara pulls the car to the side of the road. "Do you still have the running power?"

"Yes."

"That's good. You'll need to leave Canada the same way you entered—running. I'll look for you about five miles down the road."

"No problem."

I get out of the car and watch her drive away. When the coast is clear, I take off, running south. Having the diamond piece in my heart gives me a little bit of pain at first, but I use my healing ability to eliminate the pain. I can tell I'm not as fast as I was with the whole diamond, but I'm still faster than a human.

I meet up with Clara on American soil and we continue the several hour drive. Clara and I talk about the amazing powers I demonstrated on the mission and the mysterious clues she'd tried to figure out—like the fact she could tell from the beginning something was different about my ability.

She says, "I wondered if you were a new kind of Runner and thought perhaps the running power was dwindling in strength. When Chris called and reported you were displaying multiple powers, I figured it must be part of the new breed."

I chuckle. "In the end, I'm just a regular human. Ironic, isn't it?"

"Yes. I was relieved to discover you had the diamond."

"Relieved? Why?"

She takes a deep breath and lets it out slowly. "The Sanguine Diamond has been the stuff of myths for centuries. Usually when the diamond appears, an Immortal is also present."

"I thought you said Immortals weren't real."

"I never said that. The legend of Immortals and their existence has been chronicled by Spellcasters throughout many generations. Spellcasters have added their accounts of witnessing the diamond and an Immortal in action. Only other Spellcasters have access to these records. The clans have all but forgotten the real stories. I'll be adding my account of what I've witnessed, leaving out sensitive information, of course."

"You think Maetha is an Immortal, don't you?"

She looks over at me. "Yes, I do. I've known her most of my adult life as a Spellcaster. Sometimes she crosses the line of nature's will. However, her involvement with the delivery of the Sanguine Diamond and her special attention toward you leads me to believe she is an Immortal. Pretending to be a Spellcaster is the perfect disguise to hide behind."

"What do you think she wants with me?"

Clara shrugs her shoulders. "All I know is what Immortals have done in the past. My records only describe past events, not motives or overall endgame strategies."

"I'd love to read your books sometime." I smile. I wonder how being an Unaltered fits into the legend.

"I'm sure you'll get the chance." She gives me an all-knowing look, leaving me wondering what is meant behind it.

At the compound, I'm met with overwhelming applause. Runners of all ages greet me with congratulatory remarks and well wishes, and Beth attaches herself to my arm like a bodyguard. I scan the crowd for Chris, knowing even before I look that he won't be there. I can't smell him. Beth helps me wade through the sea of curious admirers and escorts me to our room.

Once inside, we both breathe sighs of relief.

"Thanks for that, Beth."

"No problem. You're our biggest celebrity! Someone needs to look out for you now, 'cause you certainly watched over us. I would never have guessed you had all those powers because you carried the real diamond. Are they gone now?"

"Yeah, pretty much," I fib.

"What can you still do?"

"I can read minds a bit. That one is my least favorite."

"Can you still heal?"

"Maetha told me if I concentrate on that power, I might be able to keep it."

"I'm so jealous, Calli."

"Don't be. What I went through in the last few days was hell. Have you seen Chris?"

"Sorry. No. Will you come back to visit us?"

"Probably not, but you can always email me." We exchange email addresses and then I say, "I need to go find Chris."

"Good luck. If you ask me, he's trying to keep from being found."

"He must hate me for lying to him over the past few days."

"Why? I don't. Clearly you'd been ordered to keep quiet. The stone did its job, and you lived, so what's the problem?"

"I really need to explain everything to him, in my own words. If you find him before I leave, will you tell him I want to speak with him?"

"Sure."

◇ ◇ ◇

Later that night I wander the halls of the compound looking for Chris. He didn't attend dinner, not surprisingly, and no one has seen him—I know, I've checked their minds. I walk around a corner and find Justin at the end of the hall. He didn't come to dinner either. He catches a glimpse of me out of the corner of his eye while he talks with some boys. I think for sure he'll run the other way, instead he excuses himself and starts walking toward me.

My mind-reading abilities are so advanced now because of the diamond in my heart I only need to be in someone's mind for a split-second, and that tiny moment in Justin's head is all I need to get the information I want concerning Chris.

"Hey, Calli," Justin calls out, "remember when we ran into each other on your first night and I called you a muck?"

"Vividly. Do you know where I can find Chris?"

"Funny thing, though, you weren't a muck after all. You are just a pathetic, plain human who doesn't belong in our world. How does it feel to have it all, then lose it?"

One thing I could count on throughout the whole ordeal would be Justin remaining a jackass. I reply with the intent to irritate him. "Hey, remember when you and I sat outside Harold Bates's office after Chris went inside? The secretary had the real diamond and tried to give it to you, but you wouldn't take it."

"What are you talking about?"

"That's when I received the diamond, right in front of you, because you were too scared to take it. When she handed me the stone, your mouth fell open, sort of like it is right now. She put a spell on your mind to make you forget the whole thing. When we passed the fake stone around inside the office, I already had the real one in my pocket. Up until that point I believed myself to be the slowest Runner, a muck, but I learned then I'm merely a human. And that's fine. Have you seen Chris?"

"Yeah, I have. What's the matter? Can't you read minds anymore? You're pathetic." He walks away laughing.

No way am I going to tell him I still have most of my powers. I will admit, I'm quite tempted to make him run to the bathroom again, but I restrain myself. I leave the hall and walk toward the front foyer. Justin's mind showed me Chris's location: Frank Kinsington's cabin, the clan's Healer.

I exit through the main doors into the bright floodlights and inhale the crisp Montana air. I catch a whiff of Chris's unique smell as I round the corner and see Frank's cabin along the edge of the property. The darkness of night brings me comfort because I will be alone on my walk. As I approach the Demons who linger beyond the

261

bright lighting, I notice new forms: white snakes. That gives me something to ponder. I've started to wonder if there's a way to eliminate the threat of the Shadow Demons. I'll be sure to ask Maetha when she comes to visit.

Frank's cabin has ill-fitting curtains in the windows which allow me a clear line of sight to Chris. I decide not to knock and make my presence known. He wouldn't be able to run because of the Demons and would be forced to talk with me, and as I know he doesn't want to see me, I choose to remain outside his vision. I peer through the window and note right away the sadness in his eyes. His hair is disheveled from the many times he's run his fingers through it. Instead of reading his thoughts, I use my intensified hearing to listen to his conversation.

"I recognized her immediately, Frank, the first time I saw her, but it was all wrong and nothing like the vision shown to me. She was supposed to be a Healer, not a Runner. Of course once her multiple powers emerged, I was relieved. But now . . . now she's powerless. In fact she never had any powers to begin with. You know, after everything went down and Maetha addressed the crowd, the whole thing made sense. Maetha was the one who gave me the vision of Calli in the first place. I thought she was a Seer, not a witch."

Frank asks, "Are you going to ask another Seer about your future?"

"Why would I want another Seer messing with my head like that? Maetha tricked me with my vision of Calli. She used me, and she used Calli. We were just little players in her game." He runs his fingers through his hair again. "It got me thinking. Wiping out the Death Clan was a good thing, but who monitors Maetha?"

"No one I've spoken with knows much about her," says Frank. "We all agreed her intentions were for the betterment of mankind, but I do wonder the same as you: who does she answer to?" He shifts the conversation. "You are aware Calli's leaving tomorrow, right?"

"Yes."

"Well, are you going to say goodbye?"

"No. We were never meant to be together, and she knew it. She even tried to tell me before she . . . anyway, I need to fix my own situation. I'm going to see my father and resign."

"What will you do after that?"

"Disappear for a while and get my head back on straight."

"You know, I'm not a Reader, but even I can tell you have feelings for the girl."

"Of course I do!" Chris slams his palm down on the table. "But they were placed in my head as part of an overall plot or goal. Maetha took advantage of my desire to find out if there was anyone out there for me."

"Yes, but perhaps this is your 'how did you two meet?' story."

"I don't know. It doesn't matter, really. She's too young and I'm too messed up."

"For the moment, but given time, she just might be your one and only whether Maetha tricked you or not."

"I don't want to think about that right now."

I step away from the side of the building feeling dejected. I think about the vision on the stone altar and feel reassured to know we do, in fact, have a future together. He is right, though, I am too young . . . for now.

He refers to himself as "messed up." I wonder why, exactly. Knowing I can perform a mind read in a split second, I use the knowledge about Chris being a spy to enter his memories. Images and scenes fly by, showing a younger Chris, maybe twelve, being studied like a lab-rat by his father after his running power surfaced. Once Chris became "certifiably abnormal," as his father put it, he was used to gather insider information on the clans. Apparently, General Harding didn't know that at some point Chris turned on him and became a double agent, working for the Runners' Clan.

This is what Chris feared I would find if I read his mind—that he's a double agent. Chris knows his father would retaliate in a "take no prisoners" kind of way. Keeping his secret was, and is, of utmost importance. It's the only way he'll be able to resign without his father coming after the Runners.

I have a better understanding of why Chris feels the way he does.

Even though Maetha warned me about looking into my own future, I make the decision to look anyway. I only want to find out when I'll see Chris again. I peek through the curtains and feel for his future. A vision opens up to me, revealing a small room similar to a hospital room. Chris lies in the bed with two broken legs. He looks to the door, and a beautiful woman enters. She walks to him and places her hands on his legs, healing them, and then she hugs him. Chris whispers, "I knew you'd come, Calli."

I pull out of his future in shock. That woman is me!

In the cabin, Chris scratches the top of his head with a confused look on his face. I turn and begin my slow walk back to the compound.

Two weeks have passed since I arrived home. After saying goodbye to everyone except Chris, I rode to the airport with Clara where she put me on an airplane bound for Ohio.

Everything's back to normal around here. I take out the trash, scrub the toilet, and go to school. The school year is almost over, summer break is approaching, and I can still do almost everything I could when I carried the diamond. I've kept my abilities hush-hush, though. The last thing I want is for anyone to find out what I can do.

Suz and I hang out a lot—at the mall of course—people-watching. However, I see everyone through different eyes after everything I've been through.

I used my healing ability for the first time yesterday. My eighty-year-old next-door neighbor fell down his front steps and broke his hip. I called 911 and hurried over to him. I searched his body, found the broken bones, and determined they were not life threatening, so I mended him. He could tell I'd done something, but when the paramedics arrived at his house his excited ramblings about miracles went unheard under the oxygen mask they placed over his face. I smiled all the way back to my house.

Last night I received an email from Beth telling me all the latest gossip about life at the Runners compound. It read:

> *Calli,*
>
> *I hope things are going good for you. Things here have been a mess. Chris left the compound, but before he did, there was a big meeting with all the leaders of the compound. They basically kicked Justin out of the clan. Justin was going to leave anyway, so it was a wasted effort. I'm glad he left. Not sure what I ever saw in him.*
>
> *Guess what? We held a new time trial and I'm now the fastest of the clan! Isn't that great?*
>
> *Maetha the Spellcaster made individual amulets from the broken pieces of the diamond you carried and gave one to each*

clan. They each look like a chandelier light bulb on a leather cord. The diamond shard magically floats inside the bulb to prevent accidental contact with its bearer, and the amulet gives small doses of each power to whomever wears it. Currently, Clara wears the Runners' Clan amulet.

Well, I hope everything is going well for you. Hope to hear from you soon.

Beth

I write Beth back and tell her how everyone here has forgotten I'd set a world record in track and everything is back to normal, just as I prefer. It's a short email, but I don't know what else to say.

I suspect Maetha played a hand in making everyone forget my supernatural moment of fame. No matter. I used to be an ordinary girl who liked to fly under the radar, but then I was pushed out in front and was forced to take on the role of a superhero. Honestly, grandeur wasn't everything I thought it would be. Being back to normal feels good.

Today, I'm going to the mall by myself to feel people. As perverse as it sounds, it's actually a great way to exercise my powers of healing and detecting problems.

As I sit on a bench in the busy mall, I enter the bodies of passersby and search for their small illnesses and disorders. Some of them I fix, while others I don't. I don't make instantaneous decisions selfishly, but more with nature in mind. I glimpse each person's future along with the defect in their body to determine the natural order of their ailment. I can't even begin to describe how disheartening it is to observe so many future deaths walking the halls of the mall.

At one point, I see a mother and teenage daughter squabbling over a purse the daughter wants to buy. In the mother's body, I find leukemia. Her future is not bright. This is a prime example of an individual who will die and one I shouldn't help. A quick mind-read tells me no one is aware of the disease yet. I am compelled to act—not to heal the illness, but to begin the healing process between mother and daughter before the hourglass drops the last few precious grains of life.

I walk over to the two bickering females, push myself between them, and turn to the girl. She isn't any older than I am. "You shouldn't be so quick to battle everything to the death with your mother. One never knows when death will come knocking on the door and take away the most important people in our lives."

The girl's response has several four-letter expletives, but she basically says "mind your own business."

I turn to the exasperated mother and say very quietly, before walking away, "Go to your doctor soon, and treasure your remaining days."

Into my mind comes the words Chris spoke in the bathroom of the motel room: "Wise Healers know when not to heal, when not to help, and when to walk away. Someday you'll be a wise Healer."

I've accepted the fact I won't be hearing from Chris any time soon. By understanding and coming to terms with this, I can move forward. He helped me learn all the different aspects of my abilities, explained the importance of respecting nature's wishes, taught me what it means to truly love someone, and how that love has nothing to do with attractiveness or lust. True love means being able to put your own selfish needs and wants aside and to be willing to sacrifice . . . or even die . . . for the other person.

He was willing to die for me, and I was willing to die for him. I did die for him. I'm still saddened when I think of the last time I saw him in the cabin. If I could have told him at that moment we would see each other again, his spirits would have lifted dramatically. But I knew then, like I do now, that everything has to play out naturally. He will find out down the road, or as Maetha said, "He'll learn soon enough." I only wish I could give him the same positive outlook on life that I have.

I'm consoled by the fact that Chris is resigning from his position with his father. However, this will forever be the skeleton in his closet. I'm saddened to learn of Chris's past and what kind of suffering he's been through. I fully appreciate how frustrated he must feel, thinking he's been "used" by Maetha. Someday he and I will both learn more about the journey we've been on together. It's not over.

When I think about the vision of Chris with broken legs, I'm always confused as to why he's in a hospital and why he hasn't had a Healer fix his legs. I guess I'll just have to wait to find the answer. Until then, I'll await Maetha's visit. I'm anxious to have her teach me about the Sanguine Diamond, Immortals, and the world of the clans—the world I never knew existed. I will live my life as an ordinary teenage girl who's been given a second chance and a gift above all gifts: a diamond in my heart.

Thank You!

I hope you enjoyed *A Diamond in My Pocket*. Please consider leaving a review on Amazon and/or Goodreads so other readers can learn what intrigued you most about the story. Reviews really matter to independent writers like me, as they help my books rise in visibility where more people can see them and, hopefully, purchase them. That's huge, as it allows me to make enough money to write full time and get more books on the market to readers like you!

Don't know how to leave a review? Send me a message using my Contact Me form on my website and I'll give you instructions.

lorenaangell.com/contact-me.html

Would you like to win a $25 Amazon Gift Card? Sign up for my Awesome Fans Newsletter on my website. The first day of every month I'll choose a name from my newsletter subscribers and reward them with $25 Amazon bucks! Plus, by signing up, you'll receive exclusive offers, freebies, news and updates before the general public does.

I'd love to hear from you and learn what you think of my books. Drop me a line and I'll do my best to respond. Visit my website lorenaangell.com and enter your message on the Contact Me form.

http://lorenaangell.com/contact-me.html

I look forward to hearing from you!

Calli's story continues in: ***A Diamond in My Heart***, book two of The Unaltered series.

Using her inherited powers, Calli detects a confusing cosmic power in a classmate who sets his eyes on her. Maetha assigns Calli to investigate the young man and teach him of his new world; before that can happen, she'll have to determine what his power actually is. At the same time, someone is systematically kidnapping the clan leaders who wear the magical amulets.

Calli is able to read minds, view the future, heal, and locate other Sanguine Diamond Bearers she didn't know existed and in doing so she'll learn of traitors who've sided with the U.S. government and threaten her new world and the lives of those she loves. She'll question her own loyalties and friendships, and ultimately be faced with the inevitable—the reuniting of the diamond shards.

Enjoy a free preview of chapter one of

A Diamond in My Heart preview
Chapter 1 - Freedom

I used to scoff at magical powers and abilities, used to have this amazing focused direction in life and didn't allow my time to be wasted on silly conspiracy theories or gossip. I certainly didn't believe in the existence of any superpowers or unnatural abilities—until I became the first person on earth to display all the known powers and abilities.

A few months ago, I learned first-hand cosmic energy rays exist and have always existed, and that nearly everyone on the planet has been affected by them in one way or another.

My mother, Dr. Charlotte Courtnae, and I belong to a rare bloodline of purity that exempts us from the effects of those cosmic energy rays. Something about our DNA protected us while we were in the womb, and we were never "altered." We are unchanged, unaffected. Unlike me, she doesn't *know* she's an Unaltered human.

Living on a planet where I'm a member of this minority isn't so bad, really. Those with powers and abilities who think they can rule the world have no control over me. My mind cannot be read by the Readers. My future remains unseen by the Seers. Healers cannot manipulate my body, and I'm untraceable to a Hunter, for I have no scent. Runners would technically have the advantage over me if I were a regular Unaltered like my mother. But I'm not regular. I'm not ordinary.

I'm an Unaltered Diamond Bearer.

I carry a piece of the Sanguine Diamond within my heart, which gives me every known power and ability plus a couple bonus powers. Maetha, my mentor and the person responsible for the jewel in my heart, hasn't admitted anything, but I suspect she bears a diamond shard in her heart as well. I plan on asking more questions when she comes to visit.

A few months have passed since I returned from the Runner's Compound in Montana. It feels like an eternity ago. I finished up my junior year in high school and welcomed the summer months as a time I could develop my powers. I've had to be more careful when using my abilities. When I healed my neighbor's broken hip right after I returned, I didn't think he would tell my parents— or the whole neighborhood, for that matter. My parents, being the doctors that they are, suspected dementia rather than believe I might have the ability to heal using my mind. Lesson learned. Now I only try to use my healing power when I'm in large crowds.

The last couple of weeks, I've been helping at my mother's counseling clinic while her regular receptionist, Evelyn, is on vacation. Today I'm supposed to take a couple files over to the Behavioral Health Center two blocks away. I could easily walk, but I figure I'll hit the Coffee Shack on the way back as an excuse to drive my new cherry-red Mini Cooper.

My parents bought me the car when I came home from Clara Winter's "Olympic" training camp. They were told I'd been in an automobile accident that resulted in injuries which had disqualified me for this go around of competition. I think they assumed I'd be bummed about being sent home and thought the Cooper would cheer me up . . . and they were right. I know I'm fortunate to be the only child of two doctors and that most kids my age would be lucky to get a rusted-out, dented, twenty-year-old car, so I try not to brag. Needless to say, any opportunity to get behind the wheel excites me to no end.

I take the files to be delivered and leave the building. I climb into my vanilla-scented car and start the engine. After making sure the mirrors are in the correct position, I carefully back the car out of the parking spot. Turning back around to put the car in drive, I see a man leaning against the building I'd just exited.

Strange. I hadn't noticed him before.

He stands around six-feet tall, with well-trimmed black hair, and I guess his age to be mid-forties. He has a square jaw line, straight nose, and his eyes are hidden behind black sunglasses. His long, black trench coat is open in front, revealing a lanky frame dressed in a T-shirt and faded blue jeans. Square-toed motorcycle boots peek out below his pant's hemline, hinting at the possibility he owns a Harley. His trench coat reminds me of what cowboys wear in the old Western movies my father loves to watch.

This man doesn't fit the profile of the normal patrons of the clinic. I decide to use my Hunter ability to smell the air around me, searching for his scent. Perhaps I'll be able to determine if he has a cosmic power. The smell of his leather duster, jeans and tee-shirt fills my nose. However, this man has no personal scent, which raises alarms.

My attention is pulled away by an approaching car. I move my car out of the way and look back for the scent-less man, but he's gone. I drive away to deliver the files, realizing I haven't met anyone other than Maetha and my mother who doesn't have a scent.

When I arrive at the Coffee Shack after delivering the files, I see the man again. This time he's leaning up against a pick-up truck with his thumbs hooked in the front pockets of his jeans. My first thought is he must be a Runner, but the fact he doesn't have a scent cancels that out. This man is clearly Unaltered. I'll be waiting for a few minutes until the two cars in front of me have their orders filled, so I decide to exercise my ability to probe his mind—one more opportunity to practice the powers of the diamond on unsuspecting subjects. I reach out with my mind to penetrate his thoughts, but find it hard to feel any kind of mind or thought process. Then, without warning I'm hit with a mental force so strong the wind is knocked out of my lungs. My fingers death-grip the steering wheel while I try to regain my breath.

A smooth, deep voice enters my head. *How is it a young girl like you is able to read minds?*

My lungs burn with the need for air as my mind swims around the realization this man is projecting his thoughts into my mind. Maetha told me this type of projection power died out over the years and the power only exists inside the complete Sanguine Diamond. The vision I had on the stone altar led me to believe there is more than one diamond. I only have a piece of the diamond now, and cannot communicate telepathically anymore. I put my thoughts at the front of my mind, figuring if he has this power he must have other powers too—he must possess a diamond.

Did Maetha send you? I ask with my mind.

Maetha? So she's behind this?

Bingo! He knows about Maetha.

Behind what? I question. My lungs finally relax and I am able to inflate them properly.

He readjusts his stance and takes off his sunglasses, revealing heavy eyebrows hovering above squinted eyes. I wonder why he removed his shades. Is he trying to get a better look at me? He puts them back on.

Who died for you? he asks, assuming I'll know what he means.

I don't know what you're talking about.

The car behind me honks to alert me to pull forward one spot. I do so.

Maetha still operates with the same deception, I see. You should take my advice, little girl. Get as far away from her as you can.

Why should I listen to you?

Because I know her better than just about anyone else!

His statement makes my hair stand on end. *What's your name?* I ask.

I don't go by one. Names are mere labels that inhibit progression. I prefer to be recognized by what I offer. Today I offer freedom. You may think of me as your freedom.

Ooh-kaaay. I am officially freaked out! *Oh, I won't be thinking of you at all, bucko!"*

The car in front of me pulls forward and I follow— only I don't stop at the window. I press the gas pedal to the floor, leaving tread marks on the pavement.

My heart races and my eyes check the rear-view mirror repeatedly as I speed through traffic on my way back to the office. My compact Mini slices through tight spots with the ease of a bobsled. The further I travel away from the creepy man, the more my clenched jaw begins to relax . . . until I arrive back at the office, where I discover "Mr. Freedom" leaning against the building in the same spot as before. I should have realized his diamond would afford him the running ability, but I'm still surprised to see him.

Calli, when you decide to utilize my help, all you'll have to do is ask. His lips part in an almost evil smile, revealing perfectly straight white teeth. Then he turns and walks away.

A couple of days have passed since I saw him, and I can't help but frequently look over my shoulder. I still experience the same panic when I think about the man I've come to refer to as "Freedom." His whole demeanor left me feeling uneasy. It's just fine with me if I never meet him again.

I wonder how he found me. Did he seek me out, or was he passing through and detected a difference in me compared to other people? I also ponder what he said.

More than anything, I wonder how many other Unaltereds have diamonds in their hearts.

Maetha said she'd come and train me to visualize auras, like my roommate, Beth, from the Runner's compound. Now that I understand all Unaltered humans have identifiable auras, I'm excited to learn how to spot other people like me. But I haven't heard from Maetha yet. I will certainly ask her more about her powers and why Freedom was familiar with her. I also want some clarity on Immortals and to know if she is one.

An important date is fast approaching: the day Chris Harding resigns as a spy.

I consider going to see him . . . to get my "Chris fix." I could watch him from a distance and he wouldn't need to know I was present. But what if he saw me? What would that do to him? He'd be reminded of the pain we suffered because of Maetha. Not only would he be tortured further, it would also be painful for me. I was several years older in the vision than I am now.

I know I will see him again, but I also know now is not that time. He, on the other hand, doesn't—and shouldn't—know I have powers. From his perspective, the whole chain of events was manipulated, just as he and I were. Not to mention the fact that in his vision I was a Healer, not the ordinary human he now believes I am.

If I were present at his resignation, he would come to the conclusion I have Seer or Reader abilities, which I would need in order to know his plans. I discard the idea of showing up to see him, but the longing to do so doesn't leave me.

Book two in The Unaltered Series, *A Diamond in My Heart* is available at Amazon and is an Amazon #1 Bestseller in the US, UK, and Germany.

Connect with Lorena Angell at:
LorenaAngell.com
Twitter: @LorenaAngell1
Facebook: The Unaltered Diamond Series
Instagram: the.unaltered.series